FURY

One morning he came in from an all-night job and smelled something strange the moment he pushed the door open. A heavy sweetness in the air, and a sharp, thick, already familiar acridness that not many Keep men would recognise these effete days.

The little dancer lay slumped against the far wall, already stiffening in her slump. Where her face had been was a great palely tinted blossom whose petals gripped like a many-fingered hand, plastering the flower tight against her skull. It had been a yellow flower, but the veins in the petals were bright red now, and more red ran down beneath the blossom over the girl's blue dress.

Beside her on the floor lay the florist's box, spilling green tissue, in which some-one had sent her the flower.

FURY

Henry Kuttner

Hamlyn Paperbacks

FURY
ISBN 0 600 33651 4

First published in Great Britain 1954
by Dennis Dobson Ltd
Hamlyn Paperbacks edition 1978
Copyright © 1947 by Street & Smith Publications, Inc.
Reprinted from *Astounding Science Fiction*

Hamlyn Paperbacks are published by
The Hamlyn Publishing Group Ltd,
Astronaut House,
Feltham,
Middlesex, England

Made and printed in Great Britain by
Cox & Wyman Ltd, London, Reading and
Fakenham

FURY

FOREWORD

This is no story for the lily-livered ...

Fury is a novel of violence. It describes the tortured struggle of the human race to aspire once again to the stars from the deeps of the Venusian seas. The struggle is organised around the career of Sam Reed, an Immortal whose insane father had him so mutilated when a baby that he had no idea he was an Immortal until he reached the age of eighty. The inward psychological warfare between his own belief in his short-livedness and his inborn, unconscious sense of the 'long view' which typifies all Immortals, is the core around which his own career, and the salvation of mankind, develops.

It is a career which finally, through chicanery, desire for self-aggrandizement, and murder – and yet, beyond it all, a distorted vision of the glowing future of man – brings all the human race up from the safe Venusian seas and out into the open terrors of the biologically furious land surface of the planet, there to struggle and achieve once again a noble destiny. In the process, Sam Reed oscillates from national hero to national villain, as he attempts to defeat the defeatism, the arrogant tranquillity, which characterise his unrecognised brethren and sworn enemies, the Immortal rulers.

This story has its own important message for our time; for today, as always, the human race cannot vegetate. It either climbs upward to new levels of social complexity and achievement, or it drifts ever downward into a universal senility. *Fury* shows how under conditions incomprehensibly different from those we now experience, mankind once again starts up the long climb from decay to greatness.

GROFF CONKLIN

INTRODUCTION

It was white night upon Earth and twilight's dawn on Venus.

All men knew of the shining darkness that had turned Earth into a star in the clouded skies. Few men understood that on Venus dawn had merged imperceptibly into dusk. The undersea lights flamed brighter and brighter, turning the great Keeps into enchanted citadels beneath the shallow sea.

Seven hundred years ago those lights were brightest. Six hundred years had passed since the destruction of Earth. It was the Twenty-seventh Century.

Time had slowed now. In the beginning it had moved much faster. There was much to be done. Venus was uninhabitable – but men had to live on Venus.

On Earth the Jurassic had passed before humans evolved into a reasoning race. Man is both tough and fragile. How fragile will be understood when a volcano erupts or the earth shakes. How tough will be understood when you know that colonies existed for as long as two months on the Venusian continents.

Man never knew the fury of the Jurassic – on Earth. On Venus it was worse. Man had no weapons to conquer the Venus lands. His weapons were either too weak or too potent. He could destroy utterly, or he could wound lightly, but he could not live on the surface of Venus. He was faced with an antagonist no man had ever known.

He faced fury . . . And he fled.

There was safety of a sort undersea. Science had perfected interplanetary travel and had destroyed Earth; science could build artificial environments on the ocean bottom. The impervium domes were built. Beneath them the cities rose.

The cities were completed . . . As soon as that happened, dawn on Venus changed to twilight. Man had returned to the sea from which he sprang.

PART ONE

DESPAIR *thy charm;*
And let the angel whom thou still hast serv'd
Tell thee, Macduff was from his mother's womb
Untimely ripp'd.

SHAKESPEARE

Sam Harker's birth was a double prophecy. It showed what was happening to the great Keeps where civilisation's lights still burned, and it foreshadowed Sam's life in those underwater fortresses and out of them. His mother Bessi was a fragile, pretty woman who should have known better than to have a child. She was narrow-hipped and tiny, and she died in the emergency Caesarean that released Sam into a world that he had to smash before it could smash him.

That was why Blaze Harker hated his son with such a blind, vicious hatred. Blaze could never think of the boy without remembering what had happened that night. He could never hear Sam's voice without hearing Bessi's thin, frightened screams. The caudal anaesthesia hadn't helped much, because Bessi was psychologically as well as physically unfit for motherhood.

Blaze and Bessi – it was a Romeo and Juliet story with a happy ending, up to the time Sam was conceived. They were casual, purposeless hedonists. In the Keeps you had to choose. You could either find a drive, an incentive – be one of the technicians or artists – or you could drift. The technologies made a broad field, everything from thal-assopololitics to the rigidly limited nuclear physics. But drifting was easy, if you could afford it. Even if you couldn't, lotus-eating was cheap in the Keeps. You simply didn't go in for the expensive pleasures like the Olympus rooms and the arenas.

Still, Blaze and Bessi could afford the best. Their idyll could make a saga out of hedonism. And it seemed that it would have a happy ending, for in the Keeps it wasn't the individual who paid. It was the race that was paying.

After Bessi died, Blaze had nothing left except hatred.

These were the generations of Harker:

Geoffery begat Raoul; Raoul begat Zachariah; Zachariah begat Blaze; and Blaze begat Sam.

Blaze relaxed in the cushioned seat and looked at his great-great-grandfather.

'You can go to the devil,' he said. 'All of you.'

Geoffery was a tall, muscular, blond man with curiously large ears and feet. He said, 'You talk like that because you're young, that's all. How old are you now? Not twenty!'

'It's my affair,' Blaze said.

'I'll be two hundred in another twenty years,' Geoffery said. 'I had sense enough to wait till I was past fifty before fathering a son. I had sense enough not to use my common-law wife for breeding. Why blame the child?'

Blaze stubbornly looked at his fingers.

His father Zachariah, who had been glaring silently, sprang up and snapped, 'He's psychotic! Where he belongs is in a psych-hospital. They'd get the truth out of him!'

Blaze smiled. 'I took precautions, Father,' he said mildly. 'I took a number of tests and exams before I came here today. Administration's approved my I.Q. and my sanity. I'm thoroughly compos mentis. Legally, too. There's nothing any of you can do, and you know it.'

'Even a two-week-old child has his civil rights,' said Raoul, who was thin, dark, elegantly tailored in soft celoflex, and seemed wryly amused by the entire scene. 'But you've been careful not to admit anything, eh, Blaze?'

'Very careful.'

Geoffery hunched his buffalo shoulders forward, met Blaze's eyes with his own cool blue ones, and said, 'Where's the boy?'

'I don't know.'

Zachariah said furiously, 'My grandson – we'll find him! Be sure of that! If he's in Delaware Keep we'll find him – or if he's on Venus!'

'Exactly,' Raoul agreed. 'The Harkers are rather powerful, Blaze. You should know that. That's why you've been allowed to do exactly as you wanted all your life. But that's stopping now.'

'I don't think it is stopping,' Blaze said. 'I've a great deal of money of my own. As for your finding ... *him* ... have you thought that it might be difficult?'

'We're a powerful family,' Geoffery said steadily.

'So we are,' Blaze said. 'But what if you can't recognise the boy when you find him?' He smiled.

The first thing they did was to give him a depilatory treatment. Blaze couldn't endure the possibility that dyed hair would grow back red. The baby's scanty growth of auburn fuzz was removed. It would never grow again.

A culture catering to hedonism has its perversions of science. And Blaze could pay well. More than one technician had been wrecked by pleasure-addiction; such men were usually capable – when they were sober. But it was a woman Blaze found, finally, and she was capable only when alive. She lived when she was wearing the Happy Cloak. She wouldn't live long; Happy Cloak addicts lasted about two years, on the average. The thing was a biological adaptation of an organism found in the Venusian seas. It had been illegally developed, after its potentialities were first realised. In its native state, it got its prey by touching it. After that neuro-contact had been established, the prey was quite satisfied to be ingested.

It was a beautiful garment, a living white like the white of a pearl, shivering softly with rippling lights, stirring with a terrible, ecstatic movement of its own as the lethal symbiosis was established. It was beautiful as the woman technician wore it, as she moved about the bright, quiet room in a tranced concentration upon the task that would pay her enough to insure her death within two years. She was very capable. She knew endocrinology. When she had finished, Sam Harker had forever lost his heritage. The matrix had been set – or, rather, altered from its original pattern.

Thalamus, thyroid, pineal – tiny lumps of tissue, some already active, some waiting till the trigger of approaching maturity started the secretions. The infant was unformed, a somewhat larger lump of tissue, with cartilage for bones and his soft skull imperfectly sutured as yet.

'Not a monster,' Blaze had said, thinking about Bessi all the time. 'No, nothing extreme. Short, fleshy – *thick*!'

The bandaged lump of tissue lay still on the operating table. Germicidal lamps focused on the anaethetised form.

The woman, swimming in anticipated ecstasy, managed to touch a summoning signal-button. Then she lay down quietly on the floor, the shining pearly garment caressing her. Her tranced eyes looked up, flat and empty as mirrors. The man who came in gave the Happy Cloak a wide berth. He began the necessary post-operative routine.

The elder Harkers watched Blaze, hoping they could find the child through his father. But Blaze had refined his plan too thoroughly to leave such loopholes. In a secret place he had Sam's fingerprints and retina-prints, and he knew that through those he could locate his son at any time. He was in no hurry. What would happen would happen. It was inevitable – now. Given the basic ingredients, and the stable environment there was no hope at all for Sam Harker.

Blaze set an alarm clock in his mind, an alarm that would not ring for many years. Meanwhile, having faced reality for the first time in his life, he did his utmost to forget it again. He could never forget Bessi, though he tried. He plunged back into the bright, euphoric spin of hedonism in the Keeps.

The early years merged into the unremembered past. Time moved more slowly for Sam then. Days and hours dragged. The man and woman he knew as father and mother had nothing in common with him, even then. For the operation had not altered his mind; his intelligence, his ingenuity, he had inherited from half-mutant ancestors. Though the mutation was merely one of longevity, that trait had made it possible for the Harkers to rise to dominance on Venus. They were not the only long-lived ones, by any means; there were a few hundred others who had a life-expectancy of from two to seven hundred years, depending on various complicated factors. But the strain bred true. It was easy to identify them.

There was a carnival season once, he remembered, and his foster parents awkwardly donned finery and went to mingle with the rest. He was old enough to be a reasoning animal by then. He had already seen glamour from a distance, but he had never seen it in operation.

Carnival was a respected custom. All Delaware Keep was shining. Coloured perfumes hung like a haze above the moving Ways, clinging to the merrymakers as they passed. It was a time when all classes mingled.

Technically there were no lower classes. Actually—

He saw a woman – the loveliest woman he had ever seen. Her gown was blue. That does not describe its colour in the least. It was a deep, rich, different blue, so velvety and smooth that the boy ached to touch it. He was too young to understand the subtlety of the gown's cut, its sharp, clean lines, the way it enhanced the woman's face and her corn-yellow hair. He saw her from a distance and was filled with a violent need to know more about her.

His foster mother could not tell him what he wanted.

'That's Kedre Walton. She must be two, three hundred yeas old by now.'

'Yes.' Years meant nothing. 'But who *is* she?'

'Oh – she runs a lot of things.'

'This is a farewell party, my dear,' she said.

'So soon?'

'Sixty years – hasn't it been?'

'Kedre, Kedre – sometimes I wish our lives weren't so long.'

She smiled at him. 'Then we'd never have met. We Immortals gravitate to the same level – so we *do* meet.'

Old Zachariah Harker reached for her hand. Beneath their terrace the Keep glittered with carnival.

'It's always new,' he said.

'It wouldn't be, though, if we'd stayed together that first time. Imagine being bound for hundreds of years!'

Zachariah gave her a shrewd, questioning stare.

'A matter of proportion, probably, he said. 'Immortals shouldn't live in the Keeps. The restrictions . . . the older you grow, the more you've got to expand.'

'Well – I am expanding.'

'Limited by the Keeps. The young men and the short-lived ones don't see the walls around them. We old ones do. We need more room. Kedre, I'm growing afraid. We're reaching our limits.'

'Are we?'

'Coming close to them – we Immortals. I'm afraid of intellectual death. What's the use of longevity if you're not able to use your skills and powers as you gain them? We're beginning to turn inward.'

'Well – what then? Interplanetary?'

'Outposts, perhaps. But on Mars we'd need Keeps, too. And on most of the other planets. I'm thinking of interstellar.'

'It's impossible.'

'It was impossible when man came to Venus. It's theoretically possible now, Kedre. But not practically so. There's no . . . no symbolic launching-platform. No interstellar ship could be built or launched from an undersea Keep. I'm speaking symbolically.'

'My dear,' she said, 'we have all the time in the world. We'll discuss this again in . . . oh, fifty years, perhaps.'

'And I won't see you till then?'

'Of course you'll see me, Zachariah. But no more than that. It's time we took our vacation. Then, when we come together again—'

She rose. They kissed. That, too, was symbolic. Both of them felt the ardour fading into grey ash – and, because they

14

were in love, they were wise enough and patient enough to wait till the fire could be rekindled again.

So far the plan had been successful.

After fifty years had passed they would be lovers again.

Sam Harker stared at the gaunt grey-faced man moving purposefully through the throng. He was wearing cheerful celoflex too, but nothing could disguise the fact that he was not a Keep man. He had been sunburned once, so deeply that centuries undersea had not bleached him of that deep tan. His mouth was set in a habitual sneering grin.

'Who's that?'

'What? Where? Oh, I don't know. Don't bother me.'

He hated the compromise that had made him don celoflex. But his old uniform would have been far too conspicuous. Cold, cruel-mouthed, suffering, he let the Way carry him past the enormous globe of the Earth, draped in a black plastic pall, which served in every Keep as a reminder of mankind's greatest achievement. He went to a walled garden and handed in an identification disc at a barred window. Presently he was admitted to the temple.

So this was the Temple of Truth!

It was impressive. He had respect for technicians – logistics, logicians . . . not logistics, that was behind him now. A priest took him into an inner chamber and showed him a chair.

'You're Robin Hale?'

'Right.'

'Well – you've collated and given us all the data we need. But there must be a few clarifying questions. The Logician will ask them himself.'

He went away. Downstairs, in the hydroponic gardens, a tall, thin, bony-faced man was pottering about cheerfully.

'The Logician is needed. Robin Hale's waiting.'

'Ah, rats,' said the tall, thin man, setting down a spray and scratching his long jaw. 'Nothing I can tell the poor fella. He's sunk.'

'Sir!'

'Take it easy. I'll talk to him. Go away and relax. Got his papers ready?'

'Yes, sir.'

'O.K. I'll be along. Don't rush me.' Muttering, the Logician shambled towards a lift. Presently he was in the control room, watching, through a visor, the gaunt sunburned man sitting uncomfortably on his chair.

'Robin Hale,' he said, in a new, deeper voice.

Hale automatically stiffened. 'Yes.'

'You are an Immortal. That means you have a life-expectancy of up to seven hundred years. But you have no job. Is that right?'

'That's right.'

'What happened to your job?'

'What happened to the Free Companies?'

... They died. They passed, when the Keeps unified under one government, and the token wars between them became unnecessary. In those days, the Free Companions had been the warriors, hired mercenaries paid to fight battles the Keeps dared not fight themselves, for fear of perishing.

The Logician said, 'Not many Free Companions were Immortals. It's been a long time since there was a Free Company. You've outlived your job, Hale.'

'I know.'

'Do you want me to find a job for you?'

'You can't,' Hale said bitterly. 'You can't find one, and I can't face the prospect of hundreds of years – doing nothing. Just enjoying myself. I'm not a hedonist.'

'I can tell you what to do very easily,' the Logician said. 'Die.'

There was silence.

The Logician went on: 'I can't tell you how to do it quite so easily. You're a fighter. You'll want to die fighting for your life. And, preferably, fighting for something you believe.' He paused. When he spoke again, his voice had changed.

'Wait a minute,' he said. 'I'm coming out there. Hang on.'

And a moment later his thin, tall form shambled from behind a curtain in the wall. Hale jumped to his feet, staring at the scarecrow figure confronting him. The Logician waved him back to his seat.

'Lucky I'm the boss,' he said. 'Those priests of mine wouldn't stand for this if they had a thing to say about it. But what could they do without me? *I'm* the Logician. Sit down.' He pulled up a seat opposite, took an odd-looking object from his pocket – it was a pipe – and stuffed it with tobacco.

'Grow it and cure it myself,' he said. 'Look, Hale. This phony stuff is O.K. for the Keeps, but I don't see the point of handing you a line.'

Hale was staring. 'But ... the Temple ... this is the Temple of Truth? You mean it's all—'

'Phony? Nope. It's on the level. Trouble is, the truth don't always come out dignified. Those old statues of Truth – naked, she was. Well, she had the figger for it. But look at me, now. I'd be a sight. There was a time when we played it straight; it didn't work. People just thought I was giving an opinion. Fair enough; I look like an ordinary guy. But I'm not. I'm a trick mutant. Come full circle. We went around through Plato and Aristotle and Bacon and Korzybski and the truth-machines – and end up right where we started, the best method in the world to use logic on human problems. I know the answers. The right ones.'

Hale found it difficult to understand. 'But ... you can't be infallible ... don't you use any system?'

'Tried the systems,' the Logician said. 'Lots of four-bit words. Boils down to one thing. Horse sense.'

Hale blinked.

The Logician kindled his pipe. 'I'm over a thousand years old,' he said. 'Kind of hard to believe, I know. But I told you I was a trick mutant. Son, I was born on Earth. I can remember the atomic wars. Not the first ones – that was how I come to be born, my parents got in the way of some secondary radiations. I'm about as close to a real Immortal as they come. But my main talent – do you remember reading about Ben the Prophet? No? Well, he was only one of a lot of prophets, in those days. Plenty of people guessed what was coming. Didn't take much logic. I was Ben the Prophet. Lucky some of the right people listened and started colonising Venus. I came along. Time the Earth blew up, I was right here being studied. Some technicians found out my brain was a little queer. There was a new sense in it, instinct, or whatever – nobody's ever found out exactly what it is. But it's the same thing that made the thinking-machines give the right answers – when they did! Brother, I just can't help giving the right answers!'

'You're a thousand years old?' Hale asked, fastening on the single point.

'Nigh. I've seen 'em come and go. I've seen how I could get to rule the whole roost, if I wanted to. But preserve me from that! I can see most of the answers to that, and I don't like any of 'em. I just sit here in the Temple of Truth and answer questions.'

Hale said blankly, 'We've always thought . . . there was a machine—'

'Sure, I know. Funny people will believe what a machine tells 'em, where they won't believe a fella like themselves. Or maybe it isn't funny at all. Look, son – no matter how you cut it, I know the answers. I turn over the information in my head, and pretty soon I see what they add up to. Common sense is all. Only requirement is that I've got to know all about you and your problem.'

'Then you can read the future.'

'Too many variables,' the Logician said. 'By the way, I hope you won't shoot off your mouth about me. The priests won't like it. Every time I show myself to some client and come off my high horse, they raise the temple roof. Not that it matters. You can talk if you want; nobody'd believe the infallible oracle's anything but a super-machine.' He grinned cheerfully. 'Main thing is, son, I got an idea. I told you I add up the numbers and get the answer. Well, sometimes I get more than one answer. Why don't you go landside?'

'*What?*'

'Why not?' the Logician said. 'You're pretty tough. Course you may get killed. Probably will, I'll say. But you'll go down fighting. Not much fighting you can do in the Keeps, for anything you believe in. There's some other people feel the way you do. A few Free Companions, I think – Immortals too. Look them up. Go landside.'

Hale said, 'It's impossible.'

'The Companies had their forts, didn't they?'

'It took gangs of technicians to keep the jungle out. And the animals. We had to keep waging a continual war against landside. Besides, the forts – there isn't much left of them now.'

'Pick one out and rebuild it.'

'But – then what?'

'Maybe you can be top man,' the Logician said quietly. 'Maybe you can get to be top man – on Venus.'

The silence drew on and on. Hale's face changed.

'Good enough,' the Logician said, getting up. He put out his hand. 'My name's Ben Crowell, by the way. Come see me if you run into trouble. Or I might even drop in to see you. If I do, don't let on I'm the great brain.' He winked.

He shambled out, sucking at his pipe.

Life in the Keeps was very much like a game of chess. In the barnyard, among fowls, social precedence is measured by length of tenancy. Extension in time is wealth. Pawns have a low life-expectancy; knights and bishops and castles have more. Socially, there was a three-dimensional democracy and a temporal autocracy. There was a reason why the long-lived Biblical patriarchs achieved power. They could hold power.

In the Keeps, the Immortals simply knew more than the non-immortals. Psychologically a curious displacement became evident. Immortals weren't worshipped as gods in those practical days, but there was definite displacement. Parents have one faculty a child cannot have: maturity. The plus factor. Experience. *Age*.

So there was displacement. Unconsciously the short-lived peoples of the Keeps began to look with dependence upon the Immortals. They knew more, of course. And, too, they were older.

Let George do it.

Besides, it is a regrettably human trait to disclaim unpleasant responsibilities. For centuries the trend had been away from individualism. Social responsibility had been carried to the point where everyone, theoretically, was his brother's keeper.

Eventually they all formed a circle and collapsed gracefully into one another's arms.

The Immortals, who knew what long, empty centuries were ahead of them, took pains to insure that those centuries would not be so empty. They learned. They studied. They had plenty of time.

As they gained in knowledge and experience, they began to take the responsibilities easily delegated to them by the collapsing multitudes.

It was a stable enough culture – for a moribund race.

He was always getting into mischief.

Anything new was fascinating to him. The Harker chromosomes took care of that. His name, though, was Sam Reed.

He kept fighting the invisible bars that he knew prisoned him. There were fourscore and ten of them. Something in his mind, something illogical and inherited, kept rebelling, seeking expression. *What can you do in ninety years?*

Once he tried to get a job in the great hydroponic gardens. His blunt, coarse face, his bald head, his precocious mind – these made it possible for him to lie convincingly about his age. He managed it for a while, till his curiosity got the better of him, and he began experimenting with botanical forced cultures. Since he knew nothing about it, he spoiled a good-sized crop.

Before that, though, he had discovered a blue flower in one of the tanks, and it reminded him of the woman he had seen at carnival. Her gown had been exactly the same colour. He asked one of the attendants about it.

'Blasted weeds,' the man said. 'Can't keep 'em out of the tanks. Hundreds of years, and they still show up. We don't have much trouble with these, though. It's the crab grass that's worst.' He pulled the weed and tossed it aside. Sam rescued it and asked more questions later. It was, he learned, a violet. The unobtrusive, pretty little plant was a far cry from the glamorous hybrid flowers grown in other sections of Hydroponics. He kept it till it broke into dust. He kept its memory after that, as he kept the memory of the woman in the violet-blue gown.

One day he ran away to Canada Keep, far across the Sea of Shallows. He had never been outside a Keep before, and was fascinated as the great, transparent globe drove upwards through the bubbling water. He went with a man whom he had bribed – with stolen money – to pretend to be his father. But after he reached Canada Keep he never saw the man again.

He was ingenious at twelve. He worked out various ways to earn a living. But none satisfied him. They were all too dull. Blaze Harker had known what he was doing when he had left the boy's mind untouched in a stunted, warped body.

It was warped only by the aesthetic standards of the time. The long-limbed, tall Immortals had set the standard of beauty. There came to be a stigma of ugliness attached to the stocky, blunt-featured, thick boned, short-lived ones.

There was a tough, violent seed of unfulfilment within Sam. It drove him. It couldn't develop normally, for it was seed of the Immortals, and he obviously was no Immortal. He simply could not qualify for work that might take training of a hundred years or more. Even fifty years training—!

He did it the hard way, and the inevitable way. He got his mentor, his Chiron-Fagin, after he met the Slider.

The Slider was a fat, wicked old man without any name. He had bushy white hair, a carbuncled red nose, and a philosophy of his own. He never proffered advice, but he gave it when it was asked.

'People want fun,' he told the boy. 'Most of 'em. And they don't want to look at a thing that hurts their tender feelings. Use your head, kid. Thieving's out. Best to make yourself useful to people who've got power. Now you take Jim Sheffield's gang. Jim caters to the right people. Don't ask questions; do what you're told – but first get the right connections.'

He sniffled and blinked his watery eyes at Sam.

'I spoke to Jim about you. Go see him. Here's the place.' He thrust a plastic disc at the boy. 'I wouldn't of got you out of that scrape if I hadn't seen something in you. Go see Jim.'

He stopped Sam at the door.

'You'll get along. Likewise, you won't forget old Slider, eh? Some people have. I can make trouble as easy as I can do favours.'

Sam left the fat, malignant old man sniffling and chuckling.

He went to see Jim Sheffield. He was fourteen then, strong, short, scowling. He found Sheffield stronger and larger. Sheffield was seventeen, a graduate of the Slider's twisted school, an independent, shrewd businessman whose gang was already becoming known. The human factor was vital for Keep intrigue. It wasn't merely politics; the mores of the era were as punctilious and complicated as the social life of Machiavelli's Italy. The straight thrust of the knife was not only illegal but in poor taste. Intrigue was the thing. In the continually shifting balance of power, the man who could outwit an opponent, wind him in webs of his own spinning, and force him to ruin himself – that was the game.

Sheffield's gang free-lanced. Sam Reed's – he didn't know the name Harker except to identify it with one of the great Families of his old Keep – first job was to go undersea, with one more experienced companion, and collect some specimens of bluish algae, illegal within the Keeps. When he got back through the secret lock, he was surprised to find the Slider waiting, with a portable ray-mechanism already set up. The little room had been sealed off.

The Slider was wearing protective armour. His voice came through a diaphragm.

'Stay right there, boys. Catch this.' He tossed a spray-gun to Sam. 'Now spray that plastibulb. It's sealed, isn't it? Right. Spray it all over – fine. Now turn around slowly.'

'Wait a minute—' said the other boy.

The Slider sniffled. 'Do what I tell you or I'll break your skinny neck,' he said conversationally. 'Raise your arms. Turn slowly, while I use the ray on you . . . that's it.'

Afterwards, the three of them met Jim Sheffield. Jim was subdued but angry. He tried to argue with the Slider.

The Slider sniffled and rumpled his white hair.

'You shut up,' he said. 'Too big for your boots, you're getting to be. If you'd remember to ask me when you get into something new, you'd save yourself trouble.' He tapped the black-painted globe Sam had set on the table. 'This algae – know why it's forbidden in the Keeps? Didn't your patron tell you to be careful when he commissioned you to get the stuff?'

Sheffield's broad mouth twisted. 'I was careful!'

'The stuff's safe to handle under lab conditions,' the Slider said. 'Only then. It's a metal-eater. Dissolves metal. Once it's been treated with the right reagents, it's innocuous. But raw like this, it could get loose and cause a lot of trouble here – and it'd be traced back to you, and you'd land in Therapy. See? If you'd come to me first, I'd have told you to have this ultraviolet set up, to burn the daylights out of any algae the boys might bring in stuck to their suits. Next time I won't be so easy on you. *I* don't want to go to Therapy, Jim.'

The old man looked innocuous enough, but Sheffield's rebellious stare wavered and fell. With a word of agreement he rose, picked up the globe and went out, beckoning to the other boys. Sam waited for a moment.

The Slider winked at him.

'You make a lot of mistakes when you don't get advice, kid,' he said.

These were only episodes among many like them along the course of his outward life. Inwardly too he was precocious, amoral, rebellious. Above all, rebellious. He rebelled against the shortness of life that made learning seem futile to him when he thought of the Immortals. He rebelled against his own body, thick and stocky and plebeian. He rebelled obscurely, and without knowing the reasons himself, against all that he had irrevocably become in that first week of his life.

There have always been angry men in the world. Sometimes the anger, like Elijah's, is the fire of God, and the man lives in history as a saint and a reformer whose anger moved mountains to improve the lot of mankind. Sometimes the anger is destructive, and great war-leaders rise to devastate whole nations. Angers like that find outward expression and need not consume their hosts.

But Sam Reed's anger was a rage against intangibles like time and destiny, and the only target it could find to explode against was himself. Granted that such anger is not normal in a man. But Sam Reed was not normal. His father before him could not have been normal, or he would never have taken such disproportionate vengeance on his son. A flaw somewhere in the Harker blood was responsible for the bitter rage in which father and son alike lived out their days, far separate, raging against far different things, but in armed rebellion all their lives, both of them, against life itself.

Sam went through many inward phases that would have astonished the Slider and Jim Sheffield and the others with whom he worked in those days. Because his mind was more complex than theirs, he was able to live on many more levels than they, and able to conceal it. From the day he first discovered the great libraries of the Keeps he became a passionate reader. He was never an intellectual man, and the unrest in him prevented him from ever mastering any one field of knowledge and so rising above his station by the one superiority he possessed – his mind.

But he devoured books as fire devours fuel, as his own discontent devoured himself. He raced through whole courses of reading on any subject that caught his quick, glancing fancy, and emerged with knowledge of that subject stored uselessly away in a chamber of the uselessly capacious brain. Sometimes the knowledge helped him to promote a fraud or consummate a murder. More often it simply lay dormant in the mind that had been meant for the storage of five hundred years' experience, and was doomed to extinction in less than a century.

One great trouble with Sam Reed was that he didn't know what really ailed him. He had long struggles with his own conscience, in which he tried to rationalise his mind out of its own unconscious knowledge of its lost heritage. For a time he hoped to find among books some answer . . .

In those early days he sought and found in them the respite of escapism which he later tried in so many other forms – drugs among them, a few women, much restless shifting from Keep to Keep – until he came at last to the one great, impossible task which was to resolve his destiny and which he faced with such violent reluctance.

For the next decade and a half he read, quietly and rapidly, through the libraries of whichever Keep he found himself in, as a smooth undercurrent to whatever illicit affair he might currently be involved with. His profound contempt for the people he victimised, directly or indirectly, was one with the contempt he felt for his associates. Sam Reed was not in any sense a nice man.

Even to himself he was unpredictable. He was the victim of his own banked fire of self-hatred, and when that fire burst forth, Sam Reed's lawlessness took very direct forms. His reputation became tricky. No one trusted him very far – how could they, when he didn't even trust himself? – but his hand and his mind were so expert that his services were in considerable demand among those willing to take the chance that their careful plans might blow up in bloody murder if Sam Reed's temper got the better of him. Many were willing. Many found him rather fascinating.

For life in the Keeps had levelled off to an evenness which is not native to the mind of man. In many, many people something like an unrecognised flicker of the rebellion which consumed Sam Reed burned restlessly, coming to the surface in odd ways. Psychological projective screens took strange forms, such as the wave of bloodthirsty ballads which was sweeping the Keeps on a high tide of popularity when Sam was in his formative years. Less strange, but as indicative, was the fad for near-worship of the old Free-Companion days, the good old days of man's last romantic period.

Deep in human minds lies the insistence that war is glamorous, although it never can have been except to a select few, and for nearly a thousand years now had been wholly terrible. Still the tradition clung on – perhaps because terror itself is perversely fascinating, though most of us have to translate it into other terms before we can admire it.

The Free Companions, who had been serious, hard-working men operating a warfare machine, became swaggering heroes in the public fancy and many a man sighed for a day he thought he had missed by a period of heartbreaking briefness.

They sang the wailing ballads the Free Companions had carried over, in changed forms, from the pioneer days on Venus, which in turn had derived from the unimaginably different days on Old Earth. But they sang them with a difference now. Synthetic Free Companions in inaccurate costumes performed for swaying audiences that followed their every intonation without guessing how wrong they were.

The emphasis was off, in words and rhythm alike. For the Keeps were stagnant, and stagnant people do not know how to laugh. Their humour is subtle and devious, evoking the snigger rather than the guffaw. Slyness and innuendo was the basis of their oblique humour, not laughter.

For laughter is cruel and open. The hour was on its way when men would sing again the old bloodthirsty ballads as they were meant to be sung, and laugh again with the full-throated heartiness that comes from the need to laugh – at one's own misfortunes. To laugh because the only alternative is tears – and tears mean defeat. Only pioneers laugh in the primitive fullness of the sense. No one in the Keeps in those days had so much as heard real laughter in its cruelty and courage, except perhaps the very eldest among them, who remembered earlier days.

Sam Reed along with the rest accepted the Free Companions – extinct almost as Old Earth's dinosaurs, and for much the same reason – as the epitome of glamorous romance. But he understood the reasons behind that emotional acceptance, and could jeer at himself for doing it. It was not Free Companionship but free endeavour which, in the last analysis, enchanted them all.

They didn't want it, really. It would have terrified and repelled most of these people who so gracefully collapsed into the arms of anyone willing to offer them moral and mental support. But nostalgia is graceful too, and they indulged themselves in it to the full.

Sam read of the pioneer days on Venus with a sort of savage longing. A man could use all of himself against an adversary like the ravening planet the newcomers had fought. He read of Old Earth with a burning nostalgia for the wider horizons it had offered. He hummed the old songs over to himself and tried to imagine what a free sky must have looked like, terrifyingly studded with the visible worlds of space.

His trouble was that his world was a simple place, made intricate only artificially, for the sake of intricate intrigue, so that one couldn't hurl oneself wholeheartedly into conflict against a barrier – because the barrier was artificial and would collapse. You had to support it with one hand while you battered it with the other.

The only thing that could have offered Sam an opponent worthy of his efforts was time, the long, complex stretch of centuries which he knew he would never live. So he hated men, women, the world, himself. He fought them all indiscriminately and destructively for lack of an opponent he could engage with in a constructive fight.

He fought them for forty years.

One pattern held true through all that time, though he recognised it only dimly and without much interest. Blue was a colour that could touch him as nothing else could. He rationalised that, in part, by remembering the stories of Old Earth and a sky inconceivably coloured blue.

Here water hemmed one in everywhere. The upper air was heavy with moisture, the clouds above it hung gravid with moisture and the grey seas which were a blanket above the Keeps seemed scarcely wetter than clouds and air. So the blueness of that lost sky was one in his mind with the thought of freedom . . .

But the first girl he took in free-marriage was a little dancer from one of the Way cafés, who had worn a scanty costume of blue feathers when he saw her first. She had blue eyes, not so blue as the feathers or the unforgotten skies of

Earth, but blue. Sam rented a little apartment for them on a back street in Montana Keep, and for six months or so they bickered no more than most domestic couples.

One morning he came in from an all-night job with the Sheffield gang and smelled something strange the moment he pushed the door open. A heavy sweetness in the air, and a sharp, thick, already familiar acridness that not many Keep men would recognise these effete days.

The little dancer lay slumped against the far wall, already stiffening in her slump. Where her face had been was a great palely tinted blossom whose petals gripped like a many-fingered hand, plastering the flower tight against her skull. It had been a yellow flower, but the veins in the petals were bright red now, and more red ran down beneath the blossom over the girl's blue dress.

Beside her on the floor lay the florist's box, spilling green tissue, in which someone had sent her the flower.

Sam never knew who had done it, or why. It might have been some enemy of his, taking revenge for past indignities, it might even have been one of his friends – he suspected the Slider for a while – afraid of the hold the girl was getting over him, to divert him from profitable business in the dark hours. Or it might have been one of the girl's dancing rivals, for the bitterest sort of struggle went on constantly among people of that profession for the too-few jobs that were open just now in Montana Keep.

Sam made inquiries, found out what he wanted to know, and exacted dispassionate justice from people who may or may not have been guilty. Sam was not very concerned with that. The girl had not been a particularly nice girl in any sense, any more than Sam was a nice man. She had been convenient, and she had blue eyes. It was his own reputation Sam was upholding when he did what he did about her murder.

After that other girls came and went. Sam exchanged the little back-street apartment for a better one in a quieter neighbourhood. Then he finished an exceptionally profitable job and forsook girl and apartment for almost elegant quarters high up in a tower looking out over the central Way. He found a pretty blue-eyed singer to share it with him.

By the time our story opens he had three apartments in three Keeps, one quite expensive, one average, and one deliberately chosen down among the port loading streets in the dimmest section of Virginia Keep. The occupants matched the apartments. Sam was an epicure in his own way. By now he could afford to be.

In the expensive apartment he had two rooms sacred to his privacy, stocked with a growing library of books and music, and an elaborate selection of liquors and drugs. This was not known among his business associates. He went here by another name and was generally supposed to be a commercial traveller from some unspecified but distant Keep. It was as close as Sam Reed could come to the life Sam Harker would have led by rights.

> *The Queen of Air and Darkness*
> *Begins to shrill and cry,*
> *O young man, O my slayer,*
> *Tomorrow you shall die . . .*

On the first day of the annual carnival which ushered in the last year of Sam Reed's life, he sat across a small, turning table and spoke practically of love and money with a girl in pink velvet. It must have been near noon, for the light filtering down through the Sea of Shallows and the great dome of the Keep fell at its dim maximum upon them. But all clocks were stopped for the three-day Carnival so that no one need worry about time.

To anyone not reared from childhood upon such phenomena as a merry-go-round café, the motion of the city around Sam would have been sickening. The whole room turned slowly to slow music within its transparent circular walls. The tables turned each upon its own axis, carrying a perimeter of chairs with it. Behind the girl's cloud of hair Sam could see all of the Keep spreading out and out below them and wheeling solemnly in parade past his unheeding vantage point.

A drift of coloured perfume floated past them in a long, airy ribbon lifted and dropped by the air currents, Sam felt tiny spatters of scented moisture beading his face as the pink fog drifted past. He dispelled it with an impatient fanning of the hand and narrowed his eyes at the girl across from him.

'Well?' he said.

The girl smiled and bent her head over the tall, narrow, double-horned lyre, streaming with coloured ribbons, which she embraced with one arm as she sat there. Her eyes were gentian blue, shadowed with lashes so heavy she seemed to look up at him through them from black eyes.

'I have another number in a minute,' she said. 'I'll tell you later.'

'You'll tell me now,' Sam declared, not harshly as he would have spoken to most other women, but firmly. The expensive apartment, high up at the exclusive peak of the Keep residential section, was vacant just now, and if Sam had his way this girl would be the next dweller there. Perhaps a permanent dweller. He was aware of an uneasy stir in his mind whenever he thought of Rosathe. He didn't like any woman to affect him this deeply.

Rosathe smiled at him. She had a small, soft mouth and a cloud of soft dark hair cut short and haloed all over her head like a dark mist. There was unexpected humour in her face sometimes, a rather disconcerting intelligence behind the gentian eyes, and she sang in a voice like the pink velvet of her gown, a small soft plaintive voice that brushed the nerves with pleasant tremors.

Sam was afraid of her. But being Sam Reed, he was reaching for this particular nettle. He dealt with danger by confronting it, and if there was any way of getting this velvety creature out of his mind, it would be through surfeit, not by trying to forget her. He proposed to surfeit himself, if he could, as soon as possible.

Rosathe plucked one string of the lyre with a thoughtful forefinger. She said, 'I heard something interesting on the grapevine this morning. Jim Sheffield doesn't like you any more. Is it true, Sam?'

Sam said without heat, 'I asked you a question.'

'I asked you one.'

'All right, it's true. I'll leave you a year's income in my will if Jim gets me first – is that what you're after?'

She flushed and twanged the string so that it disappeared in violent vibration. 'I could slap you, Sam Reed. You know I can earn my own money.'

He sighed. She could, which made it rather more difficult to argue with her. Rosathe was a more than popular singer. If she came to him it wouldn't be for the money. That was another thing that made her dangerous to his peace of mind.

The slow music which had been matching the room's slow turns paused. Then a stronger beat rang through the air, making all the perfume drifts shiver. Rosathe stood up, hoisting the tall, narrow lyre against her hip.

'That's me,' she said. 'I'll think it over, Sam. Give me a few days. I might be very bad for you.'

'I know you'll be bad for me. Go sing your song. I'll see you after Carnival, but not for an answer. I know the answer. You'll come.'

She laughed and walked away from him, sweeping her hand across the strings and humming her song as she went. Sam sat there watching, seeing heads turn and faces light up in anticipation.

But before her song was finished, he got up and went out of the turning room, hearing behind him the velvety little voice diminishing in plaintive lament for a fabled Genevieve. Every note was delicately true as she slid up and down the difficult flats which gave the old, old song its minor wailing.

'*Oh Genevieve, sweet Genevieve, the days may come, the days may go . . .*' wailed Rosathe, watching Sam's broad red-velvet back out of the room. When she had finished the song she went quickly to her dressing-room and flipped the switch of the communicator, giving Sheffield's call-signal.

'Listen, Jim,' she said rapidly when his dark, scowling face swam into the screen. 'I was just talking to Sam, and . . .'

If Sam could have listened, he probably would have killed her then, instead of much later. But, of course, he didn't hear. At the moment the conversation began, he was walking into an important coincidence which was a turning point in his life.

The coincidence was another woman in blue. Sauntering down the moving Way, she lifted an arm and threw the corner of her filmy blue robe over her hair like a veil. The motion and the colour caught Sam's eye, and he stopped so suddenly that men on both sides jolted into him, and one turned with a growl, ready to make a quarrel out of it. Then he got a better glimpse of the granite face, long-jawed, with lines of strain etched from nose to mouth, and for no clear reason turned away, giving up the idea.

Because the image of Rosathe was still vivid in his mind, Sam looked at the woman with less enthusiasm than he might have shown a few days earlier. But deep in his mind buried memories stirred and he stood motionless, staring. The breeze of the sliding Way rippled the veil above her face so that shadows moved in her eyes, blue shadows from the blue veil in the heavily shadowed blue of her eyes. She was very beautiful.

Sam brushed aside a haze of pink carnival perfume, hesitated – which was not normal to him – and then hitched his gilded belt with a gesture of decision and went forward with the long motion of a stride, but his feet falling softly, as was his habit. He didn't know why the woman's face and her violet-blue robe disturbed him. He had forgotten a great deal since the long-ago Carnival when he saw her last.

At Carnival there are no social barriers – in theory. Sam would have spoken anyhow. He came up below her on the sliding street and looked unsmilingly into her face. On a level she would have been taller than he. She was very slender, very elegant, with a look of graceful weariness much cultivated in the Keep. Sam could not know that she had set the style, or that with her weariness and grace were native, not assumed.

The blue robe was wrapped tight over a tighter sheath of flexible gold that gleamed through the filmy blue. Her hair was an extravagant cascade of blue-black ringlets drawn back from her lovely, narrow face and gathered through a broad gold ring at the crown of her head, so that they fell free from the band in a rich cascade to her waist.

With deliberate barbarism her ears had been pierced, and she wore a hooped gold bell through each lobe. It was part of the current fad that aped the vitality of barbarism. Next season might see a gold ring through the nose, and this woman would wear one with the same air of elegant disdain she turned now upon Sam Reed.

He ignored it. He said in a voice of flat command, 'You can come with me now,' and he held out his crooked arm shoulder-high before him, in invitation.

She tilted her head back slightly and looked at him down her narrow nose. She may have been smiling. It was impossible to tell, because she had the same full, delicately curved mouth so many Egyptian portrait heads once had, with the smile implicit in the contour of the lips. If she did smile, it was in disdain. The heavy waterfall of her ringlets seemed to pull her head farther back on the delicate slender neck, so that she looked down on Sam partly in weariness, partly in scorn, partly in sheer contempt for him as he was.

She stood for a prolonged moment, looking at him down her nose, so still the bells in her pierced ears did not jingle.

For Sam, at first glance merely a squat plebeian like the rest of the lower classes, at second glance offered many contrasts to the discerning eye. He had lived nearly forty years now with his all-devouring anger; if he had come to terms with it, it consumed him inwardly all the same. The marks of that violence were on his face, so that even in repose he looked like a man straining against heavy odds. It gave a thrust and drive to his features which went far towards redeeming their heaviness.

The fact that he had no hair was another curious thing. Baldness was ordinary enough, but this this man was so complely hairless that he did not seem bald at all. His bare skull had a classical quality, and hair would look anachronistic now upon the well-shaped curve of his head. Much harm had been done the infant of forty years past but in some haste and with some carelessness, because of the Happy-Cloak, so that things remained like the well-shaped ears set close against a well-shaped skull, and the good lines of the jaw and neck which were Harker lines in essence, though well disguised.

The thick neck was no Harker neck, vanishing into a gaudy crimson shirt. No Harker would have dressed even for Carnival in crimson velvet from head to foot, with a gilded belt supporting a gilded holster. And yet, if a Harker had put this costume on – somehow, subtly, this is the way a Harker would have looked in it.

Thick-bodied, barrel-chested, rolling a little with a wide stride when he walked, nevertheless there was in Sam Reed a full tide of Harker blood that showed in subtle ways about him. No one could have said why or how, but he wore his clothes with an air and moved with an assurance that was almost elegance in spite of the squatness which the upper classes so scorned.

The velvet sleeve fell back from his proffered arm. He stood there steady, holding the crooked forearm out, looking up over it at the woman with his eyes narrowed, steel-colour in his ruddy face.

After a moment, moved by no impulse she could name, the woman let her lips tuck in at the corners in an acknowledged smile, disdainful, condescending. She moved one shoulder to shrug her robe aside and stretched out a slender arm and a very slender, small-boned hand with plain, thick gold bands pushed down well at the base of every finger. Very delicately she laid the hand on Sam Reed's arm and stepped down beside him. On that thick forearm, hazed with red hair, the muscles interlacing in a hard column towards the wrist, her hand looked waxen and unreal. She felt the muscles tighten beneath her touch, and her smile grew even more condescending.

Sam said, 'Your hair wasn't black the last time I saw you at Carnival.'

She gave him an aloof glance down her delicate thin nose. She did not yet trouble herself to speak. Sam looked at her unsmilingly, inspecting her feature by feature as if this were some portrait and not a breathing, disdainful woman who was here beside him only by a precarious whim.

'It was yellow,' he said finally, with decision. The memory was clear now, wrenched out of the past in almost complete detail, so that he realised how vividly it must have impressed him at the time. 'That was – thirty years ago. You wore blue on that day, too. I remember it very well.'

The woman said disinterestedly, her head turned aside so that she seemed to be addressing someone at her other shoulder, 'That was my daughter's daughter, I expect.'

It jolted Sam. He was well aware of the long-lived aristocracy, of course. But he had never spoken directly to one before. To a man who counts in decades his own life and those of all his friends, the sudden impact of a life that spans centuries unimpaired must strike a disconcerting blow.

He laughed, a short bark of sound. The woman turned her head and looked at him with faint interest, because she had never before heard one of these lower classes make quite such a sound as that, self-assured, indifferent, the laugh of a confident man who doesn't trouble himself with manners.

Many people before Kedre Walton had found Sam rather mysteriously fascinating. Few had Kedre's perception. She knew before very long exactly why. It was the same quality that she and the world of fashion groped for when they hung barbaric ornaments through the pierced flesh of their ears and sang the wailing, forthright ballads of bloodshed and slaughter which were only words to them – yet. A quality of vitality and virility which the world of man had lost, and hungered for obscurely, and would not accept when it was next offered them, if they could avoid the gift.

She looked at him scornfully, turned her head a little to let the black cascading curls caress her shoulders, and said coldly, 'Your name?'

His red brows met above his nose. 'You don't need to know,' he told her with deliberate rudeness.

For an instant she froze. Then, slowly, an almost imperceptible warming seemed to flow down her limbs, relaxing everything about her, muscles, nerves, even the chill of her aloofness. She drew a deep, silent breath and the ringed fingers which had only touched his arm until now moved deliberately, opened out so that her palm lay against his forearm. She let the palm slide gently forward towards the thickly tapered wrist, her rings cold and catching a little in the heavy red hair that thatched his arm.

She said without looking at him, 'You may tell me about yourself – until you bore me.'

'Are you easily bored?'

'Very easily.'

He looked her up and down, liking what he saw, and he thought he understood it. In forty years Sam Reed had gained an immense store of casual knowledge about the Keeps – not only the ordinary life that anyone could see, but the devious, secret methods a race uses to whip its lagging interest in living when life has gone on longer than humans can easily adjust to. He thought he could hold her interest.

'Come along,' he said.

That was the first day of Carnival. On the third and last day, Sam got his first intimation from her that this casual liaison might not come to an end with the festival. It rather surprised him, and he was not pleased. For one thing, there was Rosathe. And for another – well, Sam Reed was locked in the confines of one prison he could never escape, but he would not submit to gyves within the confines of his cell.

Hanging without gravity in empty darkness, they were watching a three-dimensional image. This particular pleasure was expensive. It required skilled operators and at least one robot plane, equipped with special long-view lenses and televisor. Somewhere far above a continent on Venus the plane was hanging, focused on the scene it had tracked down.

A beast fought with a plant.

It was enormous, that beast, and magnificently equipped for fighting. But its great wet body was wetter now with the blood that ran from gashes opened all over it by the sabre-thorned vines. They lashed out with calculating accuracy, flirting drops of venom that flashed in the wet grey air. Music, deftly improvised to fit the pulse of the battle, crashed around them.

Kedre touched a stud. The music softened to a whisper.

Somewhere far above the plane hovered on ignored above the battle, the improviser fingered his keys unheard. Kedre, in the darkness, turned her head with a faint silken rustling of unseen hair, and said, 'I made a mistake.'

Sam was impatient. He had wanted to see the finish of the fight.

'What?' he demanded brusquely.

'You.' Out of the darkness a finger brushed his cheek lightly, with casual possessiveness. 'I underestimated you, Sam. Or overestimated. Or both.'

He shook his head to evade the finger. He reached out in the dark, feeling his hand slip across a smooth, curved cheek and into the back-drawn hair. He found the ring through which the showering curls were drawn and seized a handful of ringlets, shaking her head roughly from side to side. The hair moved softly over his forearm.

'That's enough of that,' he said. 'I'm not your pet dog. What do you mean?'

She laughed. 'If you weren't so *young*,' she said insultingly.

He released her with such abruptness he unsteadied her on the divan beside him, and she laid a hand on his shoulder to catch herself. He was silent. Then in a remote voice he asked, 'Just how old are you?'

'Two hundred and twenty years.'

'And I bore you. I'm a child.'

Her laughter was flattering. 'Not a child, Sam – not a child! But our viewpoints are so different. No, you don't bore me. That's the trouble, or part of it. I wish you did. Then I could leave you tonight and forget all this had ever happened. But there's something about you, Sam – I don't know.' Her voice grew reflective. Behind it in the darkness the music swelled to a screaming crescendo, but very softly, a muted death-note as one adversary or the other triumphed far up in the swamplands overhead.

'If you were the man you look,' Kedre Walton was saying. 'If you only were! You have a fine mind, Sam – it's a pity you must die too soon to use it. I wish you weren't one of the commons. I'd marry you – for a while.'

'How does it feel,' Sam asked her savagely, 'to be a god?'

'I'm sorry. That was patronising, wasn't it? And you deserve better. How does it feel? Well, we *are* immortals, of a sort. We can't help that. It feels – good, and frightening. It's a responsibility. We do much more than just play, you know. I spent my first hundred years maturing and studying, travelling, learning people and things. Then for a hundred years it was intrigue I liked. Learning how to pull strings to make the Council see things my way, for instance. A sort of jujitsu of the mind – touch a man's vanity and make his ego react in just the way I mean it to. I think you know those tricks well enough yourself – only you'll never live long enough to master the art as I know it. It's a pity. There's something about you that I . . . I . . . never mind.'

'Don't say again you'd marry me. I wouldn't have you.'

'Oh yes you would. And I might try it, at that, even if you are a common. I might—'

Sam leaned forward across her knees and groped for the light switch. The small, cushioned room sprang into illumination as the switch clicked, and Kedre blinked her beautiful ageless eyes and laughed half in protest and half in surprise.

'Sam! I'm blind. Don't do that.' She reached to extinguish the light. Sam caught her hand, folding the fingers together over their heavy golden rings.

'No. Listen. I'm leaving you right now and I never want to see you again. Understand? You've got nothing I want.' He rose abruptly.

There was something almost serpentine in the way she moved to her feet in one smooth, swift flow, light glinting on the overlapping golden sequins that sheathed her.

'Wait. No, wait! Forget about all this, Sam. I want to show you something. That was just talk, before. I needed to sound you out. Sam, I want you to come with me to Haven. I have a problem for you.'

He looked at her coldly, his eyes steel splinters between the ruddy lashes, under the rough, ruddy brows. He named the sum his listening would cost her. She curled her lip at him and said she would pay it, the subtle Egyptian smile denting in the corners of her mouth.

He followed her out of the room.

Haven approximated man's half-forgotten birthplace. It was Earth, but an Earth glamorised and inaccurately remembered. It was a gigantic half-dome honeycombed with cells that made a shell arched over a great public room below. Each cell could be blocked off, or a rearrangement of penetrating rays could give you the illusion of being in the midst of an immense, crowded room. Or you could use the architect's original plan and enjoy the illusion of a terrestrial background.

True, palms and pines seemed to grow out of the same surrogate soil, grapes and roses and blossoming fruit trees shouldered one another; but since these were merely clever images they did not matter except to the purist. And only scholars really knew the difference. Seasons had become an exotic piece of history.

It was a strange and glamorous thought – the rhythmic equinoxes, earth's face changing from green and brown to glittering blue-white, and then the magic of pale green blades pushing up and green buds breaking from the trees, and all this naturally, inevitably, unlike the controlled growth of hydroponics.

Kedre Walton and Sam Reed came to Haven. From the stage where they entered they could look up at the immense, shining hemisphere, crowded with glittering cells like fragments of a bright, exploded dream, shifting and floating, rising and falling in the intricate light-currents. Down below, very far away, was the bar, a serpentine black shape where men and women made centipede-legs for its twisting body.

Kedre spoke into a microphone. One of the circling cells moved in its orbit and bumped gently against the landing stage. They stepped inside, and the swaying underfoot told Sam that they were afloat again.

Leaning among cushions by the low table were a man and a woman. Sam knew the man by sight. He was Zachariah Harker, oldest of one of the great Immortal families. He was a big man, long-boned, fine of line, his face a curious mixture of – not age – but experience, maturity, contrasting with the ageless youth that kept his features fresh and unlined. He had a smoothness that came from within, smooth assurance, smooth courtesy, smooth and quiet wisdom.

The woman—

'Sari, my dear,' Kedre said, 'I've brought you a guest. Sari is my granddaughter. Zachariah, this is . . . I don't know his name. He wouldn't tell me.'

Sari Walton had the delicate, disdainful face that was apparently a family characteristic. Her hair was an improbable green-gold, falling with careful disorder loose over her bare shoulders. She wore a tight garment of the very fine fur of a landside beast, plucked down to the undercoat which was as short and thick as velvet and patterned with shadowy stripes like a tiger. Thin and flexible as cloth, it sheathed her tightly to the knees and lay in broad folds about her ankles.

The two Immortals looked up, surprise showing briefly on their faces. Sam was aware of a quick surge of resentment that they should be surprised. He felt suddenly clumsy, conscious of his thick body and his utter unlikeness to these aristocrats. And he felt, too, his immaturity. As a child resents his elders, Sam resented the superior knowledge implicit upon these handsome, quiet features.

'Sit down.' Kedre waved to the cushions. Stiffly Sam lowered himself, accepted a drink, sat watching the averted faces of his hosts with a hot resentment he did not try to hide. Why should he?

Kedre said. 'I was thinking of the Free Companion when I brought him here. He . . . what *is* your name? Or shall I give you one?'

Sullenly Sam told her. She lay back among the cushions, the gold rings gleaming softly on her hand as she raised her drink. She looked at ease, gracefully comfortable, but there was a subtle tension in her that Sam could sense. He wondered if the others could.

'I'd better explain to you first, Sam Reed,' she said, 'that for twenty years now I've been in contemplation.'

He knew what that meant – a sort of intellectual nunnery,

a high religion of the mind, wherein the acolyte retires from the world in an attempt to find – well, what is indescribable when found. Nirvana? No – stasis, perhaps, peace, balance.

He knew somewhat more of the Immortals than they probably suspected. He realised, as well as a short-lived mortal could, how complete the life that will span up to a thousand years must be. The character must be very finely integrated, so that their lives become a sort of close and delicate mosaic, an enormous one, but made up of tiles the same size as those composing an ordinary life. You may live a thousand years, but one second is still exactly one second long at a time. And periods of contemplation were needed to preserve balance.

'What about the Free Companion?' Sam demanded harshly. He knew Robin Hale, last of the warriors, was very much in public interest just now. The deep discontent which was urging popular favour towards the primitive had caught up the Companion, draped him in synthetic glamour, and was eager to follow his project towards colonisation of the landside.

Or they thought they were eager. So far most of the idea was still on paper. When it came to an actual struggle with the ravening fury that was continental Venus – well, realists suspected how different a matter that might turn out to be. But just now Robin Hale's crusade for colonisation was enjoying a glowing, irrational boom.

'What about him?' Zachariah Harker asked. 'It won't work. Do you think it could, Sam Reed?'

Sam gave him a red-browed scowl. He snorted and shook his head, deliberately not troubling to answer aloud. He was conscious of a rising desire to provoke discord among these smoothly civilised Immortals.

'When I came out of contemplation,' Kedre said, 'I found this Free Companion's project the most interesting thing that was happening. And one of the most dangerous. For many reasons, we feel that to attempt colonisation now would be disastrous.'

Sam grunted. 'Why?'

Zachariah Harker leaned across the table to set down his

drink. 'We aren't ready yet,' he said smoothly. 'It will take careful planning, psychologically and technologically. And we're a declining race, Sam Reed. We can't afford to fail. This Free Companion project will fail. It must not be given the chance.' He lifted his brows and regarded Sam thoughtfully.

Sam squirmed. He had an uncomfortable feeling that the deep, quiet gaze could read more upon his face than he wanted anyone to read. You couldn't tell about these people. They had lived too long. Perhaps they knew too much.

He said bluntly, 'You want me to kill him?'

There was silence in the little room for a moment. Sam had an instant's impression that until he spoke they had not thought the thing through quite so far. He felt a swift re-arrangement of ideas going on all about him, as if the Immortals were communicating with one another silently. People who have known each other for so many centuries would surely develop a mild ability at thought-reading, if only through the nuances of facial expression. Silently, then, the three Immortals seemed to exchange confidences above Sam's head.

Then Kedre said, 'Yes. Yes, kill him if you can.'

'It would be the best solution,' Zachariah added slowly. 'To do it now – today. Not later than forty-eight hours from now. The thing's growing too fast to wait. If we can stop him now, there's no one ready to step into his place as figurehead. Tomorrow, someone might. Can you handle it, Sam Reed?'

Sam scowled at them. 'Are you all fools?' he demanded. 'Or do you know more about me than I think?'

Kedre laughed. 'We know. It's been three days, my dear. Do you think I let myself get this involved without knowing the man I was with? I had your name before evening of the first day. I knew your record by the next morning. It's quite safe to intrust a job like this to you. You can handle it and for a price you'll keep quiet.'

Sam flushed. He hated her consciously for the first time then. No man cares to be told he has been made a fool of.

'That,' he said, 'will cost you twice what it would cost anyone else in the Keep.' He named a very high price.

Zachariah said, 'No. We can get—'

'Please, Zachariah.' Kedre lifted her hand. 'I'll pay it. I have a reason.'

He looked at her carefully. The reason was plain on her face, and for an instant Zachariah winced. He had hoped the free-marriage she had stepped out of when she went into contemplation might be resumed very soon now. Seeing her eyes upon Sam, he recognised that it would not be soon.

Sari leaned forward and put her pale, narrow hand on his arm.

'Zachariah,' she said, warning and possessiveness in her voice. 'Let her have her way, my dear. There's time enough for everything.'

Grandmother and granddaughter, almost mirror-images, exchanged a look in which Sam, who had missed nothing, thought he saw both rivalry and understanding.

Zachariah said, 'Look over there.' He moved his hand and the cell wall glowed into transparence. Floating a little distance off among the crowding cells was an inclosure in which a man sat alone. 'He's been here for two hours now,' Zachariah went on.

The cell drifted nearer. The man in it was thin, dark, frowning. He wore a dull brown costume.

'I know him by sight,' Sam said, and stood up. The floor rocked slightly at the motion. 'Drop me at the landing-stage. I'll take care of him for you.'

At the long bar he found a vacant seat and ordered a drink. The bartender looked at him sharply. This was a rendezvous for the Immortals and the upper classes; it was not often that a man as squatly plebeian as Sam Reed appeared at the bar. But there was something about Sam's scowl and the imperiousness of his order that after a moment made the bartender mutter, 'Yes, sir,' rather sullenly and bring him his drink.

Sam sat there a long while. He ordered twice more and made the drinks last, while the great shell hummed and spun above him and the crowd filled the dome with music and a vast amorphous murmuring. He watched the floating cell with the brown figure inside drift aimlessly around the vast circle. He was waiting for the Immortal to descend, and he was thinking very fast.

Sam was frightened. It was dangerous to mix in the affairs of the Immortals even politically. To get emotionally involved was sheer suicide and Sam had no illusion about his chances for survival as soon as his usefulness was over. He had seen the look of mild speculation that Zachariah Harker turned on him.

When the Free Companion's cell drifted finally towards the landing-stage, Sam Reed was there to meet it. He wasted no words.

'I've just been hired to kill you, Hale,' he said.

They were leaving Haven together an hour later when the Sheffield gang caught up with Sam.

Sam Reed would never have come this far in his career if he hadn't been a glib and convincing talker when he had to be. Robin Hale had certainly been a target for glib promoters often enough since his colonising crusade began to know how to brush them off. But here again the Harker blood spoke silently to its kindred Immortality in Hale, and though Sam credited his own glibness, it was the air of quiet conviction carried by his subsurface heritage which convinced the Free Companion.

Sam talked very fast – in a leisurely way. He knew that his life and Hale's were bound together just now by a short rope – a rope perhaps forty-eight hours long. Within those limits both were safe. Beyond them, both would die unless something very, very clever occurred to them. Sam's voice as he explained this carried sincere conviction.

This was the point at which the Sheffield boys picked him up. The two came out of the Haven portal and stepped on to the slow-speed ribbon of a moving Way. Then a deliberate press of the crowd separated them a bit and Sam, turning to fight his way back, saw too late a black bulb in the hand that rose towards his face and smelled the sickening fragrance of an invisible dust too late to hold his breath.

Everything about him slowed and stopped.

A hand slipped through his arm. He was being urged

along the Way. Globes and lanterns made patches of colour along the street until it curved; there they coalesced into a blob of hypnotic colour. The Way slid smoothly along and shining, perfumed mists curled in fog-banks above it. But he saw it all in stopped motion. Dimly he knew that this was his own fault. He had let Kedre distract him; he had allowed himself to take on a new job before he finished an old one that required all his attention. He would pay now.

Then something like a whirlwind in slow-motion struck across the moving belts of the Way. Sam was aware only of jostling, the shouts and the thud of fists on flesh. He couldn't sort out the faces, though he saw the Free Companion's floating before him time and again in a sort of palimpsest superimposed upon faces, dimly familiar, all of them shouting.

With a dreamlike smoothness he saw the other faces receding backwards along the slower ramp while the lights slipped rapidly away at the edges of the highspeed Way and Robin Hale's hand gripped his arm.

He let the firmness of the hand guide him. He was moving, but not moving. His brain had ceased almost entirely to function. He knew only vaguely that they were mounting the ramp to one of the hydroponic rooms, that Hale was clinking coins into an attendant's hand, that now they had paused before a tank where a heavy, grey-green foliage clustered.

From far off Hale's voice murmured, 'It usually grows on this stuff. Hope they haven't sprayed it too well, but it's hardy. It gets in everywhere. Here!' A sound of scraping fingernails, a glimpse of bluish lichen crushed between Hale's palms and dusted in Sam's face.

Then everything speeded up into sudden accelerated motion timed to Sam's violent sneezes. A stinging pain began in his sinuses and spread through his brain. It exploded there, rose to a crescendo, faded.

Sweating and shaking, he found he could talk again. Time and motion came back to normal and he blinked streaming eyes at Hale.

'All right?' the Free Companion asked.

'I – guess so.' Sam wiped his eyes.

'What brought that on?' Hale inquired with interest.

'My own fault,' Sam told him shortly. 'Personal matter. I'll settle it later – if I live.'

Hale laughed. 'We'll go up to my place. I want to talk to you.'

'They don't understand what they'll be facing,' the Free Companion said grimly. 'I can't seem to convince anyone of that. They've got a romantic vision of a crusade and not one in a thousand has ever set foot on dry land.'

'Convince me,' Sam said.

'I saw the Logician,' Hale began. 'The crusade was his idea. I needed – something. This is it, and I'm afraid of it now. It's got out of hand. These people are emotional deadbeats. They're pawing me like so many dogs begging for romance. All I can offer them is personal hardship beyond anything they can even dream, and no hope of success for this generation or the next. That sort of spirit seems to have bred out of the race since we've lived in Keeps. Maybe the underwater horizons are too narrow. They can't see beyond them, or their own noses.' He grinned. 'I offer not peace but a sword,' he said. 'And nobody will believe it.'

'I've never been topside myself,' Sam told him. 'What's it like?'

'You've seen it in the projectors, relayed from planes *above* the jungles. So have most people. And that's fallacy – seeing it from above. It looks pretty. I'd like to take a projector down into the mud and look up at all that stuff towering over and reaching down, and the mud-wolves erupting underfoot and the poison-vines lashing out. If I did, my whole crusade would fall flat and there'd be an end of the colonising.' He shrugged.

'I've made a start, you know, in the old fort,' he said. 'The Doonemen had it once. Now the jungle's got it back. The old walls and barriers are de-activated and useless. All that great technology is dead now. Whole rooms are solid blocks of vegetation, alive with vermin and snakes and poison plants. We're cleaning that out, but keeping it clean – well, that's going to take more than these people have got. Why, the lichens alone will eat through wood and glass and steel and flesh! And we don't know enough about the jungle. Here on Venus the ecology has no terrestrial parallel. And it won't be enough simply to hold the fort. It's got to be self-supporting.'

'That'll take money and backing,' Sam reminded him. 'The Families are dead against it – now.'

'I know. I think they're wrong. So does the Logician.'

'Are you working alone on this?'

Hale nodded. 'So far I am.'

'Why? A good promotion man could get you all the backing you need.'

'No good promotion man would. I'd be a swindle. I believe in this, Reed. With me it *is* a crusade. I wouldn't trust a man who'd be willing to tackle it, knowing the truth.'

A beautiful idea was beginning to take voluptuous shape in Sam's mind. He said, 'Would you trust me?'

'Why should I?'

Sam thought back rapidly over how much of the truth he had already told Hale. Not too much. It was safe to go ahead. 'Because I've already risked my neck to warn you,' he said. 'If I'd gone ahead with the job Harker gave me, I'd be collecting a small fortune right now. I didn't. I haven't told you why yet. I guess I don't need to. I feel the way you do about colonising. I could make some money out of promoting it – I won't deny that. But nothing like the money I could make killing you.'

'I've just told you the thing can't succeed,' Hale pointed out. But there was a light in his eyes and more eagerness in his manner than Sam had yet seen.

'Hooked!' Sam thought. Aloud, he said, 'Maybe not. All it needs is plenty of backing – and I mean plenty! I think I can provide that. And we've got to give the crusaders a substitute goal for the real one, something they think they can collect on in their lifetime. Something they *can* collect on. No cheating. Shall I try?'

Hale pinched his chin thoughtfully. At last he said, 'Come with me to the Logician.'

Sam hedged. He was afraid of the Logician. His own motives were not the kind that could stand the light of clear reason. But Hale, essentially romanticist as he was, had several centuries of experience behind him to bolster up his apparent naïveté. They argued for over an hour.

Then Sam went with him to see the Logician.

A globe spoke to them, a shining white globe on an iron pedestal. It said, 'I told you I can't foretell the future, Hale.'

'But you know the right answers.'

'The right answer for you may not be the right one for Sam Reed.'

Sam moved uneasily. 'Then make it two answers,' he said. He thought it was a machine speaking. He had let down his guard a trifle; machines weren't human. Willy-nilly, he waited uneasily, knowing the hours of his deadline were slipping away while Kedre and Harker waited for news of the Companion's death.

In the silver globe shadows swam, the distorted reflection of the Logician's long, sardonic face. Robin Hale could trace the likeness but he knew that to one who didn't know the secret the shadows would be meaningless.

'The Keep people aren't pioneers,' the Logician said unnecessarily. 'You need recruits from the reformatories.'

'We need good men,' Hale said.

'Criminals are good men, most of them. They're merely displaced socially or temporally. Any antisocial individual can be thoroughly prosocial in the right environment. Malcontents and criminals will be your best men. You'll want biologists, naturalists, geologists—'

'We'd have to pay tremendous sums to get even second-rate men,' Sam objected.

'No you wouldn't. You'd have to pay – yes. But you'll be surprised how many top flight men are malcontents. The Keeps are too circumscribed. No good worker is ever happy operating at less than full capacity, and who in the Keeps has ever used more than a fraction of his ability since the undersea was conquered?'

'You think we can go ahead then?' Hale asked specifically.

'If you and Reed can get around this current danger – ask me again.'

'Hale tells me,' Sam put in,' 'that the Logician disagrees with the Families about colonisation. Why won't you help us against the Families, then?'

The shadows moved in the globe; the Logician was shaking his head.

'I'm not omnipotent. The Families mean well – as they see it. They take a long view. By intrigue and influence they do sway the Council decisions, though the Council is perfectly free. But the Families sit back and decide policy, and then see that their decisions are carried out. Nominally the councils and the governors run the Keeps. Actually the Immortals run them. They've got a good deal of social consciousness, but they're ruthless, too. The laws they promote may seem harsh to the short-lived, but the grandchildren of the apparent victims may live to thank the Families for their harshness. From the Families' viewpoint common good covers a long period of time. In this case I think they're wrong.

'The race is going downhill fast. The Families argue we can't finance but one colonising effort. If it fails we're ruined. We'll never try again. We won't have the materials or the human drive. We've got to wait until they give the word, until they're convinced failure won't happen. I say they're wrong. I say the race is declining faster then they think. If we wait for their word, we'll have waited too long . . .

'But the Families run this planet. Not the Logician. I've opposed their opinions too often in other things for them to believe me now. They figure I'm against them in everything.'

To Robin Hale it was an old story. He said impatiently when the voice paused, 'Can you give us a prognosis, Logician? Is there enough evidence in now to tell us whether we've got a chance to succeed?'

The Logician said nothing for a while. Then a curious sound came from the globe. It was a chuckle that grew to a laugh which startled Hale and utterly astonished Sam Reed. That a machine could laugh was inconceivable.

'Landside will be colonised,' the Logician said, still

chuckling. 'You've got a chance – a good chance. And a better chance, my friend, if this man Reed is with you. That's all I can say, Hale. I think it's enough.'

Sam froze, staring at the shadows swimming in the globe. All his preconceived ideas turned over in his head. Was the Logician after all a fraud? Was it offering them mere guesswork? And if it could be this wrong on the point of Sam's dependability, of what value was anything else it said?

'Thank you, Logician,' the Free Companion was saying, and Sam turned to stare anew at Robin Hale. Why should he thank a machine, and especially as faulty a machine as this had just proved itself to be?

A deep chuckle sounded from the globe as they turned away. It rose again to laughter that followed them out of the hall, wave upon wave of full-throated laughter that had something of sympathy in it and much of irony.

The Logician was laughing from the bottom of his lungs, from the bottom of his thousand-years' experience, at the future of Sam Reed.

' "If we can get around this current danger—" ' Sam quoted the Logician. He was sitting beside a transparent plastic table, very dusty, looking at the Free Companion across it. This was a dim secret room the Slider owned. So long as they sat here they were safe, but they couldn't stay forever. Sam had a fair idea of how many of the Families' retainers were reporting on his movements and Hale's.

'Any ideas?' Hale asked.

'You don't seem much worried. What's the matter? Don't you believe me?'

'Oh, yes. I'll admit I mightn't believe just any man who came up to me in a crowd and said he'd been hired to kill me. It's easy to say, if you're working up to a favour. But I've rather been expecting the Families to do something drastic, and – I trust the Logician. How about it – have you any ideas?'

Sam looked at him from under scowling red brows. He had begun to hate Hale for this easy acquiescence. He wanted it. He needed it. But he didn't like Hale's motive. Hale wasn't likely to intrust the success or failure of his crusade to the doubtful integrity of a promoter, which was the role Sam aspired to now. Even though the Logician – moved by flawed logic – had pronounced favourable judgment and even though Hale trusted the Logician implicitly, there was another motive.

Robin Hale was an Immortal.

The thing Sam had sensed and hated in the Waltons and Harker he sensed and hated in Hale, too. A tremendous and supreme self-confidence. He was not the slave of time; time served him. A man with centuries of experience behind him must already have encountered very nearly every combination of social circumstance he was likely to encounter. He had a pattern set for him. There would have been time enough to experiment, to think things over carefully and try out this reaction and that until the best treatment for a given set of circumstances would come automatically to mind.

It wasn't fair, Sam thought childishly. Problems that shorter-lived men never solved the infinitely resourceful Immortals must know backwards and forwards. And there was another unfairness – problems the ordinary man had to meet with drastic solutions or compromise, Hale could meet simply by waiting. There was always, with the Immortals, that last, surest philosophy to fall back on: *This, too, will pass.*

The Immortals, then, were random factors. They had extensions in time that no non-Immortal could quite understand. You had to experience that long, long life in order to *know* . . .

Sam drew a deep breath and answered Hale's question, obliquely enough.

'The Families – I mean specifically the Waltons and the Harkers – won't strike overtly. They don't want to be publicly connected with your death. They're not afraid of the masses, because the masses have never organised. There's never been any question of a revolt, for there's never been any motive for revolt. The Families are just. It's only with intangibles like this colonising crusade that a question may come up, and – I hope – that may make it a dangerous question for them. Because for the first time the masses really are organised, in a loose sort of way – they're excited about the crusade.' He squinted at Hale. 'I've got an idea about how to use that, but—' Sam glanced at the dusty tele-visor screen in the wall above them – 'I can't explain it yet.'

'All right.' Hale sounded comfortable and unexcited. It was normal enough, Sam told himself, with a suddenly quick-ened pulse as he realised consciously for the first time that to this man warfare – that glamorous thing of the dead past – was a familiar story. He had seen slaughter and wreaked slaughter. The threat of death must by now be so old a tale to him that he faced it with unshaken nerves. Sam hated him anew.

'Meanwhile' – he forced him to speak calmly – 'I've got to sell myself to you on the crusading idea. Shall I talk a while?'

Hale grinned and nodded.

'We've got the unique problem of fighting off converts, not recruiting them. We need key men and we need manpower. One's expendable. The other – you *can* protect your key men, can't you?'

'Against some dangers. Not against boredom. Not against a few things, like lichens – they can get into an air vent and eat a man alive. Some of the germs mutate under UV, in-stead of dying. Oh, it isn't adventure.'

'So we'll need a screening process. Malcontents. Technical successes and personal failures.'

'Up to a point, yes. What do you suggest?' The laconic voice filled Sam with unreasonable resentment. He had a suspicion that this man already knew most of the answers, that he was leading Sam on, like a reciting child, partly to test his knowledge, partly perhaps in the hope that Sam might have ideas to offer which Hale could twist to his own use. And yet – under the confidence, under the resourcefulness that all his experiences had bred, the man showed an un-conquerable naïveté which gave Sam hope. Basically Hale was a crusader. Basically he was selfless and visionary. A million years of experience, instead of a few hundred, would never give him something Sam had been born with. Yes, this was worth a try . . .

'Of course, not all the failures will do,' he went on. 'We've got to find the reasons *why* they're malcontents. You had technicians in the old days, when the wars were going on?'

Hale nodded. 'Yes. But they had the traditions of the Free Companions behind them.'

'We'll start a new tradition. I don't know what. *Ad astra per aspera*, maybe.' Sam considered. 'Can you get access to the psych records and personal histories of those old technicians?'

'Some of them must have been saved. I think I can. Why?'

'This will come later, but I think it's our answer. Break down the factors that made them successful. The big integrators will do that. It'll give us the prime equation. Then break down the factors that make up the current crop of technicians – malcontents preferable. X equals a successful wartime technician, plus the equivalent of the old tradition. Find out who's got X today and give him the new tradition.

'It'll take careful propaganda and semantic building-up. All we need is the right channelling of public opinion now. Catchwords, a banner, a new Peter the Hermit, maybe. The Crusades had a perfect publicity build-up. I've given you a solution for your technicians – now about the manpower and the financial backing.' Sam glanced at the quiet Immortal face and looked away again. But he went on.

'We'll have to screen the volunteers for manpower, too. There are plenty of good men left in the human race. They won't all fold up at the first threat of danger. We'll set up a very rigid series of tests for every potential colonist. Phony them up if we have to. One set of answers for the public, another for us. You can't openly reject a man for potential cowardice, or the rest might not dare take the test. But we've got to know.'

'So far – good,' Hale said. 'What about money?'

'How much have you got?'

Hale shrugged. 'Pennies. I've got a foothold, cleaning out Doone Keep. But it'll take real money to keep the thing going.'

'Form a company and sell stock. People will always gamble. Especially if they get dividends – and the dividends they want aren't merely money. Glamour. Excitement. The romance they've been starved for. The reason they go in for second-hand thrills.'

'Will rejected volunteers buy stock?'

Sam laughed. 'I've got it! Every share of stock will pay a dividend of thrills. All the excitement of volunteering with none of the danger. Every move the colony makes will be covered by televisor – with a direct beam to the receiver of every stockholder!'

Hale gave him a glance in which anger and admiration were mingled. Sam was aware of a little surge of gratification at having startled the man into something like approval. But Hale's next reaction spoiled it.

'No. That's cheap. And it's cheating. This is no Roman holiday for the thrill-hunters. And I've told you it's hard work, not romance. It isn't exciting, it's drudgery.'

'It can be exciting,' Sam assured him. 'It'll have to be. You've got to make compromises. People pay for thrills. Well, thrills can be staged landside, can't they?'

Hale moved his shoulders uncomfortably. 'I don't like it.'

'Yes, but it *could* be done. Just in theory – is there anything going on landside right now that could be built up?'

After a pause, Hale said, 'Well, we've been having trouble with an ambulant vine – it's thermotropic. Body heat attracts it. Refrigerated units in our jungle suits stop it cold, of course. And it's easy to draw it off by tossing thermite or something hot around. It heads for that instead of us, and gets burned into ash.'

'What does it look like?'

Hale went into details. Sam sat back, looking pleased.

'That's the ticket. Perfectly safe, but it'll look ugly as the devil. That ought to help us screen out the unfit by scaring 'em off right at the start. We'll just have your men turn off their refrigerating units and stage a battle with the vines, while somebody stands by out of camera range with thermite ready to throw. We'll send out a message that the vines are breaking through – cover it with televisor – and that does it.'

'No.' Hale said.

'The Crusades started as a publicity stunt,' Sam remarked. But he didn't press the point just yet. Instead he mentioned the fact that both of them would be dead within thirty-six hours now unless something could be worked out. He had seen a flicker in the wall screen. It was time to bring up the next subject on the agenda.

'The Families could get rid of us both in ways that look perfectly innocent. A few germs, for instance. They've got us cold unless we do something drastic. My idea is to try a trick so outrageous they won't know how to meet it until it's had a chance to work.'

'What do you mean?'

'The Families depend tremendously on their own prestige to maintain their power. Their real power is an intangible – longevity. But public faith in their infallibility has kept them on top. Attack that. Put them in a spot where they've got to *defend* us.'

'But how?'

'You're a public darling. Harker gave me a forty-eight hour deadline because he was afraid you might turn up a henchman at any moment who could step into your shoes and carry on the crusade even if he got you out of the way.' Sam tapped his own chest. 'I'm the man. I've got to be, to save my own skin. But it offers you an out, too. We halve the danger if either of us is replaceable – by the other. It wouldn't solve anything to kill either of us if the other lives.'

'But how the devil do you expect to make yourself that important to the public in the few hours you've got left?' Hale was really interested now.

Sam gave him a confident grin. Then he kicked the leg of his chair. An opening widened in the hall and the Slider came in, sniffling.

He lowered his great bulk to a chair and looked curiously at Hale. Sam said, 'First – the Sheffield gang's after me. I can't afford to fight it out right now. Got something really big on the fire. Can you call 'em off?'

'Might manage it,' the Slider said. It was a guarantee. The old poison-master was still a top danger in the underworld of the Keeps.

'Thanks.' Sam turned in his chair to face the Slider. 'Now, the important thing. I need a quick job of sound-track faking.'

'That's easy,' the Slider assured him, and sniffled.

'*And* the faces to match.'

'That's harder. Whose faces?'

'Zachariah Harker, for one. Any other Harkers or Waltons you've got on file, but Zachariah first.'

The Slider stared hard at him, forgetting for the moment even to sniffle. "*Harkers?*" he demanded. And then chuckled unexpectedly. 'Well, I can swing it, but it'll cost you. How soon you want the job done?'

Sam told him.

Faking a sound-track was an immemorially old gag, almost as old as sound-tracks themselves. It takes only nominal skill to snip out and rearrange already spoken words into new sequences. But only recently had a technique been developed for illicit extensions of the idea. It took a very deft operator, and a highly skilled one, to break down speech-sounds into their basic sibilants and gutterals and build up again a whole new pattern of speech. It was not usually possible to transpose from one language to another because of the different phonetic requirements, but any recorded speech of reasonable length could usually be mined for a large enough number of basic sounds to construct almost any other recorded speech out of its building blocks.

From this it was, of course, only a step to incorporating the speaker visually into the changed speech. The lips that shaped each sound could be stopped in mid-syllable and the pictures transposed with the sounds.

The result was jerky to the ear and eye. There was always a certain amount of reducing and enlarging and adjustment to make the faces from various speeches into a single speech. Some experiments had been made to produce a missing full-face view, for verisimilitude, by projecting on to a three-dimensional form the two-dimensional images of profile or three-quarter views to blend into the desired face, and photographing that anew. Afterwards a high degree of skill

56

was necessary to blend the result into convincing smooth-ness.

The Slider had access to a technician who knew the job forwards and backwards. And there were plenty of Harker and Walton records on file. But at best it was a dangerous thing to tamper with and Sam knew it. He had no choice.

It took five hours to talk Robin Hale into the hoax. Sam had to convince him of his own danger first; there were Family agents by now ringing in the building where they hid, so that wasn't too hard. Then he had to convince him of Sam's own trustworthiness, which Sam finally managed by rehearsing his arguments with the straps of a pressure gauge recording his blood-reactions for conscious lies. That took some semantic hedging, for Sam had much to conceal and had to talk around it.

'You and I are as good as dead,' he told Hale, with the recording needles holding steady, for this was true enough. 'Sure, this trick is dangerous. It's practically suicide. But if I've got to die anyhow, I'd as soon do it taking chances. And it's our only chance, unless you can think of something better. Can you?'

The Immortal couldn't.

And so on the evening telecast advance word went out that Robin Hale would make an important announcement about the colony. All through the Keeps, visors were tuned in on the telecast, waiting. What they were really waiting for was a moment when the Harkers and Waltons involved in the faked reel were together and out of the way.

The private lives of the Immortals were never very private, and the Slider had a network of interlocking con-nections that functioned very efficiently. Hale's influence kept the telecast schedule open and waiting, and presently word came that the Immortals involved were all accounted for.

Then on the great public screens and on countless private ones the driving colour-ads gave place to Robin Hale's face. He was dressed for landside, and he spoke his lines with a reluctance and a haste to get it over that gave the words an air of unexpected conviction.

He said he had hoped to tell them in detail of the magnificent idea which his good friend Sam Reed had produced to make full-scale colonising possible without delay. But trouble landside had just broken out and he had been called up to offer his experience as an old Free Companion to the men who were facing a new and deadly menace up above them all, on the jungle shore. Then he offered them a stiff, quick salute and left the screen.

Zachariah Harker's face replaced Hale's. It would have taken a better than expert eye to detect the faint qualities of unevenness which might betray the fact that this was a synthesis of rearranged sound-waves and light-waves. Technically, even Zachariah, watching the screen from wherever he was just now, could not deny he had spoken the words, for every sound he heard and every motion of his own lips was genuine.

The synthetic speech was a triumph in semantics. It was typical of Sam that he could use this boldly suicidal venture not only to clear himself and Hale, if he could, but also to further his plans for the colony. So Harker was made to name Sam – brought forward with modest reluctance to stand beside the Immortal as the speech went on – as the public-spirited, adventurous philanthropist who was going to make the colonising crusade possible.

Sam Reed, man of the people, short-lived but far-seeing, would lead his fellows to success behind Robin Hale in the great crusade. Landside lay the future of the race. Even the Harkers, Zachariah said, had finally been convinced of that by the persuasions of Sam and Hale. A great adventure lay ahead. Volunteers would be accepted for examination very soon. *Ad astra per aspera!*

He spoke of danger. He went into details, each word carefully chosen and chartered to make the listeners discontented. He hinted at the stagnation of the Keeps, of growing racial debility, new vulnerabilities to disease. And most important – man had stopped growing. His destiny was no longer to be found in the Keeps. The great civilisations of Earth must not reach a dead end under the seas of this fertile planet. *Ad astra!*

Zachariah's face left the screen. Sam stepped forward to clinch the matter, nervous and deeply worried under his calm. Now that he had actually done this, he quivered with belated qualms. What would the Harkers do when they discovered how fantastically they had been tricked? How outrageously their innermost convictions had been reversed and repudiated before all the Keeps, apparently in their own words! They must be moving already; the Families were geared to rapid action when the need arose. But what they would do Sam couldn't guess.

He spoke with quiet confidence into the screen. He outlined his ideas for offering the people themselves the opportunity to join the crusade, financially if not personally. In deft words he referred to the hardships and dangers of landside; he wanted to discourage all but the hardiest from offering as personal volunteers. And to aid in that, as well as to provide a smash finale to his scheme, he made his great announcement.

Something which until today had been a plaything for the wealthy would now be offered to all who owned shares in the magnificent venture before mankind. Each participant could watch the uses to which his money was put, share almost at first hand in the thrills and perils of landside living.

Look!

On the screen flashed a dizzying view of jungle that swooped up towards the beholder with breathtaking swiftness. A ring of velvet-black mud studded the flowery quilt of tree-tops. The ring swung up towards the view and you could see an iridescent serpent slithering across the blackness. The mud erupted and a mud-wolf's jaws closed upon the snake. Blood and mud spattered wildly. Churning and screaming, the combatants sank from sight and the velvety pool quivered into stillness again except for the rings that ran out around it from time to time as bubbles of crimson struggled up and burst on the surface with dull plops which every listener in the Keeps could hear.

Sam thanked his audience. He asked their patience for a few days longer, until the first examination trials could be set up. He observed with arrogant humility that he hoped to earn their trust and faith by his service towards themselves and the Free Companion, who had left all such matters in his hands while Hale himself struggled up there on landside in the jungles he knew so well. We would all, Sam finished, soon be watching such struggles, with men instead of monsters enlisting our sympathy in their brave attempts to conquer Venus as our forebears once conquered Old Earth . . .

The Families did nothing.

It worried Sam more than any direct action could possibly have done. For there was nothing here he could fight. Profoundly he distrusted that silence. All telecast attempts to interview any of the Immortals on this tremendous subject which was uppermost, overnight, in every mind, came to nothing. They would smile and nod and refuse to comment — yet.

But the plans went on at breakneck rate. And after all, Sam told himself, what could the Harkers do? To deny the public this delightful new toy might be disastrous. You can't give candy to a baby and then snatch it away untasted without rousing yells of protest. The people of the Keeps were much more formidable than babies, and they were used to collapsing into paternalistic hands. Remove the support and you might expect trouble.

Sam knew he had won a gambit, not the game. But he had too much to do just now to let the future worry him. All this was to be a swindle, of course. He had never intended anything else.

Paradoxically, Sam trusted the judgment of the Harkers. They thought this attempt would fail. Sam was sure they were right. Of course. The Logician believed that colonising *would* succeed, and the Logician normally should be right. How can a machine err? But the machine had erred, very badly, in its analysis of Sam himself, so it isn't strange that he disbelieved all its conclusions now.

The only way to make the scheme succeed as Sam intended it to succeed was to insure its failure. Sam was out this time for really big money. The public clamoured to buy, and Sam sold and sold.

He sold three hundred per cent of the stock.

After that he had to fail. If he put the money into land-side development there'd be nothing left over for the promoter, and anyhow, how could he pay off on three hundred per cent?

But on paper it looked beautiful. New sources of supply and demand, a booming culture rising from the underseas, shaking off the water from gigantic shoulders, striding on to the shore. And then interplanetary and interstellar travel for the next goal. *Ad astra* was a glorious dream, and Sam worked it for all it was worth.

Two months went by.

Rosathe, like all the other fruits of success, dropped delightfully into his arms. Sam closed all three of his apartments and with Rosathe found a new place, full of undreamed-of luxuries, its windows opening out over the hydroponic garden that flourished as lavishly, though not so dangerously, as the jungles overhead. From these windows he could see the lights of the whole Keep spread out below, where every man danced to his piping. It was dreamlike, full of paranoid splendours, megalomaniac grandeur – and all of it true.

Sam didn't realise it yet, though looking back he would surely have seen, but he was spinning faster and faster down a vortex of events which by now were out of his control. Events would have blurred as they whirled by, if he had been given time enough to look back at them when the moment of reckoning came. But he was not given time . . .

Rosathe was sitting on a low hassock at his feet, her harp on her arm, singing very sweetly to him, when the moment finally came.

Her violet-blue skirts lay about her in a circle on the floor, her cloudy head was bent above the high horns of the lyre and her voice was very soft.

'*Oh, slowly, slowly got she up, and slowly she came nigh . . . him . . .*' How delightfully, the sweet voice soared on the last word! That dip and rise in the old ballads tried every voice but an instrument as true as the lovely instrument in

Rosathe's throat. '*But all she said*' – Rosathe reported in that liquid voice – and was stopped by the musical buzzing of the televisor.

Sam knew it must be important, or it would never have been put through to him at this hour. Reluctantly he swung his feet to the floor and got up.

Rosathe did not lift her head. She sat quite motionless for an instant, curiously as if she had been frozen by the sound of the buzzer. Then without glancing up she swept the strings with polished fingertips and sang her final line. '*Young man, I think you're dyin'*' . . .

The cloudiness of the visor screen cleared as Sam flipped the switch and a face swam out of it that rocked him back a bit on his heels. It was Kedre Walton's face, and she was very angry. The black ringlets whipped like Medusa-locks as she whirled her head towards the screen. She must have been talking to someone in the background as she waited for Sam to acknowledge the call, for her anger was not wholly for Sam. He could see that. Her words belied it.

'Sam Reed, you're a fool!' she told him flatly and without preamble. The Egyptian calm was gone from her delicate, disdainful face. Even the disdain was gone now. 'Did you really think you could get away with all this?'

'I've got away with it,' Sam assured her. He was very confident at that point in the progress of his scheme.

'You poor fool, you've never fought an Immortal before. Our plans work slowly. We can afford to be slow! But surely you didn't imagine Zachariah Harker would let you do what you did and live! He—'

A voice from behind her said, 'Let me speak for myself, Kedre, my dear,' and the smooth, ageless young face of Zachariah looked out at Sam from the screen. The eyes were quietly speculative as they regarded him. 'In a way I owe you thanks, Reed,' the Immortal's voice said. 'You were clever. You had more resources than I expected. You put me on my mettle, and that's an unexpected pleasure. Also, you've made it possible for me to overthrow Hale's whole ambitious project. So I want to thank you for that, too. I like to be fair when I can afford to be.'

His eyes were the eyes of a man looking at something so impersonally that Sam felt a sudden chill. Such remoteness in time and space and experience – as if Sam were not there at all. Or as if Harker were looking already on death. Something as impersonal and remote from living as a corpse. As Sam Reed.

And Sam knew a moment's profound shaking of his own convictions – he had a flash of insight in which he thought that perhaps Harker had planned it this way from the start, knowing that Sam would doublecross him with Hale, and knowing that Sam would doublecross Hale, too. Sam was the weak link in Hale's crusade, the one thing that might bring the whole thing crashing if anyone suspected. Until now, Sam had been sure no one did suspect.

But Zachariah Harker knew.

'Good-bye, Reed,' the smooth voice said. 'Kedre, my dear—'

Kedre's face came back into the screen. She was still angry, but the anger had been swallowed up in another emotion as her eyes met Sam's. The long lashes half veiled them, and there were tears on the lashes.

'Good-bye, Sam,' she said. 'Good-bye.' And the blue glance flickered across his shoulder.

Sam had one moment to turn and see what was coming, but not time enough to stop it. For Rosathe stood at his shoulder, watching the screen, too. And as he turned her pointed fingers which had evoked music from the harp for him this evening pinched together suddenly and evoked oblivion.

He felt the sweet, terrifying odour of dust stinging in his nostrils. He stumbled forward futilely, reaching for her, meaning to break her neck. But she floated away before him, and the whole room floated, and then Rosathe was looking down on him from far above, and there were tears in her eyes, too.

The fragrance of dream-dust blurred everything else. Dream-dust, the narcotic euthanasia dust which was the way of the suicide.

His last vision was the sight of the tear-wet eyes looking

down, two women who must have loved him to evoke those tears and who together had worked out his ruin.

He woke. The smell of scented dust died from his nostrils. It was dark here. He felt a wall at his shoulder, and got up stiffly, bracing himself against it. Light showed blurrily a little way off. The end of an alley, he thought. People were passing now and then through the dimness out there.

The alley hurt his feet. His shoes felt queer and loose. Investigating, Sam found that he was in rags, his bare feet pressing the pavement through broken soles. And the fragrance of dream-dust was still a miasma in the air around him.

Dream-dust – that could put a man to sleep for a long, long while. *How long?*

He stumbled towards the mouth of the alley. A passer-by glanced at him with curiosity and distaste. He reached out and collared the man.

'The Colony,' he said urgently. 'Has it – have they opened it yet?'

The man struck his arm away. 'What colony?' he asked impatiently.

'The Colony! The Land Colony!'

'Oh, that.' The man laughed. 'You're a little late.' Clearly he thought Sam was drunk. 'It's been open a long time now – what's left of it.'

'How long?'

'Forty years.'

Sam hung on the bar of a vending machine in the wall at the alley mouth. He had to hold the bar to keep himself upright, for his knees were strengthless beneath him. He was looking into the dusty mirror and into his own eyes. 'Forty years. Forty years!' And the ageless, unchanged face of Sam Harker looked back at him, ruddy-browed, unlined as ever.

'Forty years!' Sam Harker murmured to himself.

PART TWO

AND *indeed there will be time*
For the yellow smoke that slides along the street,
Rubbing its back upon the window panes;
There will be time, there will be time
To prepare a face to meet the faces that you meet;
There will be time to murder and create,
And time for all the works and days of hands
That lift and drop a question on your plate . . .

T. S. ELIOT

The city moved past him in a slow, descending spiral. Sam Harker looked at it blankly, taking in nothing. His brain was too filled already to be anything just now but empty. There was too much to cope with. He could not yet think at all. He had no recollection to span the time between the moment when he looked into his impossibly young face in the glass, and this current moment. Under his broken soles he felt the faint vibration of the Way, and the city was familiar that moved downwards beneath him in its slow sweep, street after street swinging into view as the spiral Way glided on. There was nothing to catch hold of and focus, no way to anchor his spinning brain.

'I need a shot,' he told himself, and even the thought came clumsily, as if along rusty channels where no thought had moved before in forty drugged years. But when he tried his ragged pockets, he found them empty. He had nothing. No credits, no memory, not even a past.

'Nothing?' he thought foggily. 'Nothing?' And then for the first time the impact of what he had seen in the mirror struck him hard. *'Nothing? I'm immortal!'*

It could not be true. It was part of the dream-dust fantasy. But the feel of his own firm cheek and hard, smooth neck muscles beneath his shaking fingers – that was no fantasy. That was real. Then the idea of forty years gone by must be the unreality. And that man at the alley-mouth had lied. Looking back now, it seemed to Sam that the man had looked at him oddly, with a more than passing interest. He had assumed the man was a passer-by, but when he forced his rusty brain to remember, it seemed to him that the man had been standing there watching him, ready to go or to stay according to the cue Sam's conduct gave him.

He groped for the memory of the man's face, and found nothing. A blur that looked at him and spoke. But looked with clinical interest, and spoke with purpose and intent beyond the casual. This was the first coherent thought that took shape in the dimness of Sam's brain, so the stimulus must have been strong. The man must have been there for a reason. For a reason concerned with Sam.

'Forty years,' Sam murmured. 'I can check that, anyhow.'

The city had not changed at all. But that was no criterion. The Keeps never changed. Far ahead, towering above the buildings, he saw the great globe of dead Earth in its black plastic pall. He could orient himself by that, and the shapes of the streets and buildings fell into familiar place around him. He knew the city. He knew where he was, where his old haunts had been, where that lavish apartment had looked down over those glittering ways, and a girl with blue eyes had blown dust in his face.

Kedre's face swam before him in the remembered screen, tears in the eyes, command in the gesture that brought about his downfall. Kedre and Rosathe. He had a job to do, then. He knew Kedre's had not really been the hand behind that poison dust, any more than Rosathe's had been. Zachariah Harker was the man who gave the orders here. And Zachariah would suffer for it. But Kedre must suffer too, and as for Rosathe – Sam's fingers curved. Rosathe he had trusted. Her

66

crime was the worst – betrayal. Rosathe had better die, he thought.

But wait. Forty years? Had time done that job for him already? The first thing he must learn was the date of this day on which he had awakened. The moving street glided towards one of the big public newscast screens, and he knew he could check the date on that when it came into view. But he thought he did not really need to. He could *feel* time's passage. And though the city had not changed, the people had, a little. Some of the men near him were bearded, so that much was new. Clothes had a more extreme cut than he remembered. Fashions change in rhythm with changing social orders, not meaninglessly but in response to known patterns. He could work it out from that alone, he thought, if his mind were clearer and there was no other way to learn.

The Way swung round slowly so that corner of the newscast screen loomed into view, and Sam noticed how few faces around him turned towards it. He could remember a time when every neck craned and people jostled one another in their hurry to read the news a little faster than the moving Way would let them. All that was over now. Apathy in direct and easily understood contrast to the extreme new styles showed upon every face. Sam was the only one here who craned to see the big screen.

Yes, it had been forty years.

There was something like a bright explosion in the centre of his brain. Immortality! Immortality! All the possibilities, all the dangers lying before him burst outwards in one blinding glow. And then the glow faded and he was afraid for a moment of maturity's responsibilities – this new, incredible maturity so far beyond anything that he had ever dreamed of before. And then the last doubts he would feel about this wonderful gift assailed him, and he searched his memory frantically for knowledge of some drug, some treatment that could produce a catalepsy like this, ageless over a span of forty years. He knew of none. No, it must be real. It could not be, but it was true.

It would wait. Sam laughed dryly to himself. This of all

things would most certainly wait. There were more urgent things to think of. Something magical had happened to him, and the result was forty years of sleep and then immortality. But what had that something been?

Dream-dust. The remembered fragrance of it was still in his nostrils, and there was an ominous dry thirst beginning to assert itself beneath his tongue, a thirst no liquid would assuage.

I've got to get cured. First of all, I've got to get cured.

He knew dream-dust. It wasn't incurable, but it was habit-forming. Worse than that, really, because once you went under the deadly stuff you didn't come out again. There were no rational periods during which you could commit yourself for cure. Not until the organism built up antibodies, and that took almost a lifetime. Even then the dream-dust virus could mutate so rapidly that the rational term didn't last. You dropped back into dreams, and eventually, you died.

Panic struck Sam for a moment. How long would this rationality last? How long had it lasted already? At any time now would the dusty dreams strike again and his newly emerged identity go under? Immortality was useless if he must sleep it all away.

He had to get cured. The thirst mounted now as he recognised it for what it was, a darker thirst than the average man ever knows. The cure took money. Several thousand korium-credits, at least. And he had nothing. He was rich beyond dreams of avarice if this immortality meant what he believed it meant, but the wealth of his endless years might vanish in any instant now because he had no material wealth at all. Paradox. He owned centuries of the future, but for lack of a few current hours he might be robbed of his treasure laid up in time.

Panic was no good. He knew that. He forced it down again and considered very quietly what he had to do. What he had to learn. How to go about it. Two things were paramount – his immortality and his dream-dust addiction.

Money.

He hadn't any.

68

Immortality.

That was an asset quite apart from the future it promised, but he didn't yet know how to spend it most wisely. So – keep it a secret.

How?

Disguise.

As whom?

As himself, of course. As Sam Reed, but not Sam Reed Immortal. Sam as he should have looked at the age of eighty. This tied in with the money angle. For the only way to get money was to return to his old haunts, his oldest practices. And he must not throw away his most precious secret there. Already a dim stirring in his brain hinted at the wonderful use he might make of this secret. Time enough for that later. Time in spilling-over plenty, if he could salvage it soon enough.

But first, a little money, a little knowledge.

Knowledge was easier and safer to acquire. It came first. He must learn immediately what had been happening in the past four decades, what had happened to himself, whether he had dropped out of the public attention, when and how. Clearly he was no longer a public figure, but where he had been the past forty years was still a question.

He stepped off on to a cross-Way and let it carry him towards the nearest library. On the way he considered the problem of money. He had been a very rich man when Rosathe blew the dream-dust in his face. Some of the credits were in his own name, but four caches privately hidden held most of the fortune. It seemed likely that at least one still remained secret, but whether he could collect the money in any identity but his own remained to be seen. That had waited forty years – it would wait a few hours longer.

He had not even the few cents required to buy the privacy of a room or a booth at the library, but he seated himself at one of the long tables and bent forward hiding his face between the sound-absorbent wings that jutted out from the middle-partition. He lowered his eyes to the viewpiece of the visor. He touched control buttons and waited.

A general newscast forty years old unrolled itself on a

magnified screen below him. It was a weekly summary that covered the last seven days he could remember.

Rip van Winkle could have helped his own disorientation by reading a twenty-year-old newspaper. It wouldn't have told him what had happened since he slept, but it would have restored the firmness of the world he woke in. In all the Keep, in all the planet, this odd newscast was the only thing that could have put solidity under San Reed's feet. Outside the library danger and unfamiliarity waited everywhere, because the frames of reference had changed so much.

The little things change most – fads, fashions, slang – and lapses from that superficial norm are instantly noticed. But a lapse from a basic can often remain undetected.

Sam watched the past unroll which seemed to vividly the present that he could almost smell dream-dust puffed freshly in his face from Rosathe's hand. When he thought of that the dryness of his thirst suddenly choked him, and he remembered anew how urgent his need for haste was. He pressed his forehead to the viewpiece and sped the roll faster.

SAM REED DREAM-DUSTS! The thin voice from the past shrilled ghostlike in his ears while the tri-di pictures moved swiftly by. *Sam Reed, promoter behind the Land Colony, today gave up his career and dream-dusted, amazing everyone who knew him ... found wandering through the city ...*

It was all there. The investigation that followed his apparent suicide, the scandal as his swindle began to emerge. Four days after Sam Reed disappeared, after a dozen reputable witnesses saw him under the influence of dream-dust, the Colony bubble burst.

Robin Hale, the Free Companion, had no answer to make. What could he say? Three hundred per cent of the stock had been sold, speaking louder than any words of the fact that the Colony's promoters had known it could not succeed. Hale did the only thing he could do – tried to weather the storm as he had weathered so many in his long lifetime, man-made storms and the violent tornadoes of landside. It was impossible, of course. Emotions had been strung too high. Too many men had believed in the Colony.

When the bubble burst, little remained.

Sam Reed's name bore the brunt of the opprobrium. Not only was he a swindler, but he had run out – given up completely and lost himself in the suicidal escape of dream-dust. No one seemed to wonder why. There was no logic behind such a step. But publicity-wise minds behind the telling of the story wasted no time that might give people a chance to think the thing out. If the Colony was foredoomed to failure, Sam had only to wait to collect his illicit three hundred per cent in safe secrecy. His suicide might have argued that he feared the Colony would succeed – but no one thought of that. It seemed only that, fearing exposure, he took the quickest way out.

Investigation followed him, back-tracked and discovered the caches of swindled money that he hadn't concealed quite cleverly enough. Not against the deductive technology of the Keeps and the Immortals. They found the four caches and emptied them – all of them. The old newscasts gave details.

Sam leaned back and blinked in the dim air of the library. Well, he was broke, then.

He could see the hands of the Harker Family moving behind this four-decade-old game. Zachariah's face came back to him like something seen an hour ago, smooth and smiling in the visor screen, remote as a god's face watching ephemeral mortals. Zachariah had known exactly what he was doing, of course. But that was only the start of the game. Sam was a pawn to be used and discarded in the opening move. He turned back to the newscast to learn how the rest of the moves had been carried out.

And he was surprised to find that Robin Hale went ahead and started the Land Colony, in the face of the lack of all popular support – in the face of actual enmity. He had only one weapon. He still had the granted charter, and they couldn't take that away from him, especially since the money Sam stole had been recovered. Doggedly Hale must have forged ahead, laying his long-term plans as the Families laid theirs, looking forward to the time when these petty scandals would have blown past and he could start anew with a fresh generation and fight the Families to win this generation over as he had won the last – for a while.

Yes, the Colony was started. But remarkably little news had been recorded about it. There was a spectacular murder in Delaware Keep and then a new play was produced that had all undersea Venus scrambling for tickets, and presently Sam found week after week of newscast spinning by with only the briefest references to the fact that a Colony had been started.

That was deliberate, of course. The Harkers knew what they were doing.

Sam stopped the newscast and thought. He would have to rearrange his tentative plans, but not much. He still needed money – fast. He swallowed dryly against the drug-thirst. The cached money was gone. What remained? Only himself, his experience, his priceless secret that must not yet be squandered – and what else? The old land charter issued in his name forty years ago was still on file, he assumed, since the charters were irrevocable. He couldn't claim it in his own name, and in any other name it would be invalid. Well, deal with that later.

Right now – money. Sam's lips tightened. He got up and left the library, walking lightly, seeking a weapon and a victim. He couldn't get two or three thousand credits by robbery without taking long risks, but he could manage a simple black-jacking up an alley for twenty or thirty credits – if he was lucky.

He was lucky. So was the man he stunned, whose skull didn't crack under the impact of a sock filled with pebbles. Sam had taken careful stock of himself, and was surprised to find that physically he seemed to be in better shape than he had any right to expect. Most dream-dust victims are skin-and-bone mummies by the time they die. It raised another mystery – what sort of life had he been leading during these forty dreaming years?

Memory of the man in the alley where Sam woke returned bafflingly. If he had only been clear-headed enough to keep his grip on that collar until he could shake the information he needed out of the watcher who had stood waiting above him. Well, that would come, too, in its time.

With forty-three credits in his pocket, he headed for a certain establishment he had known forty years ago. The attendants there kept their mouths shut and worked efficiently, in the old days, and things did not change fast in the Keeps. He thought they would still be there.

On the way he passed a number of big new salons where men and women were visible being embellished to a high point of perfection. Apparently the demand had increased. Certainly more foppery was evident in the Keep now. Men with exquisitely curled beards and ringlets were everywhere. But privacy and discretion were necessary to Sam's purpose. He went on to his semi-illegal establishment, and was not surprised to find it still in business.

His nerve shook a little as he paused before the entrance. But no one had recognised him on the Ways, apparently. Forty years ago his televised face had been thoroughly familiar in the Keeps, but now—

Rationalisation is a set pattern in men's minds. If they looked at him and saw familiarity, they decided automatically that it was a remarkable likeness, no more. The unconscious always steers the conscious towards the most logical conclusion – the one grooved by channels of parallel experience. Sometimes striking resemblances do occur; that is natural. It was not natural to see Sam Reed as he had looked forty years before, moving along a Way. And many of those he passed had been unborn at the time of the Colony fiasco, or had seen Sam Reed with the indifferent eyes of childhood. Those who might remember were old now, dim-sighted, and many faces in public life had superimposed themselves on these failing memories since then.

No, he was safe except for random chance. He went confidently through the glass door and gave his orders to the man assigned to him. It was routine enough.

'Permanent or temporary?'

'Temporary,' Sam said, after a brief pause.

'Quick-change?' There was a call for emergency quick-changes of disguise among the establishment's clientele.

'That's right.'

The artist went to work. He was an anatomist and

something of a psychologist as well as a disguise expert. He left Sam's pate bald, as directed; he dyed and bleached the red brows and lashes to pepper-and-salt that could pass for either dark or light, depending on the rest of the ensemble. With the beard, they passed for grimy white. The beard was a dirty, faded mixture.

He built up Sam's nose and ears as time would have built them had it touched Sam. He put a few wrinkles in the right places with surrogate tissues. The beard hid most of Sam's face, but when the artist had finished eighty years of hard living looked out above its greyish mask.

'For a quick change,' he said, 'take off the beard and change your expression. You can't remove the surrogate quickly, but you can iron out those wrinkles by the right expression. Try it please.' He wheeled Sam's chair around to the mirror and made him practise until both men were satisfied.

'All right,' Sam said finally. 'I'll need a costume.'

They settled on three things only – hat, cloak, shoes. Simplicity and speed were the factors behind the choice. Each item was a special article. The hat could be completely altered in shape by a pull and a twist. The cloak was opaque, but a texture so thin it could be crumpled and stuffed into a pocket. It was weighted to hang straight when worn, to hide the fact that the body beneath was not an old man's body. Sam had to practise the proper gait. And the shoes were nondescript in colour, like the hat, but their large, dull buckles could be opened to release puffy blue bows.

Sam went out by a back way. Moving stiffly, like one who felt the weight of his eighty years, he returned to the library. He was a remarkably well-preserved eighty, he concluded, watching his reflection in windows as he passed, a hale and hearty old man, but old – old. It would do.

Now he wanted to study the current crime news.

In a way the criminal classes are agrarian – if you look at them over a span as broad as Sam's. They move as they feed, drifting from pasture to greener pasture. The Blue Way had been a skid-row forty years ago, but no more, Sam realised, listening to reports from the telecast. As for the crimes themselves, they hadn't altered much. That pattern was basic. Vice, through the ages, changes less than virtue.

Finally he located the present green pasture. He bought a vial of water-soluble red dye and a high-powered smoke bomb. The instructions on the bomb told how to use it in hydroponic gardens to destroy insect pests. Sam didn't read them; he had used these bombs before.

Then he had to locate the right place for his trap.

He needed two alleys, close together, opening on a Way not too well-travelled. In one of the alleys was a cellar Sam remembered. It was deserted now, as in the old days. He hid near the entrance several fist-sized chunks of metal he had picked up, and he made a hiding-place for the smoke bomb in the cellar. After that he was ready for the next step.

He did not let himself think how many steps the stairway contained altogether. When he thought of that, he remembered that he had all the time he needed – now! – and that sent him into drunken, elated dreams far divorced from that immediate necessity of redeeming his future. Instead, he reminded himself of his drug-addiction and the need for money and curative treatment.

He went to the current green pasture and drank rotgut whisky, the cheapest available. And he kept in mind always the fact that he was a very old man. There were little tricks. He remembered never to fill his lungs with air before speaking; old men are short of breath and their voices lack resonance. The result was convincing. Also he moved slowly and carefully, making himself think of each move before he made it. A hobble doesn't indicate age, but action that is the result of old thought-processes does indicate it. The old have to move slowly because it's necessary to consider whether the stiff legs and weak muscles can manage obstacles. The world is as dangerous to the very old as to the very young, but a baby doesn't know the peril of gravity.

So Sam didn't creak or hobble. But he didn't seem to have much breath and he apparently wasn't conditioned to fast moving any more—and it was an old man who sat in Gem o' Venus drinking rotgut and getting quietly drunk.

75

It was a dive. A colourful dive, just as many of the dives of Imperial Rome must have been, the jetsam of costumes and customs drifting down from the higher levels, so that the eye caught here and there the flash of a gilded belt, the blood-brilliant scarlet of a feather-pierced cap, the swirl of a rainbow cloak.

But basically Gem o'Venus was for drinking and gaming and more sordid uses. In the upper levels men gambled with fantastic devices, tricky so-called improvements on the ancient games of chance. There you might encounter such dubious streamlined tricks as roulette which employed a slightly radioactive ball and Geiger counters; there you had the game of Empire with its gagged-up cards and counters, where men played at winning imaginary galactic empires.

In Gem o' Venus there were some gadgety games too, but the basics remained constant – dice and cards. Faces were not familiar to Sam here, but types were. Some of the customers didn't care where they sat, other always faced the door. These interested Sam. So did a card game on the verge of breaking up. The players were too drunk to be wary. Sam picked up his drink and kibitzed. After a while he slid into the game.

He was rather surprised to find that the cards they were using were not the familiar pipped and face cards of the old days. They were larger, patterned with the esoteric pictures of the tarot. The old, old cards of Earth's cloudy past had been drifting back into favour in Sam's earlier life, but it was a little surprising to find they had reached such depths as these in forty years.

He had chosen these players carefully, so he was able to win without making it obvious, though the cards were distracting enough to lend verisimilitude to his game. It was confusing to play with pentacles and cups instead of diamonds and hearts, though, when you thought of it objectively, no more exotic.

These stakes weren't high, but Sam didn't expect to make his killing here. Cards were too uncertain, in any case. He needed only enough money to make an impression, and he managed to put over the idea that he had quite a lot more tucked away in his pockets. Shabbiness was no criterion of a man's financial status in this fluctuating half-world.

He let the game break up presently, protesting in his thin old voice. Then he made his way slowly out of Gem 'o Venus and stood considering, letting himself sway a trifle. To the man who followed it must have appeared as though libation had induced libration.

'Look, Grandpa – want to sit in on another game?'

Sam gave him a wary glance. 'Floater?'

'No.'

Sam was pleased. The backer of a floating game might be too penny ante for his needs. He let himself be talked into it, remaining obviously wary until he found the destination wasn't a dark alley, but a third-rate gambling-and-pleasure house he remembered as a restaurant forty years past.

He was steered into poker, this time with more familiar cards. Playing against sober men, he tried no tricks, with the result that he lost what money he had and ended up with a stack of chips he couldn't pay for. As usual, Sam Reed had sold three hundred per cent of his stock issue.

So they took him to a man named Doc Mallard, a short, neckless man with curly fair hair and a face bronzed with scented skin-oil. Doc Mallard gave Sam a cold look. 'What's this about? I don't take IOU's.'

Sam had the sudden, strange realisation that forty years ago this man had been a raw kid, learning the angles that he himself had mastered long before that. He knew a queer moment of toppling, almost frightening psychological perspective, as though, somehow, he looked down at Mallard from the enormous height of years. *He was immortal*—

But vulnerable. He let the drunkenness die out of his voice, but not the age. He said, 'Let's talk privately.' Mallard regarded him with a shrewdness that made Sam want to smile. When they were alone he said deliberately, 'Ever hear of Sam Reed?'

'Reed? Reed? Oh, the Colony boy. Sure. Dream-dust, wasn't it?'

'Not exactly. Not for very long, anyhow. I'm Sam Reed.'

77

Mallard did not take it in for a moment. He was obviously searching his memory for details of that long ago scandal of his boyhood days. But because the Colony bubble had been unique in Keep history, apparently he remembered after a while.

'Reed's dead,' he said presently. 'Everybody knows—'

'I'm Sam Reed. I'm not dead. Sure, I dream-dusted, but that can be cured. I've been landside for a long time. Just got back.'

'What's the angle?'

'Nothing's in it for you, Mallard. I've retired. I just mentioned it to prove I'm good for my IOU's.'

Mallard sneered. 'You haven't proved a thing. Nobody comes back rich from landside.'

'I made my money right here, before I left.' Sam looked crafty.

'I remember all about that. The government found your caches. You haven't got a penny left from *that*.' Mallard was goading him.

Sam made his voice crack. 'You call seventy thousand credits nothing?' he cried in senile anger.

Mallard grinned at the ease with which he was trapping the old fool.

'How do I know you're Sam Reed? Can you prove it?'

'Fingerprints—'

'Too easy to fake. Eyeprints, though—' Mallard hesitated. Clearly he was of two minds. But after a moment he turned and spoke into a mike. The door opened and a man came in with a bulky camera. Sam, on request, looked into the eye-piece and was briefly blinded. They waited in silence, a long time.

Then the desk-mike buzzed before Mallard. Out of it a tiny voice said, 'O.K., Doc. The patterns check with the library files. That's your man.'

Mallard clicked the switch and said, 'All right, boys, come on in.' The door opened and four men entered. Mallard spoke to them over his shoulder. 'This is Sam Reed, boys. He wants to give us seventy thousand credits. Talk him into it, will you?'

The four moved competently towards Sam Reed.

Third-degree methods hadn't changed much. Here along Skid Row you depended on the basic, physical pain, and generally it worked. It worked with Sam. He stood it as long as an old man might, and then broke down and talked.

There had been one bad moment when he was afraid his beard would come off. But the artist knew his business. The surrogate tissue stuck firm and would continue to do so until Sam used the contents of the bottle in his pocket, the bottle that looked like the stub of a stylus.

Breathing short and hard, he answered Doc Mallard's questions.

'I had — double cache. Opened with a korium key—'

'How much?'

'One point . . . one point three four—'

'Why haven't you got that seventy thousand before now?'

'I just . . . just got back from landside. They'd found — all the other caches. All but that — and I can't open it without the korium key. Where can — I get that much korium? I'm broke. Seventy thousand credits — and I can't buy the key to open the lock!' Sam let his voice break.

Mallard scratched his ear.

'That's a lot of korium,' he said. 'Still, it's the safest kind of lock in the world.'

Sam nodded with an old man's eager quickness at the crumb of implied praise. 'It won't open – without the exact amount of radioactivity – focused on the lock. I was smart in the old days. You've got to know just the right amount. Can't stand the exposure – hit-or-miss. Got to know—'

'One point three four, eh?' Mallard interrupted him. He spoke to one of his men. 'Find out how much that would cost.'

Sam sank back, muffling his smile in his beard. It was a cold smile. He did not like Mallard or Mallard's methods. The old, familiar anger with which he had lived his forty earlier years was beginning to come back — the familiar impatience, the desire to smash everything that stood in his path. Mallard, now – he curled his fingers in the depths of his cloak, thinking how satisfying it would be to sink them into that thick bronze-oiled neck.

And then a strange new thought came to him for the first time. Was murder satisfactory vengeance – for an Immortal? For him other methods lay open now. He could watch his enemies die slowly. He could let them grow old.

He played with the idea, biding his time. Time – how much of it he had, and how little! But he must take it step by step, until he could use his immortality.

One step at a time he went with the gang to the cache.

One stiff, eighty-year-old step at a time.

In the cellar, Sam reluctantly showed Doc where to expose the korium key. Korium was U233 – activated thorium – and definitely not a plaything. They didn't have much of it. Not much was needed. It was in a specially-insulated box, just too big to fit in a man's pocket, and Doc had brought along a folding shield – the only protection necessary against a brief one-time exposure. He set it up at the spot Sam indicated.

There were four men in the cellar besides Sam – Doc Mallard and three of his associates. They were all armed. Sam wasn't. Outside, in the alley, was another man, the lookout. The only preparation Sam had been able to make was to seize an opportunity to rub the 'defixer' liquid into the roots of his beard. That appendage would come off at a tug now.

It was so silent the sound of breathing was very audible. Sam began taking long breaths, storing the oxygen-reserve he would probably need very soon. He watched Mallard's careful adjustment of the shield and the korium box, which looked like an old-fashioned camera, and, like a camera, had a shutter and a timing attachment.

'Right here?' Mallard asked, jabbing his finger at the plastic brick wall.

Sam nodded.

Mallard pressed the right button and stepped back, behind the shield. *Click – click!*

That was all.

Sam said hastily. 'The cache is over here, where I said. Not by the lock.' He stumbled forward, reaching, but one of the men caught his shoulder.

'Just show us,' he said. 'There might be a gun stashed away with the dough.'

Sam showed them. Mallard tested the loose brick with his finger tips. He exhaled in satisfaction.

'I think—' he began – and pulled the brick towards him.

Sam drew a long breath and kept his eyes open just long enough to see the smoke cloud begin to explode outward from the cache. With the tail-end of his glance he made certain of the korium box's location. The he moved.

He moved fast, hearing the sound of startled voices and then the explosive *sssssh-slam* of a gun. The beam didn't touch him. He felt the sharp corners of the korium box against his palm, and he bent and used his free hand to pull another loose brick from the wall. The korium went into this emergency cache, and the brick slipped back easily into its socket.

'Hold your fire!' Mallard's voice shouted. 'Head for the door. *Pollard!* Don't come in here! Stop Reed—'

Sam was already at the door and had opened his eyes. He could see nothing at all in the thick smoke that was billowing across the threshold, but he could hear a plaintive query from the look-out – Pollard. He crouched, searching for the jagged lump of metal he had planted here. It was gone. No – he found it; his fingers curled lovingly around the cold, hard alloy, and he brought his arm up and back as, through the thinning edges of the smoke, he saw Pollard.

The man's gun was out. Sam said, 'Where's Reed? Did he—'

That was enough. It made Pollard's finger hesitate on the trigger button, as he tried to make certain of the identity of the vague figure emerging from the smoke. Sam's weapon was already poised. He smashed it into Pollard's face. He felt the crunching of bone and he heard a muffled, choking bleat as Pollard arched backward and began to fall. Sam hurdled the body before it struck. He ran fourteen feet and whipped around the corner. Instantly he snatched off his cloak and beard. They went into his pockets, making no noticeable bulges. He was still running. He tore off his hat, twisted it deftly, and thrust it back on his head. It had a new shape and a different colour. He dropped to the pavement and spun around, facing in the direction from which he had come. Two hasty motions opened the buckles on his shoes so that the bright bows leaped out, disguising them. There was no need for the surrogate red dye; he had blood on his hand – not his own. He wiped this across his mouth and chin.

Then he twisted his head and looked behind, until he heard thudding footsteps.

Doc Mallard and one of his associates burst out of the alley mouth. They paused, staring around, and, as they saw Sam, sprinted towards him. Another man came out of the alley and ran after Mallard. His gun was out.

Sam dabbed feebly at his chin, blinked, and made a vague gesture behind him. He said, 'Wh ... what—' His voice wasn't senile any more.

The fourth man came out of the alley. 'Pollard's dead,' he called.

'Shut up,' Mallard said, his mouth twisting. He stared at Sam. 'Where'd he go? The old man—'

'That passage up there,' Sam said, pointing. 'He bumped into me from behind. I ... my nose is bleeding.' He dabbed experimentally and eyed his wet fingers. 'Yes. That passage—'

Mallard didn't wait. He herded his men on and turned into the alley Sam had indicated. Sam glanced around. The Way wasn't crowded, but one man was coming crosswise towards Sam.

He got up and waved the good Samaritan back. 'It's all right,' he called. 'I'm not hurt.' Wiping the blood from his face, he started to walk away.

He turned back into the alley from which he had emerged. There was no special hurry. Mallard would be chasing an old man, and feeling certain he could overtake the slow-moving octogenarian. Later he would return to the cellar, but not immediately, Sam decided.

Smoke was still billowing out. He stumbled over Pollard's body, and that gave him the location of the door. Inside the cellar, he oriented himself in the darkness and then found the loose brick. He prised it out, removed the korium box, and replaced the brick. Carrying the korium, he went out, and thirty seconds later was on the fastest Way-strip, moving rapidly away from Doc Mallard and company.

What next?

Korium was negotiable. But on a no-questions-asked basis. This loot would have to be disposed of through illegal channels. Sam was no longer recognisable as the old man who had bilked Mallard. Nevertheless, he dared not appear in this transaction – not until he had fortified his position. Mallard would be watching for an underground korium sale, and he could check back.

What channels would have remained unchanged after forty years?

The same ones – but administered by different individuals. That was no help, since in such transactions it was vital to know the right people. The right ones wouldn't be at the top any more – after forty years. Except, of course, the Harkers – the Immortal families. Sam grimaced and licked his lips, conscious again of the dry thirst under his tongue.

Who, then?

He rode the Ways for three hours, increasingly furious at this simple, easy problem that had him stopped cold. He had swindled Doc Mallard out of several thousand credits. He had the korium under his arm. But he had lost all his contacts.

Hunger grew, and thirst grew. He had no money at all. He had lost it all at the gaming table. To be distracted by such a trivial matter as hunger was infuriating. He was an Immortal!

Nevertheless Immortals could starve.

These petty details! There was so much to do, so much he could do – an endless road opening down for his feet — and he couldn't do a thing till he got cured of the dream-dust addiction.

So, groping, he came at last to the one man who had stood *in loco parentis* to him many years before.

It was not surprising that the Slider still lived in the same dingy apartment in a corner of the Keep. What was surprising was the fact that the Slider still lived.

Sam hadn't expected that. He had expected it so little, unconsciously, that he hadn't put on his disguise again.

The Slider was in bed, a monstrously corpulent figure sagging the mattress, his dropsical face bluish. He sniffed painfully. His malevolent little eyes regarded Sam steadily.

'All right,' he wheezed. 'Come on in, kid.'!

The room was filthy. In the bed the old man puffed and blinked and tried to prop himself upright. He gave up the impossible task and sank back, staring at Sam.

'Give me a drink,' he said, breathlessly.

Sam found a bottle on the table and uncapped it. The invalid drank greedily. A flush spread over the sagging cheeks.

'Woman never does anything I tell her,' he mumbled. 'What you want?'

Sam regarded him in distance and amazement. The monstrous creature seemed almost immortal as the Immortals themselves, but a Tithonian sort of immortality that no sane man would covet. He must be close to a hundred years old now, Sam thought, marvelling.

He stepped forward and took the bottle from the Slider's lax hand.

'Don't do that. Give it back. I need—'

'Answer some questions first.'

'The bottle – let's have it.'

'When you've told me what I want to know.'

The Slider groped among his dirty bedding. His hand came out with a needle-pistol half engulfed by the flesh. The tiny muzzle held steady on Sam.

'Gimme the bottle, kid,' the Slider said softly.

Sam shrugged and held it out, feeling reassured. The old man hadn't quite lost his touch, then. Perhaps he had come to the right place, after all.

'Slider,' he said, 'do you know how long since you saw me last?'

The shapeless lips mumbled a moment. 'Long time, son. Long time. Thirty – no, close to forty years, eh?'

'But – you knew me. I haven't changed. I haven't grown older. And you weren't even surprised. Slider, you must have known about me. *Where have I been?*'

A subterranean chuckle heaved the great wallowing bulk. The bed creaked.

'You think you're real?' the Slider demanded. 'Don't be a fool. I'm dreaming you, ain't I?' He reached out and patted an opalescent globe the size of a man's fist. 'This is the stuff, kid. You don't need to feel any pain no matter what ails you, long as you got Orange Devil around.'

Sam stepped closer, looking down at the bright powder in the globe.

'Oh,' he said.

The Slider peered up at him out of little shrewd eyes in their fat creases. The eyes cleared a bit as they stared. 'You're real, ain't you?' he murmured. 'Yes, I guess you are. All right, son, now I'm surprised.'

Sam eyed the orange powder. He knew what it was, yes. A drug of sorts, weakening the perception between objective and subjective, so that a man's mental images and ideations became almost tangible to him. The hope that had roused for a moment sank back in his mind. No, he was not likely to learn from the Slider where he had spent that vanished forty years.

'What's happened to you, Sam?' the Slider wheezed. 'You ought to be dead long ago.'

'The last thing I remember is having the dream-dust blown in my face. That was forty years ago. But I haven't changed!'

'Dream-dust – that don't keep you young.'

'Is there anything that will? Any sort of preservation at all that could have kept me – like this?'

The bed heaved again with the enormous chuckling.

'Sure,' he said. 'Sure! Get yourself born of the right stock – you live a thousand years.'

'What do you mean?' Suddenly Sam found that he was shaking. Until now he had had no time to reason the thing out. He awoke, he was young when he should have been old – ergo, he was immortal. But how and why he had not yet considered. Out of some unconscious well of sureness, he had assumed that like the long-limbed Immortals, he, too, was the heir of a millenium of life. But all Immortals until now had been slender, tall, fine-boned . . .

'You've always been bald?' the Slider asked obliquely. At Sam's mystified nod he went on. 'Might have been sickness when you were a baby. Then it might not. When I first knew you, you had a few little scars here and there. They're mostly gone now, I see. But the Slider's smart, kid. I heard some talk a long time ago – didn't connect it with you till now. There was a woman, a medic, who did some work on a baby once and got herself a happy-cloak for pay.'

'What kind of work?' Sam asked tightly.

'Mostly glands. That give you any ideas?'

'Yes,' Sam said. His voice was thick. His throat felt tight and the blood throbbed in his temples and his neck. He took two forward steps, picked up a plastic chair and broke it across his knee. The tough plastic broke hard, cutting his hands a little, bruising his knee. The final snap as the chair gave way was satisfying. Not enough, but satisfying. With a tremendous effort he choked back his useless rage, fettering it as Fenris Wolf was fettered, to bide its time. Carefully he set down the chair and faced Slider.

'I'm an Immortal,' he said. 'That's what it means. I'd have grown up like them if . . . if someone hadn't paid that medic. Who paid her?'

A vast seismographic shrug rippled the bedding. 'I never heard.' The Slider wallowed restlessly. 'Give me another drink.'

'You've got the bottle,' Sam pointed out. 'Slider – forget about this immortality. I'll take care of – everything. I came to you about something else. Slider, have you still got your contacts?'

'I'm still with it,' the Slider said, tilting the bottle.

Sam showed him the box he had taken from Mallard's men. 'This is korium. I want two thousand credits. Keep all you get above that. Make sure the transaction can't be traced.'

'Hijacked?' the Slider demanded. 'Better give me a name, so I can play it close.'

'Doc Mallard.'

The Slider chuckled. 'Sure, kid. I'll fix it. Shove that visor over here.'

'I'm in a hurry.'

'Come back in an hour.'

'Good. One thing more – you're the only one who knows I'm young.' Sam pulled the ragged beard from his pocket and dangled it.

'I get it. Trust the Slider, kid. See you in an hour.'

Sam went out.

At the hospital he would have to give a name. Would they recognise him as the old-time Colony swindler? Someone might. His eye-pattern records were on file, so must his other identifying marks be recorded. The average man, seeing a baffling familiarity in Sam, would chalk it up to some accidental resemblance. But in the sanatorium he would be under much closer observation. Too close to maintain the octogenarian disguise – that was certain.

Suddenly it occurred to Sam that there was one man who could very logically resemble him and yet seem the age he looked now. His own son.

He had none, it was true. But he might have had. And everyone knew that short physiques weren't Immortal, couldn't tap the fountain of youth. He could preserve his precious secret and get by with a minimal disguise as Sam Reed's son.

What name? Out of the depths of his omnivorous reading in those years which still seemed hardly an hour ago he dredged up the memory of the prophet Samuel, whose eldest son was Joel. *Now the name of his first-born was Joel.*

As good a name as any. He was Joel Reed . . .

Thirty-five minutes after that he stood before the hospital reception desk, shocked into immobility with surprise, able only to stare, while the circuits of his brain tried frantically to close their contacts again. But the disorientation was too abrupt and complete. All he could do was stand there, repeating stupidly, 'What? What did you say'?

The competent young man behind the desk said patiently, 'We discharged you as cured early this morning.'

Sam opened his mouth and closed it. No sound came out.

The young man regarded him thoughtfully. 'Amnesia?' he suggested. 'It hardly ever happens, but – do you want to see one of the doctors?'

Sam nodded.

'Six weeks ago,' the man in the quiet office said, 'you were brought here for the regulation cure. A man who gave the name of Evans delivered you and signed you in. He gave us no permanent address – said he was a transient at one of the hotels. You can try to trace him later if you like. The fee was paid anonymously, by special delivery, just before you arrived. You seemed in good physical condition on admission.' The doctor referred again to the ledger page before him. 'Apparently adequate care had been taken of you while you were dream-dusting. You were discharged this morning. You seemed quite normal. Another man called for you – not the same one, though he gave the name of Evans, too. That is all I can tell you, Mr Reed.'

'But' – Sam rubbed his forehead dazedly – 'why have I forgotten? What does it mean? I—'

'There are a good many amnesic preparations on the underworld market, unfortunately,' the doctor said. 'You left here in a suit of good clothes, with a hundred credits in your pocket. Did you wake with them?'

'No. I—'

'You were probably robbed.'

'Yes, I . . . of course that was it.' Sam's eyes went blank as he thought of many ways in which a man might be rendered unconscious – a puff of dust in the face in some alleyway, a crack on the head. Robbers rarely bother to stuff a stripped victim into their own discarded rags, but aside from that the story was plausible enough.

Except for that man who had been waiting when he woke.

He got up, still slightly dazed. 'If I could have the address the Evans man gave you—'

It would lead nowhere, he knew, looking down on the scrawled slip as the moving Way glided slowly beneath him, carrying him away from the hospital. Whoever was responsible for the chain of mysteries which had led him here would have covered any tracks efficiently.

Someone had fed him dream-dust forty years ago. Zachariah Harker – that much he knew. Kedre Walton gave the signal, but Zachariah was the man behind her. *The voice is Jacob's voice, but the hand is the hand of Esau.*

Had Harker watched over him these forty years? Had Kedre? Someone did a careful job of it, according to the doctor. Someone paid to have him cured at last, and discharged – and robbed and stripped, so that when he woke he possessed materially as little as he had possessed when he came into the world.

Less – for then he came with a birthright. Well, of that they had not cheated him after all. And if there were a Joel Reed, Sam realised with a sudden gust of pride, he would stand head and shoulders above his father, on long, straight legs slender and elegant as Zachariah himself – an Immortal in body as well as in heritage.

The stretching of his mind was almost painful as he surveyed the years before him. And when he thought now of the Slider he saw him through a new temporal perspective that was almost frightening. It was oddly similar to the attitude he might have towards a cat or a dog. There was always, and there must always be from now on, the knowledge that the life-span of an ordinary man was too short.

No wonder the Families had formed a tight clique. How could you feel deep friendship, or love untouched by pity, except for an equal? It was the old, old gulf between gods and men. Nothing – immortal – was alien.

That didn't solve his current problem. He was here on sufferance – by grace of somebody's indulgence. Whose? If only he had kept his grip on the collar of that unknown man in the alley until his own wits returned to him! Someone had deliberately redeemed him from oblivion and set him free, penniless and in rags – why? To watch what he would do? It was a godlike concept. Zachariah? He looked around hopelessly at the uninterested crowds that moved with him along the Way. Did one of these faces mask an absorbed interest in his behaviour? Or had his unknown guardian tired of the burden and set him on his own feet again, to go his own way?

Well, in time he would know. Or he would never know.

One excellent result of the past few hours was the money in his pocket, two thousand credits, free and clear. He had hurdled the next step without realising it. Now there were a few old scores to settle, a few details to attend to, and then – immortality!

He refused to think of it. His mind shrank from the infinite complexities, the fantastic personal applications of his new, extended life. Instead, he concentrated on the two men named Evans who had shepherded him to and from the hospital. The Slider would start investigations on those – he made a mental note. Rosathe. The Slider would be useful there, too. Other things he would attend to himself.

His throat was dry. He laughed to himself. Not the pseudo-thirst of dream-dust, after all. He had simply played a trick on himself. Water could have quenched his thirst at any time, had he allowed himself to believe it. He stepped off the Way at the nearest Public Aid station and drank cool water, freshly cold, ecstatically quenching, until he could drink no more.

He looked up at the brightness of the Way, the towering buildings beyond, twinkling with lights, and something within him began to expand, growing and growing until it seemed the Keep could not contain this strange vastness. He stared up at the impervium dome and pierced the shallow seas above it, and the clouds and the twinkling void beyond which he had never seen. There was so much to do now. And no need to hurry. He had time. All the time in the world.

Time to kill.

His bones are full of the sin of his youth, which shall lie down with him in the dust. Though wickedness be sweet in his mouth . . . – JOB

He turned from his contemplation of the city and into the arms of the two men in uniform who had come up behind him on the Way platform. The uniforms had not changed – they were private government police and Sam knew before a word had been uttered that there was no point in trying to argue.

In a way he was rather more pleased than otherwise as the older of the two flashed an engraved plaque at him and said, 'Come along.' At least, someone else had finally made a tangible move. Perhaps now he would learn the answers to some of the questions that had been tantalising him.

They took him along the high-speed Ways towards the centre of the Keep. People glanced curiously at the three as the city flashed past around them. Sam held the railing to keep steady, aware of an unaccustomed flutter around his face as his red wig blew in the wind of their speed. He was watching with interest and anticipation the destination towards which they seemed headed.

The Immortals of every Keep lived in a group of high, coloured towers built at the city's centre and guarded by a ring of walled gardens. The police were taking Sam straight towards the tall, shining quarters of the Harker Family. Sam was not surprised. It seemed unlikely that Zachariah would have ordered his ruin forty years ago and then let him wander unguarded for the next forty. On the other hand, it seemed unlikely that Zachariah would have let him live at all. Sam shrugged. He should know the truth, soon.

They took him in through a small door at the back of the highest tower, down transparent plastic steps under which a stream of grey water flowed towards the gardens beyond. Red and gold fish went by with the stream, a long blue ribboneel, a strand of flowering seaweed.

At the foot of the steps a small gilded lift was waiting. The two policemen put Sam into it, closed the door without a word behind him. He had glimpse through the glass of their impassive faces sliding down outside; then he was alone in the gently sighing cage as it rose towards the height of the Harker tower.

The lift's walls were mirrored. Sam considered himself in the role of Joel Reed, feeling rather foolish about it, wondering whether whoever it was that waited him above knew him already as Sam Reed. The disguise was good. He couldn't look exactly like his supposed father, but there was a naturally strong likeness. A red wig matched the heavy red brows, trimmed and smooth a little now. A set of tooth caps altered the contour of his lower face. There were eye shells with bright blue irises instead of grey. Nothing else.

The eye shells served the same psychological purpose as dark glasses – unconsciously Sam felt himself masked. He could look out, but nobody could look in. It is difficult to meet a straight stare, unprotected, when you have something to hide.

The pressure on Sam's soles decreased; the lift was slowing. It stopped, the door slid open and he stepped out into a long hall whose walls and ceiling were a constant rustle of green leaves. A glow of simulated daylight poured softly through them from luminous walls. The vines sprang from hydroponic tanks under the floor and met in a trellis-like tunnel overhead. Flowers and fruits swayed among the leaves in a scented, continuing breeze that soughed down the arbour. To Keep-bred man it was exotic beyond all imagining.

Sam went warily down the silent hall, shrinking a little from the leaves that brushed his face. Like all Venus-bred people he feared and mistrusted by instinct the dangerous products of the landside world.

From the other end of the hall came the pleasant tinkle and splash of falling water. Sam paused on the threshold of the room upon which the trellis opened, staring in amazement.

This room was an arbour, too. Vines looped down festooned with clustering blossoms; the air was heavy with their fragrance. And the floor of the room was water. Blue water, a shallow lake of it perhaps a foot deep, filling the room from wall to wall. Flowers mirrored themselves in its surface, other flowers floated upon it. Tiny fish darted among their drifting leaves. A luminous jellyfish or two lay motionless on the blue water, dangling dangerous-looking jewelled webs.

There was a bridge of filigreed glass, insubstantial-looking as frost, that spanned the pool. One end lay at Sam's feet, the other at a low platform, cushion-covered, on the far side of the room. A woman lay face-down among the cushions, elbow on the edge of the pool, one arm submerged to the elbow as she splashed in the shining water. Her hair hid her face, its curled ends dipping in the ripples. The hair was a very pale green-gold, wholly unreal in its colour and its water-smooth lustrousness.

Sam knew her. The long lines of Kedre Walton's body, her leisured motions, the shape of her head and her hands, were unmistakable even though the face was hidden. Why she should be here in the Harker stronghold, and why she had summoned him, remained to be seen.

'Kedre?' he said.

She looked up. Sam's mind spun dizzily for an instant. It was Kedre – it was not. The same delicate, narrow, disdainful face, with the veiled eyes and the secret Egyptian mouth – but a different personality looking out at him. A malicious, essentially unstable personality, he thought in his first glimpse of the eyes.

'No, I'm Sari Walton,' the pale-haired woman said, smiling her malicious smile. 'Kedre's my grandmother. Remember?'

He remembered. Sari Walton, leaning possessively on Zachariah's shoulder long ago, while Zachariah spoke with him about the murder of Robin Hale. Sam had scarcely noticed her then. He searched his memory quickly – antagonism was what returned to it first, antagonism between Sari and Kedre, submerged but potent as the two beautiful women watched each other across the table with mirror-image faces.

'All right,' he said. 'What does that mean?' He knew well enough. Joel Reed could not be expected to remember a scene in which Sam Reed had figured. She knew who he was. She knew, then, that he, too, was immortal.

'Come here,' Sari said, gesturing with a dripping white arm. She sat up among the cushions, swinging her feet around beneath her. Sam looked dubiously at the glass bridge. 'It'll hold you. Come on.' Derision was in Sari's voice.

It did, though it sang with faint music at the pressure of every step. At Sari's gesture he sank hesitantly to a seat among the cushions beside her, sitting stiffly, every angle of his posture rejecting this exotic couch, this fantastic, water-floored bower.

'How did you locate me?' he demanded bluntly.

She laughed at him, putting her head to one side so that the green-gold hair swayed between them like a veil. There was something about her eyes and the quality of her laughter that he did not like at all.

'Kedre's had a watch out for you for the past forty years,' she said. 'I think they traced you through an inquiry at the library archives about your eye patterns today. Anyhow, they found you – that's all that matters, isn't it?'

'Why isn't Kedre here now?'

Again she laughed, that faintly malicious laughter. 'She doesn't know. That's why. Nobody knows but me.'

Sam regarded her thoughfully. There was a challenge in her eyes, an unpredictable capriciousness in her whole manner that he could not quite make up his mind about. In the old days he had known one solution for all such problems as that. He reached out with a quick, smooth gesture and closed his fingers about her wrist, jerking her off balance so that she fell with an almost snakelike gracefulness across his knees. She twisted, unpleasantly lithe in his grasp, and laughed up at him derisively.

There was a man's aggressive sureness in the way she reached up to take his cheek in the cup of her palm and pull his head down to hers. He let her do it, but he made the kiss she was demanding a savage one. Then he pushed her off his knee with an abrupt thrust and sat looking at her angrily.

Again she laughed. 'Kedre's not such a fool after all,' she said, running a delicate forefinger across her lip.

Sam got to his feet, kicking a cushion out of the way. Without a word he set his foot on the ringing bridge and started back across it. From the corner of his eye he saw the serpentine twist with which Sari Walton got to her feet.

'Come back,' she said.

Sam did not turn. An instant later he heard a hissing past his ear, felt the searing heat of a needle-gun's beam. He stopped dead still, not daring to stir for fear another beam was on the way. It was. The hiss and the heat stung his other ear. It was fine shooting – too fine for Sam's liking. He said without moving his head, 'All right, I'm coming. Let me hear the gun drop.'

There was a soft thud among the cushions and Sari's laughter sounded almost as softly. Sam turned and went back to her.

When they were standing like this he had to tip his head back to look into her eyes. He did not like it. He liked nothing about her, least of all her air of self-confident aggressiveness which from time immemorial has belonged to man, not woman. She looked as fragile as the frost-patterned bridge, as delicately feminine as the most sheltered woman alive – but she was an Immortal and the world belonged to her and her kind. There had been generations of time for her to set in this pattern of malice and self-assurance.

Or – had there been? Sam squinted at her thoughtfully, an idea beginning to take shape in his mind that blotted everything else out for a moment. In contrast to Kedre, this beautiful, fragile creature seemed amazingly immature. That was it – immaturity. It explained the capriciousness, the air of experimental malice he had sensed in her. And he realised that for the Immortals maturity must be a long, long time in forming fully. Probably he himself was very far from it, but his early training had hardened him into the pattern of an adult.

But Sari – sheltered and indulged, wielding almost godlike powers – it was no wonder she seemed unstable in these years before her final matrix of centuries-old maturity had set. It would never set quite properly, he thought. She was not essentially a stable person. She would never be a woman to like or trust. But now she was more vulnerable than she knew. And one of Sam's devious schemes for making use of an adversary's weakness started to spin a web in his mind.

'Sit down,' Sam told her.

She lifted both hands over her green-gold head to pluck a cluster of pale fruit like grapes that dangled from a vine. Sam could see her cradling fingers through them, they were so nearly transparent, the blue seeds making a pattern of shadows inside the tiny globes. She smiled at him and sank to her knees with her unpleasantly boneless litheness.

Sam looked down at her. 'All right,' he said. 'Now. Why did you get me up here? If Kedre sent the orders out, why isn't she here instead of you?'

Sari put a pale, glassy globe into her mouth and bit down on it. She spat out blue seeds. 'Kedre doesn't know, I told you.' She looked up at him under heavy lashes. Her eyes were a paler blue than Kedre's. 'The warrant's been out for forty years. She's in Nevada Keep this week.'

'Has she been notified?'

Sari shook her head, the lustrous, improbable hair swinging softly. 'Nobody knows but me. I wanted to see you. If Zachariah knew he'd be furious. He—'

'Zachariah ordered me dream-dusted,' Sam broke in impatiently, eager to get the story clear in his head. 'Was Kedre behind it?'

'Zachariah ordered you poisoned,' Sari corrected, smiling up at him. 'He meant you to die. Kedre said no. They had a terrible quarrel about it.' Her smile grew secret; she seemed to hug herself with a pleasant memory. 'Kedre made it dream-dust,' she went on after a moment. 'No one could understand why, really. You wouldn't be any use to her after that, alive or dead, young or old.' Her voice failed gently; she sat with a transparent fruit between thumb and finger halfway to her lips, and did not move for a long second.

Sam had a sudden, dazzling idea. He dropped to his knees before her and put a finger under her chin, turning her head towards him, looking into her eyes. And a surge of triumph made his throat close for an instant.

'Narco-dust!' he said softly. 'I'll be damned! Narco-dust!'

Sari gurgled with laughter and leaned forward to rub her

forehead against his shoulder, her eyes glazed with that strange luminous lustre which is unmistakable in the addict.

It explained a great deal – her instability, her curious indifference, the fact that she had not yet quite realised Sam's strange youth. How odd, he thought – and how significant – that the two people he had met who remembered him from long ago were both under a haze of drug-induced dreams.

Sari pushed him away. She put the fruit in her mouth without knowing her gesture had been interrupted, and spat out the seeds and smiled at him with that sharp, glittering malice that had no reason behind it. Of course his inexplicable youth had not struck her. She was quite accustomed to seeing unchanging faces about her as the decades went by. And under narco-dust a serene, unquestioning acceptance of all one sees is a major factor. But at any moment now she might have a flash of clarity. And Sam still had much to learn.

'Kedre substituted dream-dust for the poison,' he said. 'Did she have someone guard me after that?'

The greenish hair spread out like a shawl as Sari shook her head.

'She meant to. Zachariah fixed that, I think. Kedre always thought he did. You'd disappeared when her men went to look for you. You've been missing ever since – until now. Where were you, Sam Reed? I think I could like you, Sam. I think I see now what was in Kedre's mind when she sent her people out to find you and cure you.'

'What are you doing here, in the Harker house?'

'I live here.' Sari laughed, and then an ugly timbre crept into the laughter and she closed her delicate, long fingered hand suddenly over the cluster of fruit. Colourless juice spurted through her fingers. 'I live here with Zachariah.' She said. 'He wants Kedre. But if he can't have her – I'll do instead. Some day I think I'll kill Zachariah.' She smiled again, sweetly enough, and Sam wondered if Zachariah knew how she felt about him, and that she was a narco-addict. He rather doubted it. The combination was dynamite.

He was beginning to realise what a ripe plum of opportunity had dropped into his lap – but an instant later the familiar doubt crept in. How opportunely had it dropped, after all? How much reasoned planning lay behind all that had happened to him since he woke? There was still no explanation of the watcher in the alley. And that man had known what he was doing. There was no drug-dream behind the precise pattern of what had so far happened to Sam Reed.

'Why did you send for me?' he demanded. Sari was splashing her hand in the water to wash away the sticky juice. He had to ask her twice before she appeared to hear him. Then she looked up and smiled her bright, vacant smile.

'I was curious. I've been watching Kedre's private visor for a long time now. She doesn't know. When word came in that they'd found you I thought I'd see . . . I thought I could use you. Against Kedre or against Zachariah – I'm not sure yet. After a while I'll think about it. Not now. I'm thinking about Zachariah now. And the Harkers. I hate the Harkers, Sam. I hate all Harkers. I even hate myself, because I'm half a Harker. Yes, I think I'll use you against Zachariah.' She leaned forward, brushing Sam's shoulder with a fan of green-gold hair, looking up at him with a pale-blue flash under the heavy lashes.

'You hate Zachariah too, don't you, Sam? You should. He wanted you poisoned. What do you think would hurt him most, Sam? I think for Kedre to know you're alive – alive – and young. Young?' Her narrow brows drew together in brief bewilderment. But that was a subject that required thought, and she was in no condition now to attack serious problems. Her mind was not working except in its deepest levels at this moment, the primitive levels that move automatically, without conscious effort.

Suddenly she drew back her head and laughed, choked on the laughter, looked at Sam with swimming eyes. 'It's wonderful!' she said. 'I can punish them both, can't I? Zachariah will have to wait until Kedre's tired of you, now that you're alive again. And Kedre can't have you if she doesn't know where you are. Could you go away and hide, Sam? Some place where Kedre's men couldn't find you? Oh, please, Sam, do go and hide! For Sari. It would make Sari so happy!'

Sam rose. The bridge rang musically as he crossed it, a series of faint, sweet undernotes to Sari's laughter. The scented breeze blew in his face as he went back down the trellised hall. The lift stood waiting where he had left it. There was no one in sight when he came out at the foot of the shaft and went back up the glass steps over the swimming stream and into the street.

Moving almost in a daze, he stepped on to the nearest Way and let it carry him at random through the city. The episode just past had all the qualities of a dream; he had to focus hard upon it to convince himself it had happened at all. But the seed of a great opportunity lay in it, if he could only isolate what was important.

The Harkers had a weakness they did not suspect – Sari. And beyond that lay implicit an even deeper weakness, if Sari was really a Harker, too. For she was definitely not a normal person. The narco-dust and the possible immaturity of her mind explained only partly that shuddering instability at the very core of her being. It opened new vistas for Sam's thought. So even Immortals were not wholly invulnerable, even they had hidden weaknesses in the fabric of their heritage.

There were two secret paths now by which he might ambush Zachariah. The paths would need exploring. That must come later.

Just now the most important thing was to hide while he thought things over. And the more he considered this, the more inclined Sam felt to visit the Colony where Robin Hale administered his sterile jurisdiction.

Hale would probably shoot him on sight. Or would he, as Joel Reed? No one knew Sam yet except Sari, but who could guess what wild caprices might move her between now and the time he was face to face with Hale? He had better act fast.

He did.

The most striking thing about the Colony was that it might just as well have been undersea.

At no time since Sam Reed had left the Keep was the open sky ever above his head. First there was the Keep's impervium dome and above that a mile of water. Then the plane, with its alloy and plastic shell. After that, the great Colony locks, with their safeguards against infection – UV, acid spray, and so on –and now he stood on the land of Venus, with a transparent impervium dome catching rainbows wherever the fugitive sun broke through the cloud blanket. The air smelt the same. That was a tip-off. The free air of Venus was short on oxygen and long on carbon dioxide; it was breathable, but not vintage atmosphere. And it was unmistakable. Here, under the dome, the atmospheric ingredients were carefully balanced. Necessary, of course – just as the impervium shell itself seemed necessary against the fecund insanity that teemed the Venusian lands – flora and fauna bursting up towards the light, homicidally and fratricidally determined to bud and seed, to mate and breed, in an environment so fertile that it made its own extraordinary imbalance.

On the shore stood the old Fort, one-time stronghold of the Doonemen Free Companions. It had been rehabilitated. It, too, was enclosed under the impervium, the great shell a quarter of a mile in diameter. There were small houses arranged here and there, with no attempt at planning. The houses themselves were of all shapes, sizes, and colours. With no rainfall or winds here, the architects had a free hand. The only limitations were those of natural gravity, and paragravitic shields made even Pisa-towers possible. Still, there was nothing really extravagant in material or design. No lavishness. The whole Colony had an air of faint attrition.

There was no open land visible beneath the dome.

The ground had been floored over with plastic materials. Protection against the ground-lichens? Probably. Great hydroponic tanks were the gardens, though a few shallow tanks held sterilised soil. Men were working, rather lazily. It seemed a siesta hour.

Sam walked along one of the paths, following the sign that

pointed towards Administration. A mild agoraphobia afflicted him. All his life he had dwelt under an opaque dome, knowing the weight of water above it, shutting out the upper air. Now through the translucent impervium above he had glimpses of watery sunlight, and the illumination was not artificial, though it seemed a bad imitation of the surrogate daylight of the Keep lamps.

His mind was very busy. He was taking in all he saw, evaluating it, packing facts and impressions away against the moment when his innate opportunism saw its chance. He had for the moment dismissed Sari and the Harkers. Let that group of ideas settle and incubate. How Robin Hale would receive Sam Reed, or Sam's son, was the important question now. He did not consider that he owed Hale any debt. Sam did not think in terms like that. He thought only in terms of what would best benefit Sam Reed – and the Colony was something that still looked promising to him.

A girl in a pink smock, bending over a tank of growing things, looked up as he passed. It was curious to see the effect even diluted sunlight made upon the faces of these Landsiders. Her skin was creamy, not milk-white as Sari's in the Keep. She had smooth brown hair, brushed sleek, and her eyes were brown, with a subtly different focus from the eyes of Keep people. An impervium dome shut in her life as fully as any undersea Keep life, but light from the sun came through it, and the jungle pressed ravenously against the gates – a hungry, animate jungle, not the dead weight of sea water. You could tell by her eyes that she was aware of it.

Sam lingered a little. 'Administration?' he asked unnecessarily.

'That way.' Her voice was pleasant.

'Like it here?'

She shrugged. 'I was born here. The Keeps must be wonderful. I've never seen a Keep.'

'You wouldn't know the difference – there isn't any,' Sam assured her, and went on with a troubling thought in his mind. She had been born here. She could be no more than twenty. She was pretty, but not wholly to his taste. And the idea had come to him if she had only partially the qualities he liked in a woman, he could afford to wait for her daughter, or her daughter's daughter – if he chose the parents of the final product with reasonable care. An Immortal could work out a strain of humanity as a mortal could breed for elegance in cats or speed in horses. Except that the product would be only a cut flower, lovely but perishing in a day. He wondered how many of the Immortals did just that, maintaining in effect a harem in time as well as in space. It would be excellent, so long as one's emotions remained unengaged.

The Governor of the Land Colony should have been busy. He wasn't. A minute after Sam sent in his assumed name, the door opened with an automatic click and he walked into Robin Hale's office.

'Joel Reed?' Hale said slowly. His stare was intent, and it took all Sam's hardihood to meet it without shrinking a little.

'Yes. Sam Reed was my father.' He said it with a bit of bravado.

'All right,' Hale said. 'Sit down.'

Sam looked at him through the thin protection of his eye shields. It might have been yesterday they met last, Hale had changed so little. Or – no, he had changed, but in ways too subtle for the eye to catch. The voice told more of the story. He was still thin, still brown, still quiet, a man whose mind was attuned to patience because of the years behind him and the centuries ahead. He could accept any defeat as temporary, and any victory as evanescent.

This change in him was temporary too, but no less real for that. He had not quite the quiet enthusiasm of voice and manner that Sam remembered. The thing he had been working towards with high hope when they parted was an accomplished fact now, and a finished failure. But it was so brief a thing in the total of Hale's experience – that was it, Sam realised, staring at the man.

Robin Hale remembered the Free Companion days, the long war years, the time generations past when the last vestiges of mankind had been free to roam the seas, free to face danger. It had been matter-of-fact enough, Sam knew. A business, not a swashbuckling romance. But emotions had run high and the life the Free Companions led was nomadic, the last nomads before mankind returned wholly to the shelter of the Keeps, the stagnation of the underseas. The Keeps were the tomb, or the womb, or both, for the men of Venus, who had begun their life as wild tribesmen on Earth.

Sam was beginning to feel the first stirrings of interest in his own kind as a long-term investment for a long-lived Immortal.

'Are you a volunteer?' Hale asked.

Sam came back to himself with something of a jolt. 'No,' he said.

'I didn't know Sam Reed had a son.' Hale was still looking at him with that quiet, speculative stare that Sam found hard to meet. Could one Immortal know another, through any disguise, simply by those mannerisms no man could wholly hide? He thought it likely. It didn't apply to himself – yet, for he was not yet immortal in the sense that these others were. He had not acquired the long-term view with which they kept life at bay.

'I didn't know myself until just lately,' he said, making his voice matter-of-fact. 'My mother changed my name after the Colony scandal.'

'I see.' Hale was non-committal.

'Do you know what happened to my father?' That was pushing things. If Hale said, 'Yes – you're Sam Reed,' it would at least settle this uncertainty. But if he didn't, it need not mean he had failed to recognise Sam.

The Free Companion shook his head. 'He dream-dusted. I suppose he's dead by now. He'd made enemies after the bubble burst.'

'I know. You . . . you must have been one of them.'

Hale shook his head again, smiling faintly. Sam knew what the smile meant. One neither hates nor loves the ephemeral short-lived. Temporary annoyance is the worst they can evoke. Nevertheless Sam was not tempted to reveal himself. Olympians had the god-prerogative of being unpredictable. Zeus tossed thunderbolts on impulse.

'It wasn't Sam Reed's fault,' Hale said. 'He couldn't help being a swindler. It was born in him and bred in him. Anyhow, he was only a tool. If it hadn't been Sam, it would have been someone or something else. No, I never hated him.'

Sam swallowed. All right, he had asked for that. Briskly he moved on to the next point. 'I'd like your advice, Governor Hale. I've only learned who I really am lately. I've been checking up. I know my father was a crook and swindled, but the government found his caches and paid back everything – right?'

'Right.'

'He left me nothing – not even his name, for forty years. But I've been investigating, just in case. There was one asset my father had when he dream-dusted, and that wasn't taken away from him. A land-grant. Forty years ago the government issued him a patent on certain Venusian land areas, and that grant's still valid. What I want to know is this: Is it worth anything?'

Hale tapped his fingers on the desk. 'Why did you come to me?'

'My father was with you when the Colony started. I figured you'd know. You'd remember. You're an Immortal; you were alive then.'

Hale said, 'I knew about that patent, of course. I tried to get hold of it. But it was in your father's name, absolutely watertight. The government wouldn't release. As a matter of fact, land-grants aren't revokable. There's a reason. On Venus all colonies presumably have to depend for existence on Keeps, and it would be easy to cut off supplies if necessary. So you've inherited that patent, eh?'

Sam said, 'Is it worth anything?'

'Yes. The Harkers would pay you a good deal to suppress the information.'

'The Harkers? Why?'

'So I couldn't start a new colony,' Hale said, and his hand on the desk opened slowly from a tightballed fist. 'That's why. I started this Colony, after your father – after the collapse. I went ahead anyway. The good publicity we'd built up boomeranged. We had to start on a skeleton crew. Just a few, who believed in the same things I did. Not many of them are still alive. It was a tough life in the beginning.'

'It doesn't look so tough,' Sam said.

'Now? It isn't. The Colony's been emasculated. You see what the Harkers did was try to stop me from even starting the Colony. They couldn't stop me. And after I'd started, they didn't dare let me fail. Because, eventually, they want to colonise Venus, and they don't want the psychological effect of a failure chalked up in history. They couldn't let me fail once I'd started, but they wouldn't let me succeed either. They didn't believe I *could* succeed. So—'

'So?'

'Attrition. Oh, we worked hard the first year. We did it with our fingernails. We didn't lick the jungle, but we started. We got the Colony cleared and built. It was a fight every step, because the jungle kept pushing back in. But we kept going. Then we were ready to reach out – to establish a new beach-head. And the Harkers stopped us cold.

'They cut off our supplies.

'They sat in the Keeps and made sure there wouldn't be any volunteers.

'The equipment dwindled. The power dwindled. The machines stopped coming.

'According to the original charter, we had to show an annual profit. Or the government could step in as administrator till matters got on an even basis again. They couldn't take my grant away from me, but they could cut down the blood supply so the Colony wouldn't be able to show a profit. That's what they did, thirty-four years ago. Since then, the government has been administrator here – maintaining the *status quo*.

'They administer. They give us enough supplies so we won't fail. But not enough so we can go forward. They don't want us to go forward – because there's the risk of failure. They want to wait until there's no risk. And that time will never come.'

Hale looked at Sam, a deep fire beginning to glow far back

in his eyes under the scowling brows. Was he talking to Joel Reed – or to Sam? It was hard to be sure. Certainly he was saying more than he would say to the casual visitor.

'My hands are tied,' Hale went on. 'Nominally I'm Governor. Nominally. Everything here has come to a full stop. If I had another patent – if I could start another colony—' He paused, looking at Sam from under meeting brows. 'They won't grant me a patent. You can see how important yours is. The Harkers would pay you very well to suppress it.'

That was it, then. That was the reason behind his freedom of speech. He had finished, but he did not look at Sam. He sat motionless behind his bare-topped desk, waiting. But he made no plea and no argument.

For what could he offer the man before him? Money? Not as much as the Harkers could offer. A share in the new colony? By the time it would begin to pay off any short-term man would be long dead.

On impulse Sam said suddenly, 'What could you do with the patent, Governor?'

'Start over, that's all. I couldn't pay you much. I could lease the patent from you, but there'd be no profit for many years. They'd be eaten up by the costs. On Venus a colony has to keep moving, spreading out. It's the only way. I know that now.'

'But what if you failed? Wouldn't the government come in again as administrator – the same thing over again? Wouldn't they see you did fail?'

Hale was silent.

Sam hammered at him. 'You'd need a big stake to start a new colony. You—'

'I'm not arguing,' Hale said. 'I told you you'd get more money from the Harkers.'

It was Sam's turn for silence. A dozen possibilities were already taking shape in his sind – ways to raise money, to cir- cumvent the Harkers, to spread propaganda, to make the next colony a success in spite of all opposition. This time he thought he could do it. He had all the time in the world and it would be worthwhile now to invest in it a successful colony.

Hale was watching him, a flicker of hope beginning to show through the fatalistic inertia which had dulled all he said until now. And Sam was a little puzzled by the man. With all that long life behind him, all that unthinkable maturity which must be the sum of his experiences, still he had turned once and was ready to turn again to Sam Reed, short-lived, immature to the point of childishness from an Immortal's view. Hale was ready to let his most cherished venture fail for lack of ideas and initiative, unless this man before him, short-lived as a cat and as comparatively limited in scope, could take over for him.

Why?

A vague parallel with the social history of Old Earth swam up in Sam's memory. Somewhere in his reading he had encountered the theory that those countries on Earth which the Mongol hordes invaded in very ancient times had been so completely vitiated by the terrible experience that they had never again been able to regain their initiative. With all the resources their countries offered, the people themselves remained helpless to use them or to compete with other peoples who had not been robbed of that essential spark.

Perhaps the same thing had happened to Robin Hale. He was the only man alive now who had fought with the Free Companions. Had he expended in those wild, vigorous years the spark that would move him now if he still possessed it? He had the centuries of experience and knowledge and accumulating maturity, but he no longer had the one essential thing that could let him use them.

Sam had it, in abundance. And it occurred to him suddenly that perhaps of all men alive he alone did possess it. Hale had the long life but not the will to use it. The other Immortals had initiative enough, but—

'If we wait on the Families, the time will never come to move,' Sam said aloud, in a marvelling voice, as if he had never heard the idea before.

'Of course not.' Hale was calm. 'It may be too late already.'

Sam scarcely heard him. 'They think they're right,' he

went on, exploring this new concept which had never dawned on him before. 'But they don't want a change! They'll go right on waiting until even they recognise they've waited too long, and then maybe they'll be a little bit glad it *is* too late. They're conservatives. The people on top are always conservatives. Any change has to be for the worse where they're concerned.'

'That applies to the Keep people, too,' Hale told him. 'What can we offer any of them to match what they already have? Comfort, security, plenty of entertainment, a complete, civilised life. All we have up here is danger and hardship and the chance that maybe in a couple of hundred years they can begin to duplicate on land what they already have undersea, without working for it. None of them would live to cash in on the rewards even if they saw the necessity for changing.'

'They responded once,' Sam pointed out. 'When . . . when my father promoted the first Colony scheme.'

'Oh, yes. There's plenty of discontent. They know they're losing something. But it's one thing to talk about romance and adventure and quite another to endure the danger and hardships that make up the total sum. These people lack a drive. Pioneers are pioneers because conditions at home are intolerable, or because conditions elsewhere look more promising or . . . or because there's a Grail or a Holy Land or something like it to summon them. Here it's simply a small matter like the salvation of the race of man – but intangibles are beyond their grasp.'

Sam wrinkled red brows at him. 'Salvation of the race of man?' he echoed.

'If colonisation doesn't start now, or soon, it never will. Our korium supplies will be too low to support it. I've said that over and over until the words come out whenever I open my mouth, it's that automatic. The race of man will come to an end in a few more centuries, huddled down there in their safe Keep-wombs with their power-source dwindling and their will to live dwindling until nothing remains of either. But the Families are going to oppose every move I make and go on opposing like grim death, until it's too late to move at all.' Hale shrugged. 'Old stuff. It's out of fashion even to think in those terms any more, down in the Keeps, they tell me.'

Sam squinted at him. There was conviction in the Immortal's voice. He believed Hale. And while the ultimate destiny of the race was far too vague a concept to worry Sam at all, his own increased life-span made the next few hundred years a very vital subject. Also, he had a score to settle with the Harkers. And there were almost unlimited possibilities in this colonising project, if it were handled by a man like Sam Reed.

He was beginning to see the dawning flicker of a magnificent idea.

'The patent's yours,' he said briskly. 'Now look—'

Robin Hale closed the shuttered door of Administration behind him and walked slowly down the plastic path, alone. Overhead the glowering greyness of the Venusian day lightened briefly with a flash of blue sky and sun, filtered diffused through the impervium overhead. Hale glanced up, grimacing a little against the brightness, remembering the old days.

A man in brown overalls some distance away, was leisurely moving a hoe around the roots of growing things in one of the broad beds of soil dug from Venus' over-fertile ground. The man moved quietly, perhaps a bit stiffly, but with the measured motions of one who knows and enjoys his work. He lifted a gaunt, long-jawed face as Hale paused beside the shallow tank.

'Got a minute?' Hale asked.

The man grinned. 'More than most,' he said. 'What's on your mind?'

Hale put a foot on the rim of the tank and crossed his arms on the lifted knee. The older man leaned comfortably on his hoe. They looked at each other for a moment in silence, and a faint smile on the face of each told quietly of the things they had in common. These two, of all the men now alive, remembered life under an open sky, the succession of night and day, sun and moon, the natural rhythms of a world not ordered by man.

Only the Logician remembered a day when the soil of an open planet had not been man's deadly enemy. Only he of all the workers here could handle his hoe in leisurely communion with the turned dirt, knowing it for no enemy. For the others, the very sight of soil meant dangers seen and unseen, known and unknown – fungi in the brown grains they hoed, bacteria of unguessable potentialities, mysterious insects and tiny beastlings lurking ready for the next stroke of the blade. This soil, of course, had been processed and was safe, but conditioning dies hard. No one but the Logician really liked these beds of open ground.

Hale had been surprised only superficially when he first thought he recognised the gaunt figure wielding the hoe as he backed slowly along a path between brown seed beds. That was not very long ago – a few weeks, perhaps. He had paused beside the tank, sending his subordinates on ahead, and the older man had straightened and given Hale a keen, quizzical look.

'You're not—' Hale had begun hesitantly.

'Sure.' The Logician grinned. 'I'd have come topside a lot sooner, but I've had a job needed finishing. Hello, Hale. How are you?'

Hale had said something explosive.

The Logician laughed. 'I used to be a dirt farmer back on Earth,' he explained. 'I sort of got the itch. That's one reason, anyhow. I'm a contingent volunteer now. Used my own name, too. Didn't you notice?'

Hale hadn't. Much had happened to him since he last stood in the temple of Truth and listened to this man's voice coming impressively from the oracular globe. The name of Ben Crowell hadn't caught his eye, though the volunteer lists were scanty enough these days that he should be able to recite them from memory.

'Somehow I'm not very surprised,' he said.

'Needn't be. You and I, Hale, we're the only men left now who remember the open air.' He had sniffed elaborately, and then grinned up at the impervium dome. 'We're the only ones who know this isn't. Did you ever locate any more of the Free Companions? I've wondered.'

Hale shook his head. 'I'm the last.'

'Well' – Crowell struck off a random runner with his hoe – 'I'll be here a while, anyhow. Unofficially, though. I can't answer any questions.'

'You haven't done that even in the Temple.' Hale was reminded of a grievance. 'I've been to see you maybe a dozen times in the last forty years. You wouldn't give me a single audience.' He looked at the Logician and for a moment illogical hope quickened in his voice. 'What made you come landside – now? Is something going to happen?'

'Maybe. Maybe.' Crowell turned back to his hoe. 'Something always does sooner or later, doesn't it? If you wait long enough.'

And that was all Hale had been able to get out of him.

Hale was remembering that conversation now as he told the Logician what had just happened.

'Is that why you came up here?' he demanded at the end of his story. 'Did you know?'

'Hale, I just can't tell you. I mean that. I can't.'

'Don't you know?'

'That hasn't got anything to do with it. Don't forget every talent's got its drawbacks, too. It's not so much prescience I've got as it is infallibility – and that's fallible by definition. I told you once it was more horse sense than anything else.' Crowell seemed mildly irritated. 'I'm not God. Don't start thinking like the Keep men – wanting to shift every responsibility. That's one thing wrong with Venus today. The leave-it-to-George fallacy. George isn't God either. And God Himself can't change the future – and still *know* what's going to happen. Minute He meddles, you see, He introduces a new factor into the equation, and it's a random factor.'

'But—'

'Oh, I've interfered a time or two,' the Logician said. 'Even killed a man once, because I figured nothing worse could happen than letting that particular fella live. Turned out I was right, too – in that case. Only I don't interfere any more than I can help. When I do, I step in as the random factor, and, since I'm *in* it, it isn't easy to look at the whole equation from outside. I can't predict *my* reactions – see?'

'More or less,' Hale said thoughtfully. 'Yet you say you've interfered when you had to.'

'Only then. And afterwards I've tried to make things come out even again. The way it is, there's a balance. If I step into the right-hand pan, the balance shifts in that direction. So afterwards I try to give the other pan a little push – so x will equal x again. If I add y to one side, I try to subtract y from the other. I admit it don't look too sensible from where you're sitting, but it sure does from my perch, son. Like I say, I'm not God. Not the God the Keeps want today, certainly. They expect God to come down and push 'em around in a wheel chair.'

He paused, sighed, glanced up at the impervium dome where a streak of blue sky let sunlight glow briefly through the Colony. 'What did Reed want?' he asked. 'He's got some ideas, I take it. What are they?'

'I don't see why I need to tell you,' Hale said irritably. 'You probably know more about it than I do.'

The Logician struck his hoe handle a light blow with his closed fist. 'No, son, not strictly speaking. There's the best reason in the world why I can't tell you what I know. Some day maybe I'll take time to explain it. Right now I'd be mighty glad to hear what young Reed's up to.'

Hale replied, 'We looked over the maps. His patent covers a three-hundred-mile area with about a hundred miles of seacoast. I asked for that originally because one of the Free Companion Forts stood on the shore there. It's a good base. I remember it was chosen for its harbour. A chain of islands shields it and curves out westward in a long sweep.'

In spite of himself, Hale's voice quickened. 'There won't be an impervium dome over this colony. You've got to adapt to colonise. And you can't have a balanced ecology with one atmosphere outside and another inside. Still, we'll need protection from the landside life. I think water's our answer to that. The islands make natural stepping stones. We'll bring them under control one after another and move along to the next.'

'Um-hum.' The Logician pinched his long nose thoughtfully. 'Now what's going to stop the Families from the same tricks they used to kill *this* Colony?'

Hale coughed. 'That remains to be seen,' he said.

Even nightfall had its own strange, exotic quality to a Keep-bred man. Sam clutched the chair arms in the tossing plane that carried him back to Delaware Keep and looked out fascinated at the deep darkness gathering over the sea. Venus air currents are treacherous; few planes attempt flight unless really necessary, and even those flights are short ones. Sam's view of the scene below was intermittent and jolted. But he could see, far off in the gathering darkness, the great submerged glow that was the Keep, spreading its stain of light upon the water. And he was aware of an unaccustomed emotional pull. That vast spreading glow was home – safety, companionship, lights and music and laughter. The Colony behind him was sterile by contrast, the dwelling place of danger and defeat.

It wouldn't do. He would have to think of something very good to counteract this emotion which he himself was heir to, and all the rest of the Keep's numbered thousands. A pioneer needs bad home conditions and the promise of a Grail or a City of Gold beyond the wilderness to draw him on. Push plus pull, Sam thought. But in this case the bad conditions were all on the wrong side of the scale, from the promoter's viewpoint. Something would have to be done.

Success would require korium, enthusiastic recruits and Harker acquiescence if not actual Harker backing. So far he had nothing. And he would have to work fast. At any moment, once he landed, private police might come up beside him as they had come before, and Sam Harker would drop out of sight, quite possibly forever. He had little money, no prestige, no friends except one old man dying of drugs and senility, and even that friendship had to be bought.

Sam laughed softly to himself. He felt wonderful. He felt exultantly confident. He was perfectly sure of success.

'The first thing I've got to do,' he said to the Slider, 'is get myself before the public. Fast. I don't care how, but I've got to go on record in opposition to the Families so fast they won't have time to snatch me. Afterwards I'll take care to make it plain if I do vanish they'll be responsible.'

The Slider wallowed and sniffled. The small room was stifling, but it was comparatively safe. So long as Sam stayed here in these underworld haunts he still knew well, he was unlikely to vanish into the Harker stronghold. Once he stepped out, the tale might be quite different.

'Give me another drink,' was all the Slider said in answer.

'I've got two thousand credits,' Sam told him, pushing the bottle closer. 'Hale can raise maybe another two thousand. We've got to make a fast start on that. You tell me where I can spend it to stretch it farthest. I'll want newscast time and a good semantics man to dope out our opening speeches. Once we're started, enough money will come in to keep us going. And this time I'm not going to pour it all down a rat-hole. It's going to go where it'll do the most good.'

'Where?' The Slider cocked an inquiring, hairless brow above his bottle.

'Into a fleet,' Sam said grimly. 'This time the new colony will be an island-chain. We're going to stay mobile. We're going to fight the sea beasts for the islands, and fortify them and settle in. We'll need good fast boats, well armoured, with good weapons. That's where the money's going.'

The Slider sucked at his bottle and said nothing.

Sam didn't wait for his propaganda machine to start paying off before he began placing orders to outfit his boats. He cut corners wherever he could, but most of his four thousand credits went under assumed names into secret orders for the materials Hale had figured as basic necessities.

Meanwhile the propaganda got under way. There wasn't time or money for a subtle approach such as Sam would have preferred. A long campaign of cunningly devised songs stressing the glamour of landside life, of the open skies, the stars, the succession of night and day – that would have helped. A successful play, a new book with the right emphasis would have made it much easier. But there wasn't time.

The televisors carried paid-for commercials. Robin Hale announced a new colony under a separate charter. And boldly, openly, because it could not be helped or hidden, Joel Reed's connection with the scheme was made public.

Joel on the screen spoke frankly of his father's disgrace. He disclaimed all knowledge of his father. 'I never knew him,' he said, putting all of his considerable persuasive powers behind the words. 'I suppose a great many of you will discount everything I say, because of my name. I haven't tried to hide it. I believe in this colony and *I can't afford to have it fail*. I think most of you will understand that. Maybe it'll help prove that I mean what I say. I wouldn't dare come before you, using my right name with all the disgrace you know belongs to it, if I didn't know the colony *must* succeed. No one named Reed would dare to try the same thing twice. I'm not. If the colony fails it'll mean my own ruin and I know it. It won't fail.' There was quiet conviction in his voice, and something of his enthusiasm carried over to the listeners. He was telling the truth this time. Some of them believed him. Enough of them believed him, for his purposes just now.

The same urges and stresses which had made the first colonisation plans successful were still present. Subtly men sensed the losses Keep life imposed upon them. They yearned obscurely for lost heritages, and there were enough of the yearners to give Sam and Hale the finances they needed to meet immediate demands. It wasn't very much, but it was enough. The rest sat back and waited to be convinced.

Sam moved to convince them.

The Harkers, of course, were not idle. After the first startled hour, they moved too, quite rapidly. But here they operated at a slight disadvantage. They couldn't openly oppose the colonisation scheme. Remember, they were supposedly in favour of colonisation. They could not afford to have a colony actually fail. So all they could do was start counter-propaganda.

Word went out of a mutated virulent plague that had begun to develop landside. A robot plane crashed spectacularly on the news screens, torn apart by the violent wind tides of the upper air. It was dangerous up there on the land, the rumours increasingly declared. Too dangerous, too uncertain . . .

And then Sam made his next bold stroke. Almost openly he attacked the Harkers. Almost specifically he accused them of responsibility in the failure of the present Land Colony. 'There are powerful forces at work,' Sam declared, 'to prevent the colonisation of the land. You can see why. Anyone could see. Put yourself in the place of a powerful man, a powerful group of men. If you were governing a Keep, wouldn't you be perfectly contented with things as they are? Would you want any changes made? Wouldn't you do all you could to discredit those who offer opportunities landside to men like us?' Sam leaned to the screen, fixing his audience with a steady, significant gaze. 'Wouldn't you try to silence anyone who fought to give the common man a chance?' he demanded, and then held his breath, waiting to be cut off the air.

But nothing happened. Perhaps the technicians were too stunned. Perhaps even the Harkers dared not challenge public opinion that far. Sam went on while he could. 'I hope to continue working towards the new colony,' he said. 'I'm working for myself, yes – but for all of you others, too, who are *not* rulers in the Keeps. As long as I'm alive I'll keep on working. If I don't come on the air again tomorrow to report our new plans – well, you people of the Keeps will know why.'

There was an extraordinary, soft, rumbling murmur in the streets of Delaware Keep as Sam signed off, leaving those words still humming in the air. For the first time in many decades, crowds had begun to gather again beneath the big public news screens, and for the first time in human history on Venus, the murmur of the crowd-voice had lifted from Keep Ways. It was in its way an awe-inspiring sound – the faintest murmur of surprise rather than menace, but a murmur that could not be ignored.

'The Harkers heard it. And bided their time. They had so much time – they could afford to wait.

So Sam had his temporary insurance against the private police. He made rapid steps towards consolidating his position. He had to find some hold over the Harkers stronger than this gossamer lever based on the unpredictable masses.

Sari was his only key. Sari Walton, half Harker by blood – and certainly abnormal. Why? Sam tried hard to find out. There was little material on file about the Immortals – only vital statistics and names and brief histories. It was true that the Immortals, by their very longevity, were spared many of the stresses that drive a short-termer into neuroses. But that very longevity must in its way impose other stresses incomprehensible to men of normal life.

Sam searched and pondered, pondered and searched. He traced many ideas up blind alleys and abandoned them. Eventually he came across one small factor that looked promising. At best it was not conclusive – only indicative. But it pointed an interesting path.

The reproductive cycle of the Immortals was a curious one. They had successive periods of fertility, usually at intervals of fifty to seventy-five years and covering only a brief time. The child of two Immortals had never yet failed to show all the traits of long life. But the children were not strong. Their mortality rate was high, and most of them had to be reared almost under glass.

Sam was interested to discover that at the time of Sari Walton's birth a son had been born to the Harker family too – a son named Blaze. These two children were the only surviving offspring on record for that particular period in Delaware Keep.

And Blaze Harker had apparently vanished.

With increasing interest Sam traced through the records, searching for some explanation of what had happened to the man. No death date appeared. The usual records of education and various duties and enterprises for Blaze went steadily along up to a date seventy years past. And then vanished.

Sam filed the information away with a sense of profound excitement.

'This one ought to do,' the Free Companion said, stepping back from the view-glass. 'Look.'

Sam crossed the pitching deck unsteadily and bent to the eyepiece. He felt half drunk with this unaccustomed atmosphere, the motion of the boat, the wet wind in his face. There was so much about open air that took getting used to – even the feel of the breeze was faintly alarming, for in the Keeps a wind meant entirely different things from the random winds of landside.

The milk-white water heaved around under the milky sky. On shore the great festooned hulk of a ruined fort seemed to stagger under the weight of jungle rioting over it. There was a constant murmur from the jungle, punctuated by a pattern of screams, flutings, hisses, roars from invisible beasts. The sea lapped noisily at the boat's sides. The wind made meaningless noises in Sam's ears. Landside was strangely confusing to the Keep-bred.

He put his forehead in the head rest and looked down.

Another world sprang into being, a world of wavering light and wavering weed, threaded by the wavering shapes of underwater things, fish with shivering fins, siphonophores trailing their frostlike streamers, jellyfish throbbing to a rhythm of their own. Anemones clenched into brilliantly striped fists with a dreamlike slowness. Great fans of dazzling coloured sponge swayed to the random currents.

And buried in this bright, wavering world, visible only in rough outlines beneath the weeds, lay the hulk of a sunken ship.

It was the third they had found which Hale seemed to think worth salvaging. 'And they're in better shape than you think,' he assured Sam. 'Those alloys are tough. I've seen worse wrecks than this rehabilitated in the old days.' His voice trailed off and he looked out over the empty water, remembering.

You could almost see it peopled by the fleets of the Free Companions as Hale must be seeing it, very clearly over the generations already gone. The Keeps had been sacrosanct then as now, for only under their impervium domes did civilisation survive. But the token wars had raged between them, on the surface of the grey seas, between fleets of hired mercenaries. The Keep that backed the loser paid its korium ransom, sometimes only after token depth bombs had been dropped to remind the undersea people of their vulnerability.

It all passed. The jungle ate up the great forts and the sea giants sank at their moorings. But they did not crumble. That much was apparent now. The weeds grew over and through them and the lichens nibbled at their fabric, but the strong basic structure remained.

Hale and Sam had searched the coasts of Venus where the old forts stood. Hale had known the forts when they were alive. He knew the harbours and could still quote the battle strength of the Companies. The first two hulks they had salvaged were already nearly seaworthy again. And there was a new enthusiasm in Hale's voice and in his eyes.

'This time they won't pin us down under impervium,' he told Sam, gripping the rail and grimacing as spray blew in his face. 'This time we'll stay mobile no matter what it costs us.'

'It'll cost plenty,' Sam reminded him. 'More than we've got. More than we're going to get, unless we do something very drastic.'

'What?'

Sam looked at him thoughtfully, wondering if the time had yet come to take Hale into his confidence. He had been building towards the revelation for weeks now, leading Hale step by step towards a solution he would have rejected flatly at their first interview.

Sam was applying to his current problem exactly the same methods he had applied – almost by instinct – when he worked in the alley with dream-dust still fragrant in his nostrils. In the weeks since that wakening he had retraced in swift strides the full course of a career that paralleled the career of his earlier life, condensing forty years' achievements into a brief two weeks. Twice now he had come into the world penniless, helpless, every man's hand against him. Twice he had lifted himself to precarious success. This time his foot was only the first rung of a ladder that leaned against the very stars. He assured himself of that. Failure was inconceivable to him.

By misdirection and cunning he had tricked Doc Mallard into a catspaw play and seized the korium he needed to start him on his upward climb. It was korium he wanted again now, but the Harkers were adversaries this time and they were a much more difficult problem.

Remembering his method with Doc Mallard, he had searched in vain for some lure he could dangle to tempt them out on a limb. He could think of nothing. The Harkers already had everything they could desire; their position was almost impregnable. There was, of course, Sari. Sam knew that it he could plan some subtle but strong irritation for her, and make sure she had narco-dust at the time, she was almost certain to kill either Zachariah or herself – or both. That was one weapon. But it was terrifyingly uncertain, and it was too strong. He meant to kill Zachariah, eventually. But death was no solution to this current problem.

There was a parallel here between weapons at Sam's command and the weapons men had with which to attack the Venusian landside. In both cases the only available weapons were either too weak or too strong. Utter destruction was no answer, but the only alternative would leave the adversary essentially untouched.

Sam knew he must either give up entirely or take a step so bold it would mean total success or total ruin.

'Hale,' he said abruptly, 'if we want enough korium to colonise the land, we've got to do something that's never been done before. We've got to bomb the Keeps.'

Hale squinted at him and then laughed. 'You're joking.'

'Maybe.' Sam hunched his shoulders and glanced at the smothered fort across the water. 'You know anything better?'

'I don't know anything worse.' Hale's voice was sharp. 'I'm not a murderer, Reed.'

'You were a Free Companion.'

'That's a different matter altogether. We—'

'You fought the Keeps' battles, at the Keeps' orders. That was necessary, under the circumstances. You did what you had to in the way of killing, plundering – piracy, really. The losing Keep paid up in korium or faced bombing. It was a bluff, I suppose. None of them were ever really bombed. Well, what I'm suggesting is a bluff, too. The Families will know it. We'll know it. But we've got to outbluff them.'

'How can we?'

'What have we got to lose? They're at that much of a disadvantage – they have everything to lose. We have everything to gain.'

'But they'll *know* we don't dare do it. People won't even take the threat seriously. You know the Keep people. They're – inert. They've never known a menace. It won't be conceivable that we could bomb them. They'll laugh at us. The race has outlived the fear of danger. We'd have to bomb one Keep and kill thousands of people before we could convince them we meant business. I—'

Sam's laugh interrupted him. 'I'm not so sure. We're still human beings. It's true there's been no war or danger for a good many generations – but men still wake up with a dream of falling as old as the first arborean who lost his grip on a tree limb. Men's nostrils still dilate when they're angry, because when the pattern was first set they had to ... to breathe – because the mouth was full of the enemy! I don't think we've shed our fears quite so easily as you think.'

'Well, I won't do it,' Hale said firmly. 'That's going too far. It's out of the question—'

The threat, when it first sounded over the news screens, was as shattering as a bomb itself. There was dead silence in every Keep for a long moment after the words had rung out from the big screens. Then tumult. Then laughter.

Hale had been right – in part. No one believed in the threat of the rehabilitated fleet. The colonies depended for their very existence on the support of the Keeps. They would not dare bomb their sources of supply. And if they were mad enough to do it, every man reasoned in those first few minutes, the chances were strong that it would be some other Keep that got the depth-charges – not his own.

Then Sam on the public screens named the Keep – Delaware. He named the time – now. He named his price – korium.

And the battle of wills was on.

But Sam had a weapon before he launched his bluff that gave him confidence. It was not a very strong weapon, but that simply meant he must use more skill in wielding it. It had to succeed. This was a point from which no turning back was possible.

The weapon, like all the most effective weapons man can use against man, was personal.

He had found Blaze Harker.

In the final analysis the whole struggle was a conflict between two men – Sam and Zachariah. The Families of the Immortals ruled the Keeps, the Harkers set the pattern for all other Families, and Zachariah was the head of the Harker clan. Zachariah may or may not have realised himself just where the point of greatest stress lay, but Sam knew. He was gambling everything on the hope that with this lever, and a plan he had made very carefully, he could outbluff Zachariah Harker.

He realised, of course, that the Families must be laying plans of their own. Last time they had worked quietly away in secret until the moment for action came, and in the resulting explosion Sam and all his schemes had been swept away in unimportant fragments. This time it would be different.

It was the Slider who found Blaze for Sam. When the message reached him, Sam went as quickly as the Ways would carry him to the small, foul-smelling den in the slums of Delaware Keep. The Slider was sunk in an Orange-Devil dream when he came in, and for a few minutes addressed Sam hazily as Klano and spoke of ancient crimes that not even Sam remembered.

He gave the Slider a drink, and presently the mists faded

and the vast bulk heaved itself up in bed, chuckling and sniffling.

'On that Harker deal, son – I got an address for you.' He gave it, grunting.

Sam whirled towards the door.

'Wait a minute, son – hold on there! Where you think you're going?'

'To find Blaze.'

'You'll never get in. That place is guarded.'

'I'll make a way!'

'Son, you'd need six weeks buildup. You'll have to ferret out somebody who'll take bribes before you could get within a city block of that place. You'll need at least one ringer. You'll need a fast getaway organisation afterwards. You'll—'

'All right, all right! Let's get started, then. Could you work it?'

'Maybe. I could try.'

'Then begin! How long will it take? I can't wait six weeks, Can you do it in three?' He paused, interrupted by the vast, increasing chuckles that sent earthquake waves over the bulk beneath the blankets.

'Forget it, kid. It's already done.' Sam stared. The Slider choked on his own laughter. 'The old hand hasn't lost its cunning, my boy. Don't think the job wasn't hard – but it's done. Raise that shutter over there – turn off the light. Now watch.'

A square of dim illumination appeared on the far wall. Shadows moved across it, blurred by the wall's irregularities. They were looking at the product of a tiny spy camera, apparently carried about waist-high at the belt of someone who progressed at uneven speed. Sometimes he walked, and the film went along in smooth, rhythmic rocking motion; sometimes he ran and then the pictures flashed by jerkily. When he stopped the eye seemed to stop with him. It resulted in an irregular but very convincing motion picture.

The first seconds of the film showed the little camera apparently staring at an iron grille, very close to the lens. White trousered legs appeared, the grille swung open, a vista unfolded briefly of garden paths and fountains playing. One of the Immortal strongholds, obviously.

There was a feeling of quick, furtive alertness to the pace of the film, the way it kept swinging right and left in tiny arcs as the man who carried it scanned his surroundings. Twice it was apparent that the carrier had ducked into hiding; the film went dark for several seconds when a door or a curtain closed to conceal him. There was a dizzying amount of corridor-walking, all of it quick and giving the impression of stealth.

Then the speed of the carrier increased suddenly – the man was running. Walls bobbed up and down, swung sharply as he whipped around a corner. The film went almost totally dark and walls slid downwards before it. A glass-walled lift was rising. More corridors, at a run.

A pause before another grilled door, this substantial looking – bars with adornment. The bars grew enormous, blurred, apparently melted. The lens was pressed close against the door looking through into the room beyond.

And this, the key scene, ran very fast. There was only a flash of a richly furnished room and a man in it with two others bending over him. The man appeared to be struggling with his companions.

Abruptly the picture swung sidewise, jarred so that everything vibrated. There was a sweeping glance upwards, along soaring walls, a flash of ceiling, a flash of scowling face swooping towards the lens and an arm uplifted with something that flashed.

The picture went white and clicked noisily to a halt.

Then it began again. Time retraced itself. The lens was floating towards the bars again. Very slowly indeed the room inside came into focus. In nightmarish slow motion, which gave watchers the opportunity to study every detail, the struggling man and his two companions moved upon the wall.

The room was cushioned everywhere. The carpeting looked soft and sank under the pressure of the three men's feet; the walls were panelled head-high with beautifully quilted patterns of velvet. The furniture was thick and soft, no edges showing.

The man who struggled was tall, slender, fine-boned. He had a beautifully shaped head and even in this convulsive activity his motions were curiously smooth and graceful. It was at first impossible to guess what sort of features he had, they were so contorted in a rapid series of violent grimaces. Blood flecked his face from bitten lips and his eyes were rolled back until no iris showed.

His two adversaries were trying to pull a strait-jacket over his flailing arms.

Little by little they were succeeding. It all happened in that strange slow motion that gave the whole performance a look of calculated rhythm, like a ballet, robbing the struggle of any spontaneity because it happened so slowly. The tall man beat his prisoned arms against his sides, threw back his head and laughed wildly and soundlessly, blood running down his chin. The laughter changed without a break into sheer rage and he hurled himself sidewise with a cunning lurch and carried one of his attendants with him to the floor. The other bent over them, and the whole scene jigged furiously and swept upwards, and the film clicked to a halt.

'That was Blaze Harker,' the Slider said in the brief silence that followed. 'Give me a drink, son. Have a shot yourself – you look like you need one.'

'—and so it's come down to this,' Sam said over the seawide newscast, to the listening thousands. 'Give us the korium we have a right to, or take the consequences. The time's past for bargains and promises. This is the showdown. What's your answer, Harker?'

Under all the seas, under all the impervium domes, a breathless silence held as the multitudes watched Sam's magnified face, multiplied many times upon many screens, turn and wait for his reply. And in nineteen of the Keeps as the waiting lengthened a murmur began to grow. To them it was at the moment an academic problem.

But in Delaware Keep the problem was a vital one. There was not a sound in the streets, and for the first time, perhaps since a Keep had been reared beneath its bubble dome you could hear the deep, soft humming of the Ways as they glided on their endless rounds.

Zachariah kept them waiting exactly long enough. Then with a perfect sense of timing, just as the delay grew unbearable, he gave his signal in his distant study. Sam's face grew indistinct upon the screens of all the Keeps; it hovered in the background like a shadow. Superimposed upon it the serenely handsome Harker face grew clear.

'Reed, you're a fool.' Zachariah's voice was calm and leisurely. 'We all know this is a childish bluff.'

The shadow that was Sam flashed into clarity; Zachariah's face went translucent. Sam said, 'I expected you to say that. I suppose you believe it. My first job's to convince you all. There isn't much time, so – look.'

Sam and Zachariah alike blurred and vanished from the screen. In their stead a shining seascape grew. Sunlight shafted down through clouds, touching grey water to blue dazzle. And ploughing through the dazzle, tossing glittering spray over their mailed snouts, a fleet of five ships moved head-on towards the observer.

They were small ships, but they were built for business. Impervium sheathed them in everywhere and their lines were smooth and low and fast. They looked grim. They were grim. And the thing about them that most effectively struck fear to the hearts of the watchers was their complete inhumanity. No man's outlines showed anywhere, except as vague, alarming shadows moving purposefully inside the shells. These were machines for destruction, moving forward to fulfil the purpose for which they had been made.

From beyond the screen Sam's disembodied voice said, 'Watch!' and a moment later, at a distance behind the last ship, the sea boiled suddenly into a white tumult, erupted high, rained down in diamond showers.

Then the ships grew dim. The screens went briefly blank, and another scene took shape upon it. This time it was a water-world, full of wavering light, greenish-yellow because it was near the surface. Looking up, you could see the water-ceiling as a perfectly tangible thing, quilted and puckered all over with the foreshortened shadows of the waves. Breaking it, the long, sharp bellies of the ships came gliding – one, two, three, four, five – mailed and darkly shining.

The illumination darkened, the ship keels rose and vanished as the scene plunged downwards, following the course of a dark, cylindrical something which shot from the last ship in the line. The telefocus stayed constant on the bomb as it slipped silently down through the Venusian sea. Every watcher in the Keeps felt his skin crawl coldly with the question: *What target?*

The sea was deep here. The depth-bomb dropped eternally. Very few watched the missile itself; most eyes were intent on the lower edges of the screens, avid for the first sight of the bottom . . . It was sand.

As it came into view, the bomb struck, and instantly the telefocus changed so that the results of the explosion could be visible. Yet not much could be seen. Perhaps that was the most terrifying – the swirling, inchoate undersea chaos, the blinding blur on the screen, and the deep, thundering boom of the explosion that carried clearly over the sound beam.

It crashed out and lingered.

Not only through the visors. In Delaware Keep, through fathoms of water, the sound waves rushed and struck with a deep impact on the great impervium shell. Was there the faintest tremor – the slightest possible vibration – in the Keep itself?

Did the Keep – *the Keep!* – shiver a little as the undersea Titan smashed his hammer against the sea bottom?

The sound died. There was a stillness.

Far above in the flagship, Sam flipped sound-absorbent panels into place and turned to the auxiliary screen. He was getting a report.

No face showed on this tight-beam circuit connection. No voice sounded. But Sam automatically translated the scrambled code into an understandable message.

'Kedre Walton left Montana Keep an hour ago. She's just entered Delaware.'

Sam instinctively looked down. He used his own scrambler.

'Does she know the situation'?

'Not sure. She'll find out from the public televisors in Delaware.'

'Has Sari got the special stuff?'

'As soon as we got word Kedre left Montana. She'll have taken it by now.'

The other screen was calling insistently. Robin Hale's voice came from another auxiliary.

'Reed! Are you handling it?'

'I've got it,' Sam said, and went back to his Keep connection. But he waited a second, looking into Zachariah's eyes, while he marshalled his thoughts. He couldn't quite repress a twisted, triumphant smile in the face of the Immortal's godlike – but fallacious – confidence.

For his schemes were working. He had chosen the time very carefully indeed. The vital key, the zero hour, depended on just when Kedre Walton returned to Delaware Keep. The psychological hammer blows were far more useful against Immortals than any bomb.

By now Sari should have in her hands the narco-dust Sam had conveniently provided for her, through his new underworld connections. A narco-addict asks few questions. She would have taken the powder the instant it reached her – and this was not ordinary narco-dust.

There was another drug mixed with it.

By now Sari's nerves should be jolting with shock after shock. By now her brain should be building up a high potential, temporarily crumbling away the mortar of caution, of reserve that had held the bricks of sanity together. By now she should be ready to explode, when the hair trigger was touched. And the direction of her explosion had already been channeled by her own conditioning and environment. Besides, she was born under the same star as Blaze Harker. Not Mars – it was the more baleful star of Earth that glared coldly above the Venus clouds, the star that had given Sari her dangerous heritage of mental instability.

'Reed,' Zachariah said calmly, 'we can't be bluffed. You won't destroy Delaware Keep.'

'That was the first bomb,' Sam said. 'We're heading for Delaware. A bomb will be dropped every five minutes, till we anchor above you. But we won't stop dropping them then.'

'Have you thought of the results?'

'Yes,' Sam said. 'We have radar and anti-aircraft. We have guided missiles. And none of the Keeps is armed. Besides, they're undersea. It's safe undersea – as long as you're not attacked. Then there's no way to strike back. You can only wait and die.'

His voice went out over the public telecast. Sam switched on an auxiliary to focus on one of the great public televisors at a clover-leaf meeting of Ways. A crowd had gathered, he saw. From all directions the Keeps were like arteries carrying the people to their listening posts. Red cells, not white – builders, not fighters. Well, they needed builders to colonise Venus.

At present, however, he was fighting the Keeps.

He began to worry, a little, over Hale. He wasn't sure about the Free Companion. If it came to a final showdown, would Hale actually drop a bomb on Delaware? Would he himself?

He mustn't let matters go quite that far.

By now Kedre must be on her way to the Harker stronghold. She would have learned what had happened; the televisors all over the Keep were carrying the news. She would be hurrying to Zachariah's side. Zachariah, whom she had loved for hundreds of years, not with the unflickering glow of a radium lamp, but as a planet inevitably swings towards the sun at perihelion, swinging away towards other planets, but returning whenever the orbit took her close. Yes, she would want to be beside Zachariah in this crisis.

'Another bomb,' Sam said.

Again the telefocus shifted. Again a bomb dropped. This time it struck rock. The explosion came in long, rolling thunders through the public visors, and the crowds swayed with the tides and currents of vibration, as seaweed moves in water.

Again the roar continued as underwater sound waves moved in the track of televised sound waves.

And this time men were surer. Delaware Keep shivered slightly.

Silence dropped. The Ways hummed. People of the Keep waited, in greater throngs than had gathered in the Ways since man first reached Venus, a herd that always, until now, had been guided by the Immortals – watching the duel between Zachariah Harker and the pirate.

Sam said, 'Suppose you surrender? The Families may lose a little, but the common people won't. Are you afraid of letting the short-termers go landside? Afraid you won't be able to rule them out there?'

'Any man who wishes to volunteer for your colony is free to do that,' Zachariah said. 'Just as every man in the Keeps is free. You're trying to get slaves. Men won't go landside yet; it isn't time. It's too dangerous just now. You can't get volunteers. You say you want korium. But I think that will be only your first demand. Later you'll want colony conscription – peonage.'

'The time's past for abstruse arguments,' Sam said, knowing his voice was heard in every Keep on Venus. 'Listen! Pay us the korium we want or we'll bomb Delaware Keep!'

'You won't bomb the Keep. Half a million people would die.'

'A cheap price for you to pay if you can stop the colony – is that it? Perhaps you're willing to die with Delaware, but what about the Delaware Immortals? There's a rumour all the Harkers but you have already left the Keep – and that you've got a getaway ship waiting. Where are you vising from?'

Zachariah dared not let that challenge drop. Beside him, too, as Sam knew, was a scanning screen that showed the throngs in the Keep. All the Harker prestige – the Immortal prestige – depended on keeping the trust of the commoners. And they would not follow rulers who were not leaders.

Zachariah turned his head and spoke briefly. He said to Sam, and to the Keeps, 'No Immortal has left Delaware. I'm speaking from the Harker Council Room. As you see.'

The image on the screen changed; it showed the well-known Council Room, empty except for Zachariah, who was seated at the head of a long table before a broadcasting unit.

But now the door opened, and men and women began to come in. Sam recognised Raoul. He was watching for another face he knew.

Was his timing correct?

'The other Families—' Zachariah said. 'We'll scan them quickly.'

Other Council Rooms showed on the screen – the sanctums of the great Families of Delaware Keep. They were all filling rapidly, the Randolphs, the Wood clan, the Davidsons and Mawsons – but the Harkers were the real rulers of Delaware, as everyone knew. The focus returned to Zachariah. It was the long view, showing Geoffrey and Raoul and a few others seated at the table. Sam looked for Sari and saw her. He wished he could get a closer view. Had she taken the hopped-up narco-dust?

She sat motionless. But suddenly her hands moved together on the table top and clenched violently, and Sam knew.

'Your bluff won't work,' Zachariah said. 'No Immortal has left the Keep.'

'So you're all willing to die rather than give up a little korium,' Sam said. 'That's your affair – your own lives. But the korium isn't yours. It belongs to the Keep people. They made it and they own it – or should. You've no right to decide whether they should live and die.'

'We are the people,' Zachariah said.

'You lie,' Sam said. 'What do you know about us? You're gods. You don't know a thing about the common people, who have to work blindly for reward we'll never lay our hands on. But you'll get those rewards. You'll get them by waiting and doing nothing, while the short-termers work and have children and die – and their children do the same. You can wait to colonise landside, because you'll live long enough to walk under the stars and the sun and know what it was like on Earth in the old days. You'll go out in ships to the planets. You'll get the rewards. But what about us? We'll die, and our children will die, and our children's children – sweating to build a pyramid we'll never see complete. You're

131

not the people!' His voice raised in a shout. 'You're not even human! You're Immortals!'

'We rule by will of the people. Because we're best qualified.'

'Qualified?' Sam asked, and then, 'Where is Blaze Harker?'

'Not in Delaware Keep at the moment—'

'Tight beam,' Sam said.

There was a pause. Then Zachariah made a gesture. All over the Keeps the screens dimmed and went blank. Only two visors carried the conversation now – Sam's, and the Harkers'.

Sam, too, had adjusted to the private tight beam. He said: 'I know where Blaze Harker is. I've got telepictures of him. I can broadcast them, and you know what that will do to Harker prestige if the people learn that an Immortal can go insane.'

Sam heard signals begin to click behind him. Automatically he translated. '*Kedre Walton entering Harker grounds—*' Almost time.

The signals suddenly began again. Mystified, Sam heard them say, 'Listen to the Keeps! Tune back! Listen!'

He didn't want to. This distraction was something he hadn't counted on. There was so much depending on his own split-second timing just now, and on chance and luck – if anything went wrong he was ruined. He didn't want to deflect his attention for a single instant from this flood of pressure he was pouring on the Harkers. But he switched his private screen on briefly – and then for a moment stood tense, listening.

Down there in the Keeps the screens were blank. The people had been cut off from this fascinating and vital debate just at the moment when it was reaching a climax.

And the people didn't like it.

A low roll of anger was rising from the packed thousands. The crowd was shifting uneasily, restlessly, surging in little eddies around the screens as if pressing closer could make the image come back. And the murmur of their anger deepened as the seconds ticked by. Voices rose in thin shouts now and then – the imperative commands of the mob. They would have to be answered. Quickly – very quickly.

Sam whirled to the tight beam where the Harkers waited. From their council room came a distant echo of that same rising murmur of anger. They, too, were watching the temper of the crowds. They, too, knew time was going too fast. Sam grinned. It was perfect. It couldn't be better. He had them on the run now, whether they had realised it yet or not. For until this moment no Immortal had ever known such pressure. They weren't used to coping with it. And Sam had lived under pressure all his life. He was adjusted to fast thinking. Now if he could only talk fast enough—

'Immortal prestige!' he said rapidly into their private beam. 'You've lost all touch with human beings. What do you know about human emotions, you Immortals? Faith – loyalty – do they look so different after a few hundred years? I'm glad I'm a short-termer!'

Zachariah gave him a bewildered look as Sam paused for breath. This didn't ring quite true, and Zachariah was quick to hear the false note. It was all very well to orate when the mob was listening, but these high, abstract things were irrelevant on the private beam. False heroics were for the small minds of the crowd, you could all but hear him thinking. Or for a small mind here, clouded and confused—

Sam saw understanding break across the Immortal's face – too late. Sam had a few more words to hurl into the transmitter, and as he gathered himself to do it he saw the door behind Zachariah swinging open, and knew he had timed himself almost too closely.

'So it's all right for people like you,' he shouted, 'to pick up some gullible fool of a woman for awhile and kick her out again when you're ready to go back to—'

Kedre Walton came quietly through the door and into the Council Room. From the corner of his eye Sam caught the flash of green-gold hair as Sari's head flung up, saw the hunched tenseness of her shoulders under a gleaming shawl. But his eyes were for Kedre.

She did not seem to have heard. She came quickly across

the room, tall, exquisitely fine, holding her head back under the weight of her cascading hair as if it were too heavy for the slender neck. She was unclasping her long cloak as she came, and she let it slip to the floor in shining folds and hurried forward, her narrow white hands outstretched to Zachariah.

Sam had been sure it would happen so. Between her and Zachariah lay too many decades of past intimacy for her to ignore the tie now. They had created between them in the long orbits of the past a communal flesh and a communal mind that functioned most highly only when they were together. If Zachariah had ever needed this completion, he needed it now. She had come as quickly as she could. Every eye in the room could see that these two were as nearly one, and in their crises must always be, as any two humans can become.

Sam's gaze swung back to Sari. So did Zachariah's – but just too late. Both of them knew what was coming a split second before it came, but by then it was too late to stop her. The timing was perfect. Shock after shock had hammered upon Sari, already fighting down the cumulative neural explosions of the adulterated narco-dust Sam had supplied.

And Sari's action was already channeled. She hated Zachariah and Kedre. This was the moment of critical mass.

She was born under the star of exploded Earth. Sari, too, seemed to explode into an incandescence of madness and rage.

Within seconds the assembly of Immortals had degenerated into a primitive struggle as they swarmed to loosen Sari's homicidal grip on Kedre's throat.

Sam threw a switch and saw his face appear in minature far below, on the great public televisors. The sullen muttering of the crowd, which had been increasing slowly but steadily, fell to abrupt silence as Sam called,

'Harker! Harker, I can't reach you! Tune in!'

How could they? There was no answer.

'Harker, Harker! *Are you leaving the Keep?*'

Another depth bomb dropped.

Above the rolling thunders of the explosion, above the

ominous creaking of tortured impervium over the city, Sam's voice called again.

'Harker, where are you? If the Harkers have left, who's next in authority? *Answer me!*'

Zachariah's face came into sudden, swift focus. He was breathing hard. Blood trickled down his cheek from a long scratch. His face was icily calm.

He said, 'We have not left the Keep. We—'

He did not finish. For the roar of the crowd drowned him out. It was Montana Keep that roared. It was the first time in all Venusian history that the voice of a mob had lifted under a city dome, the first time since the Immortals had assumed control of human affairs that a crowd dared dispute that control.

They disputed it now. If the sound meant anything, they rejected it. Zachariah mouthed silently at them from the screen, no words coming through the vast, voiceless roaring.

For to the crowd it must have seemed that the Keep was already falling. Zachariah, coming back from the urgency of some hidden crisis, breathing hard, blood running down his face – it was a terrifying sight to see. The dome still groaned above them under the impact of the bombs and even this imperturbable Immortal looked panic-stricken at last.

It was terror that made the crowd roar. Surrender was what they roared for, and the volume of the noise mounted.

And then Sam made his first mistake.

He should have stood back and let events go their way. But the sight of Zachariah's ice-cold calm, even in this tumult, made him want suddenly to smash his fists into the flawless, ageless face, batter it to a more nearly mortal aspect – force the acknowledgment of defeat upon the inflexible Immortal. If there was anything there to admire, Sam did not recognise it.

And because he could not reach Zachariah with his fists, Sam lashed out with his voice.

The first few words he roared at the Immortal no one heard. But when his blunt, redbrowed face forced itself into focus upon the screens the shouting of the crowd quieted a little, slowly, until Sam's message came through.

'—surrender now!' Sam was roaring. 'No Harker's fit to rule! Give us what we ask, or show us what happened just now in your Council Room! Show us! Show us how sane any Harker is when a crisis comes! No – wait, *I'll* show you! People of the Keeps, wait until you see Blaze Harker and what he—'

The shadow that was the waiting Zachariah made an impatient gesture, and Sam's face and voice faded into the background, still gesturing, still shouting. Zachariah came clear before them, leaning forward, seeming to look down, godlike, over the panic-stricken throngs.

'I have news for you, people of the Keeps,' he said quietly. 'You're still safe. No bombs have fallen here. No bombs will. This man is – not what he seems. Until now I've kept his secret for him, but this is the time to speak. Joel Reed has told you he never knew his father. He's sworn to wipe out the dishonour of his name and give you a second chance at landside life that Sam Reed robbed you of.' He paused.

'This man *is* Sam Reed,' he said.

A bewildered buzzing followed the silence when Zachariah's voice ceased. He let them murmur for a moment, then lifted a hand and went on.

'We have definite proof of that – the eye prints and finger prints match. Our investigators don't make mistakes. This is Sam Reed, the swindler, the dream-duster, who's promising you so much. Can you believe anything he says, knowing that? Sam Reed – speak to the Keeps! Make more promises! Speak to the people you've swindled! Or do you deny who you are? Shall we show the proof now? Answer us, Sam Reed!'

Sam let his face swim into clear focus on the screen. In shadow behind him Zachariah waited, lips a little parted, still breathing hard and the blood running down his cheek.

Zachariah had lost his head.

For an instant no one knew it, not even Sam. Sam only knew that he must do the fastest thinking he had ever done in his life. He had perhaps fifteen seconds that would look like a deliberate pause. Then he must speak. In the back of his brain was the answer. He knew it was there, he could almost touch it. But for ten of the fifteen seconds he groped in vain.

And then it came to him. Zachariah had made one vast and fatal mistake. The Harkers were not used to quick thinking. For too many centuries they had not been called upon to see all sides of a threatening danger in one glance, evaluate all possibilities and choose by instinct the safest out. And Zachariah was an Immortal. He did not think as normal men think. Zachariah's mind worked by decades and scores – not by the days and weeks of ordinary living.

Sam laughed. 'No,' he said, 'I won't deny it. I wanted to prove myself. I owed you that. I made a bad mistake and I've got to make amends. But Harker's right – *I am immortal.*'

He waited a moment to let that sink in. 'I was forty years old when they blew dream-dust in my face,' he said. 'For forty years I've been away. Do I look like a man of eighty? Here – look! Am I eighty years old?'

He ducked his head and pushed the eye shells loose, slipped them out, spat out the tooth-cap shells. He pulled the red wig from his head and grinned at them, burning with a confidence that seemed to pour out upon all the Keeps from the thousand screens that mirrored his face.

It was a strong, square, hard-featured face, lines of violence upon it, but no lines of age. Even the bareness of his head was not the bareness of age – the shape of his skull was too sculptured in the strong, full curves of his Harker heritage. It was a vital, virile face – but it was certainly not the face of an Immortal.

'Look at me!' Sam said. 'You can see I'm no Immortal. I'm a man like the rest of you. No immortal was ever born built like me. But I've lived eighty years.' He stepped back a little, paused, turned upon them a keen, grey, angry stare.

'I was a man like you,' he said. 'But I've been landside. I've made a great discovery. I've learned why it is the Immortals don't dare let landside colonies get started. You all know how hard they've worked to stop us – now I'm going to tell you *why*!

'You can all be immortal!'

It was nearly five minutes before the tumult died. Even then, Sam was very nearly the only listener who heard Zachariah Harker say wearily:

'All right, Reed. You'll get your korium. Now, is this another swindle? If not – *go ahead and give them immortality!*'

PART THREE

When Israel out of Egypt came
Safe in the sea they trod;
By day in cloud, by night in flame,
. . Went on before them God . . .
I see the country, far away,
Where I shall never stand;
The heart goes where no footstep may
Into the promised land.

— HOUSEMAN, *circa 1900*

The wall was painted with a running mural of fantastic green seas banded with purple and white, washing the feet of velvety brown hills. There had been shores like that, once, long ago, on an incandescent world. The artist who painted these walls had never seen bare hills or a coloured sea. There was a curious off-beat focus about his rendition of these imaginary things, and it showed all the more clearly now because in the centre of his mural a square of brightly tinted moving shadows showed a real sea and a real shore, smothered in jungle, and a boat shooting forward on V-spread wings of water.

Two people sat quietly in the painted room, watching the images of the landside world rehearse in duplicate the action far above them. Kedre Walton, cross-legged on a flat cushion on the floor, was laying out a game of tarot solitaire on the low glass table before her, glancing only now and then at the flickering screen. But Zachariah Harker in his deep chair never moved his eyes from the flying boat.

'There they go, poor fools. There they go,' he said, almost to himself. He held a little censer of burning vine-dust in one hand, moving it gently to and fro under his nose occasionally. The vine had once run heavy with white sap that dripped poison on any landside animal rash enough to pass beneath it. Dried and burned, it gave out a slightly narcotic fragrance that soothed the senses and the mind. Zachariah inhaled a deep breath of the smoke and blew it out again towards the screen. 'This time,' he said, 'Sam Reed's bitten off more than he can chew.'

'How vulgar,' Kedre murmured, flashing him a smile. It was a smile that literally flashed, for she had adopted today an extreme of a current fashion. Her heavy black ringlets were gilded, each separate hair sheathed in a film of gold and twisted into a great braided coronet like a helmet above her narrow Egyptian face. Even her brows were delicate arcs of gold, and a bead of gold winked at the tip of every lash.

'You look ridiculous,' Zachariah assured her, blinking.

'Of course I look ridiculous. I'm just testing how far I can go. You'll see. Every woman in—'

'Look!' Zachariah sat up suddenly in his chair, eyes on the screen. Kedre turned, holding a card poised above the table, and the two of them sat motionless, watching the mimic action on the wall. It did not look very real.

The boat was swerving in to a landing inside a long, encircling arm of breakwater, where a white pier jutted out into the pale sea. There were ten passengers in the boat, ten young men and women on their way to a promised immortality. Their head turned this way and that in quick, nervous motions, watching the strange upper world that had always meant danger and improbable romance to the people of the Keeps. Like the youths and maidens traditionally borne to the Minotaur, they watched in excited apprehension the mighty wall of jungle drawing nearer and nearer, and the low, polished white walls of Plymouth Colony encircling the first island to be subdued.

It was no Minotaur that rose from the water in their path, but it was bent on exacting sacrifice. There were many saurian monsters in these seas. Not many yet had names, and the one that came dripping out of the milky water before the boat was unfamiliar to every watcher. Its darkly gleaming neck rose twenty feet with leisurely speed, water sliding like ragged silk from both sides of the great, gracefully bending arch. It opened a mouth that could encompass a man's head, opened it wide and hissed terribly. The mouth was solidly lined with fangs, rim, roof and sides jagged with them.

A chorus of shouts and screams, thin over the water, rose from the rocking boats as frantic passengers scrambled futilely towards the far side. The head dived down towards them, the neck looping after it like thick rope. There was infinite grace in the long, smooth, curving motion. The beast seemed to have chosen a girl near the front of the boat as its immediate victim. She had yellow hair and she wore a rose-red tunic, bright against the pale sea water.

For a moment pandemonium reigned in minature in the little boat. Then its pilot, moving with rather elaborately scornful precision, leaned forward and pushed a lever. From both sides of the boat translucent impervium slid upwards, half-shells that met overhead with a click, shutting in the passengers and the crew in impregnable protection.

The diving head struck hard against the dome. The boat heeled far over, dipping its impervium arch deep into the water, tossing the men and women into a frantic tangle. The sharp keel flashed into daylight and the long dark neck of the monster struck it squarely.

An ear-piercing scream soared across the water. The saurian's fang-studded mouth gaped towards the clouds. Its curved neck straightened rigidly and from the gashed dark throat a jet of rose-red blood spurted, fantastically identical in colour with the rose-red tunic of the girl.

The scream sounded again, more shrilly; blood gurgled in the long throat and gushed from the gaping mouth. The dark neck beat the sea twice and then slid downwards out of sight. A beautiful carmine stain spread outwards in circles from the spot where it sank.

The boat righted itself and swung in towards the pier.

Kedre laughed, laying down her card in its proper place.

'That pilot!' she said. 'How bored he was with it all! It wouldn't surprise me in the least if Sam Reed had tied the beast out there for a nice spectacular welcome to his recruits. What a tale they'll have to tell!'

'Don't underestimate Sam Reed, my dear,' Zachariah said, gravely, moving the censer under his nose again. 'He'd do exactly that, or something even more elaborately dangerous, if he saw any profit in it. He's a very dangerous person, Kedre – not because he's resourceful but because he's irresponsible.'

Kedre nodded her glittering braided helmet. 'You're right, of course. It's no laughing matter, really. Whoever would have dreamed he'd go so far as piracy! I think we can look for another act of violence the next time anything thwarts him and he can't see any legal way out. We've got a problem, Zachariah.'

'Have you lost your taste for him, then, my dear?'

She did not look up, hearing that note of query in his voice. Instead she stirred the cards beside her with a pointed fore-finger until she had uncovered the tarot called The Hanged Man. It was a beautifully wrought card like the rest. The Hanged Man hung by his right ankle from a T-shaped tree against a background of elaborate gold-diapre work. A golden halo radiated around his serene face and hanging hair, which was red. Kedre reversed the card and looked at the small painted face thoughtfully.

'Don't ask me that, Zachariah,' she said.

'You'll have to find an answer some day, my dear. It isn't just a matter of passing fancy, now. The man's an Immortal.'

'I know.'

'Do you know who he is?'

She looked up quickly. 'Do you?'

Zachariah nodded, inhaled more smoke and fanned the cloud away from his face. Through it he said, 'He's a Harker, Kedre. Do you know the story of Blaze?'

'I do now. I suppose everyone does. Sam didn't leave much to the imagination when he decided to tear down Harker prestige. Does *he* know, Zachariah?'

The Immortal laughed softly. 'That's a very fine paradox. No, he doesn't know. He's put a great deal of energy and thought into the problem of discrediting us so that no one is likely to believe anything a Harker says. When he finds it's his own name he's destroyed, I'd enjoy watching his face.'

' "Destroy" is hardly the word, is it?'

'Oh, it isn't irreparable. We can win opinion back. We may have made mistakes – I'm beginning to think that we were mistaken about opposing colonisation, for one thing – but our long-term motives have always been sound, and I think everyone knows it. Sam still thinks in short-term schedules. When we want to swing public opinion our way, we'll do it. Just now I'm inclined to watch and wait. Give him rope. The colonies have got to succeed now, of course. Much as I dislike the thought, we'll have to work with Reed on that.'

Kedre turned up a card, started to lay it in place on the board and then hesitated, regarding it with a faint smile. Still looking at the picture on its face, she said,

'For a while, yes. He's a bad man, Zachariah. However I feel towards him I realise that. He's got a way to go yet before he reaches the top. Until he gets there he'll do a better job than any of us could do. With the worst possible motives he'll do quite heroic things to establish a sound pyramid under him, something he can use as a basis for power. He'll establish the foundation for a working social system. But only the foundation. Beyond that he can't go. He has no conception of constructive society. We'll have to stop him, then.'

'I know. Have you any idea how?'

'Use his own methods, I'm afraid. Misdirection. Exploit his weaknesses and turn his strength against him. Tempt him with some irresistible bait, and then—' She smiled and flipped the card with a delicate finger.

Zachariah waited.

'I don't have a plan yet,' Kedre said, 'but I think I have

the beginning of one. I must think about it for a while. If it's possible, it's the one weapon for which he'd have no defence.'

'A weapon?'

Her gold-lacquered brows rose. She looked up at him under the heavy casque of gold, her mouth tucking in at the corners with that faint Egyptian smile that might be no smile at all, but a look of pain. The gold brows gave her face a masklike expression and again she flicked the card with her nail. As well as he knew her, Zachariah could not fathom the things that went on behind her eyes when she wore that look. He had never seen it before.

Wordlessly he leaned forward to see the card. It was the Ten of Swords. It showed a grey amorphous seascape and a dark sunset sky, with the hilts of ten swords sharply outlined against it. Their ten blades stood upright in the body of a dead man.

The day came when Plymouth Colony got the first full quota of volunteers. Sam had waited for that day with a certain eagerness and a certain shrinking, but the eagerness was stronger. He had always preferred to come to grips with a problem – perhaps because so many of his enemies had proved irritatingly elusive in the past. The immediate hurdle was purely psychological. He had to make a speech, and he had to say exactly the right things to the thousands of immortality-seekers.

Facing the battery of visor screens, he drew a long breath while he studied his audience. Then he was ready.

Sam said:

'You're a specially selected group. You've been screened carefully, and all of you have passed the basic tests. They were hard tests. We wanted the smartest, toughest, strongest material in the Keeps because you're the shock troops of immortality.'

He paused, glancing from screen to screen, at the thousands of faces intent on his own televised face.

'Not everyone can have immortality. After a certain time of biological life, senescence begins to set in. It doesn't necessarily show right away, and it comes sooner to some than to others. We still don't know what causes age, though we know how to stop it. Age may simply be a virus. Some day we'll find out. At present all we know is that there's a treatment that will arrest aging. But it seldom works on those over forty – perhaps because the balance has swung too far towards obsolescence by that time.'

He let his gaze flicker again across the screens. There was danger latent in those waiting thousands. He held a live grenade in his hand. And he had to keep on holding it, till the last possible moment.

'You've all been screened and tested, physically and psychologically. You're the cream of the Keeps. You'll be the first to get immortality. Later, others will too, but you're the advance guard. You'll make it safe for the others – and they'll keep it safe while you enjoy the rewards of your work. It will be work. It will be hard. You must live landside for some years befor you gain immortality.'

Five years, he thought. Perhaps longer – but five years was the maximum he had allowed himself. Bearing that deadline in mind, he had supervised the tests, rigging them, watching for vital points.

Screening thousands – later it would be millions – would have been a long, difficult job except that the machinery was already set up for Sam. The bureaus of vital statistics had records of most of the population with all pertinent information, including psychology, heredity, probably longevity – an important point! – and pathological propensity. Sam wanted smart, tough, strong men and women certainly – but one other factor was even more important. On that the success of this scheme depended.

He needed youngish, mature people. Because they wouldn't age visibly in five years.

The only way to prove or disprove immortality is by the empirical method unless—

He had allowed for that possibility, too.

He said, 'You must live landside. Remember, I lived landside for nearly forty years. The treatment takes six or seven years for the average mature man. There, again, it may be because age is a virus, and the older a man is, the longer it takes to destroy it. If a child is exposed to the radiations at birth, as the Immortals' children have been, only a few treatments are necessary. There once more, it may be because the age-virus is not present in the newly-born. In such a case, the child grows, reaches maturity – and stops at that point, living for hundreds of years, but growing no older.

'Babies born in the Keeps from now on will have that opportunity. With adults, it's another matter. You'll have the chance, but you'll have to work and fight for it. Because you must be continually exposed to the radiation for six or seven years, and that can't be done in the Keeps.

'We don't know too much about the radiation yet. The radioelement itself is present in the soil and air of Venus, but in microscopic quantities. For reasons we don't understand yet, exposure to solar and cosmic-ray radiation is necessary too. Later we'll learn more. Right now, we know this: we can give you the immortality treatment, but it will take years, and you must spend those years landside, so that the action will be cumulative.

'The process is too complicated to explain in detail.

'It works only on humans. We know that much. Like the ancient *bacillus leprae*, it affects humans but not animals. Guinea pigs couldn't be given leprosy, which was why researchers took so long to discover the cure.

'Immortality is for humans – for you. For all the Keeps. For everyone who isn't already too old to take the treatment. But to be immortal you must live landside for a time. There isn't room in Plymouth Colony for you all.

'You must build new colonies.

'It's the only answer. We had thought of rotating the population in groups at seven-year intervals, but, to be fair, we would have to take the oldest men and women still able to benefit by the radiation. And they would remain at that age, while the rest grew older. We feel it best to choose people at the peak of their powers mentally and physically, so that they will remain so for hundreds of years. This way, too, the others won't have to wait seven years or fourteen or twenty-one. As soon as you've expanded the colony sufficiently, another batch will come in from the Keeps – and expand the colony farther. Thus everyone will benefit equally.'

Sam studied the screens. They were swallowing it. Perhaps after five years they wouldn't, but until then no signs of age should appear that couldn't be explained away on the grounds of environmental influences. Colonising Venus naturally would change a man.

'You've got to earn immortality,' Sam told the thousands. 'You may be a bit confused at first in the transition from Keep life; the administration will allow for that. But remember you must live landside for six years or more, and only by adapting to Colony tradition can you succeed.

'Those in charge here have learned how to cope with landside. They have authority, and you must obey them. We have our own laws – not Keep laws. This is landside. Landside is trying to kill us all every minute of the day and night. You are colonists now, not Keep men, and you are subject to Colony law. According to the contracts you signed, you cannot become a Keep man again until formally discharged by the Colony. That will be when you are – immortal.

'Generally speaking, it won't be hard for anyone to readjust. Know your job. Be ready to step into the job of the man ahead of you. Promotion is going to be very rapid in the colony. Be ready for it.

'Immortality must be earned. The next six or seven years may be hard ones for us all. But you won't be giving up onetenth of your life, you'll be giving up less then one-hundredth. Remember that. Seven years in the colony is the equivalent of *less than a month* after you're immortal.

'*Remember that!*

'Every time you feel discouraged, think of it. You'll be immortal. And there's no hard work a strong man can't endure for – one single month!'

Sam switched off the teleunit. He was alone in the room. He sat silent for a moment or two, watching the throngs who could no longer see or hear him.

Then he said softly, 'Sugar-coated pills. But it always works. Always.'

The crowds were still watching their screens, getting new orders from their individual unit commanders – members of Plymouth Colony's original settlers, the tough, trained men who had already worked under Hale and Sam. They were falling in line – figuratively and actually.

Expanding the Colony – sure. But along rather different lines. As raspberry plants expand and root by canes, so landside would be colonised. Not in five years – it would take far longer than that. But from now on new settlements would appear along the coasts, supported and guarded by Plymouth till they were self-supporting. Plymouth had to remain compact and strong.

The other colonies, the new ones that were to come—

There was a problem. They couldn't be vulnerable, or they couldn't exist against the interminable fury of the continent. Yet, Sam knew, they would have to remain vulnerable to *him*.

And Plymouth Colony had to become completely invulnerable.

He had five years before the pack could be expected to turn and tear him.

Link by strong link they forged the island chain. There was no time for relaxation. Even minutes were grudged. Nevertheless Sam thought Hale was dodging him.

When he walked into the Free Companion's office and found it empty, he made an angry noise in his throat and clicked on the desk televisor. 'Where's the Governor?' he demanded.

'He's directing Operation Clearing, Island Six.'

'Switch me over.'

Presently the screen blanked – apparently Hale didn't have a visual hookup where he was – and the Governor's voice said, 'Hale speaking.'

'Sam Reed. We had an appointment, didn't we?'

'Oh,' Hale said, and his tone changed. 'I'm sorry. Things are moving so fast – some new equipment we needed came in, and I found we could start on Six right away. Make it later.'

Sam grunted and broke the connection. He went outside and commandeered a flitterboat. This time he was certain that Hale had been dodging him.

The pilot was one of the old Plymouth colonists; he gave Sam a soft salute and turned the little boat's prow seaward. They made a big, fast semicircle and swung towards Island Six. The other islands they passed were already colonised, the monstrous forests gone, planting already in progress. Huts were here and there. Quays jutted out at intervals, guarded by pillboxes. Islands One to Five were an odd combination of agrarian and military.

Five islands, only five, balanced against the huge continent of Venus that teemed with ravening life. Yet they were the beginning. Step by step the progress would continue.

Sam studied the pilot's face. He could read nothing there. When the danger came, it probably wouldn't come from the old Plymouth men; the late recruits from the Keeps would be the malcontents. And that time hadn't arrived yet; it wouldn't, Sam hoped, for years. By that time he should have established the tight control he wanted.

And Hale?

Where did Hale stand? Where would he be standing five years from now? That was beginning to worry Sam a good deal. The Keep Families he could cope with, because they were his enemies. But Robin Hale had all the cryptic potentialities of immortality plus a position that could become extremely dangerous to Sam. The pair were nominally fighting as comrades, back to back – which implied vulnerability. He couldn't figure Hale out. That was the real difficulty. How much did the Free Companion know or guess? Had Hale known, all along, that 'Joel Reed' was really Sam Reed? And how much did Hale suspect about the phoniness of the Immortality treatment?

For all Hale knew, Sam might be telling the truth. If, as Sam argued, Immortals were exposed to the radiation soon after birth, no Immortal could actually remember such experiences. Yet the Free Companion wasn't gullible. Even his willingness to follow Sam's lead was somehow suspect.

Hale's passivity, of course, might be due to attrition following arduous experiences; yet, even if that were true, the parallel warned Sam. Metal can become tired – but it can recover. A sword is metal.

Metal – metal. A new thought came to Sam. The Keep recruits – tough, strong, but so far malleable in his hands. They would go through hard struggles landside. When metal becomes work-hardened—

The Sword again.

I must keep my back armoured, too, Sam thought.

The flitterboat raced in towards Island Six. The jungles hid most of the land, except for a high knoll at one end. There was a copter there, and a man's figure silhouetted against the pearly sky. Barges and lighter craft were moving at temporary beachheads on the shore. Sam pointed; the pilot nodded and swung the flitterboat deftly aside, threading his way among the craft. The V-spray of water rushed up along the transparent prow-shield like rain.

It would not rain today, Sam decided, glancing up at the cloud blanket. That was good. Meteorology played an important part in Plymouth – landside conditions were bad enough anyway, without battling torrential rains, so jobs were apportioned according to the weather predictions. There should be a few clear days to work on Island Six and establish a base. Later, much later, a bridge would be constructed to Island Five, and the chain extended by one more link.

Sam stood up as the flitterboat grated against a quay. He jumped lightly on the jetty, instantly in the midst of confusing, ordered activity. A crusher rolled on its caterpillar treads from a barge and lurched monstrously up the beach. Lighter, mobile landcraft followed in its wake, specialised weapons for fighting the jungle mounted on huge-wheeled carriages. The men wore light protective suits and respirators. Heavy armour would only be a handicap at this point.

A tapir-masked figure touched Sam's arm and extended a bundle. 'Better wear these, sir. There may still be bugs around – and the poison plants are pretty bad on this hunk of land.'

'All right,' Sam said, and donned suit and respirator. 'I want to get up to the Governor. Is he on that hill?'

'Yes, sir. There's no road yet, though. He came in by copter.'

'Find me another one, then.'

The man thought for a moment, turned and shouted a question. After a while a twin-screwed gyro came down from somewhere and picked Sam up. Four minutes later he jumped out on the summit of the knoll from the hovering copter and waved to the pilot to proceed.

Hale wasn't wearing an aseptic suit or respirator, so Sam took his off. Up here, above the jungle, there was less danger of infection. Besides, both Sam and Hale had built up a good deal of resistance and immunity in the last few months.

Hale gave Sam a nod. He carried binoculars and a portable microphone, wired from his own grounded copter near by. He had no other equipment except for a large-scale map pinned out on a camp table before him.

'How's it coming?' Sam asked.

'Fair,' Hale said. 'The five-spray treatment hit the tolerance levels of most of the bugs. But you never know with mopping up.'

Anything under a foot long was classified as a bug. That left the fauna – critters – and the flora – the green stuff. The operation meant a little more than merely mopping up, since the fauna was big and the flora unpredictable and perilous.

But the five-spray treatment helped considerably. They had learned much in colonising five islands. The first step now was to shower the island very thoroughly with solutions that didn't like bugs. One formula hit the lichens chiefly – a vital matter. Another damaged a good deal of the flora. The critters, at best, got slightly sick, but they charged at you and bared fangs and you could shoot them, if you were fast; they didn't have the unpleasant trick of infiltrating your lungs and sprouting quickly into a spongy mass that paralysed your respiratory apparatus.

Island Six didn't look like the colonised islands or the raw ones now. It looked sick. The jungle wasn't a blazing green riot. It seemed to hang, like Spanish moss draped across the great boles, and occasionally slow, lethargic movements stirred in it. Sam could get a better picture now.

'There's another pair of binoculars in the plane,' Hale suggested.

Sam got them. He studied the island below. He studied the men. There was something about the patterns of their movements that interested him – a briskness unfamiliar in the first Colony, certainly almost unknown in any Keep. Sam's interest in the jungle was purely superficial and subsidiary. To him the only truly interesting thing was his own kind and he spent long, absorbed thought on the motives behind every act that seemed out of the ordinary in his fellow creatures, his unconscious mind faithful to the concept that there might be something in it for Sam Reed.

These men were very happy in their work. It was something new on Venus. Sam knew their muscles must be aching at the still-unaccustomed toil, the sweat must be running uncomfortably down their bodies inside the protective suits. There was danger in every breath they drew and every move they made. But they were happy. The work was new and absorbing. They were creating. They could see the great strides of their progress simply by glancing behind them. This was the proper occupation of mankind – bringing order out of chaos in the sweat of their brows. It was good and right, and mankind had for long lacked any pleasure in physical toil. Sam filed the thought away for that day when the pleasure in work gave way to boredom.

Then he glanced sideways at Hale, still holding the binoculars to his eyes to hide the fact that he was studying his partner.

Abruptly he said, 'Hale, what are we going to do about the Harkers?'

Hale spoke crisply into his microphone, waving one arm in perfectly futile gestures of direction to the invisible crusher, and then turned to Sam.

'What do you want us to do?' he asked mildly.

'They're too quiet. They let us win – maybe too easily. Once before they let us think we were winning, until they were ready to strike. I know – that was my fault. I was younger then. I didn't have much sense. This time I'm on the level – I know I've got to be. But I still don't trust the Harkers.'

Hale regarded him with a quiet gaze that gave nothing away.

'Maybe,' he said enigmatically. 'How far ahead have you planned, Reed?'

It was Sam's turn to hedge. 'What do you mean?'

'I mean there's going to be trouble in a few years – five or ten, wouldn't you say? Or have you figured on that yet?'

Sam sighed with some relief. So that much of it had emerged into the open, then. Since his triumph on the tele-cast, when he had forced the Immortals to surrender to his demands and snatched victory from defeat by a promise he could not keep, he had not spoken privately with Hale.

That was Hale's doing. He had taken care that there were always others present. And now it had somehow become im-possible for Sam to ask him openly whether or not he had recognised Joel Reed from the start. There was a psycho-logical pressure there Sam recognised and did not like. It meant that Hale had more power latent in him than Sam had quite counted on.

At least, one thing was emerging now – the immortality question. And Hale knew. Obviously he knew the truth. Still – he had tacitly accepted the fraud. He was making use of re-cruits who could have been won no other way, lending his name to a swindle beside which Sam's original deceit was nothing.

Realising that clearly for the first time, Sam felt surer of himself.

'Yes, I figured on it,' he said. 'I wish I didn't have to. Maybe the end justifies the means – we couldn't have worked in any other way, could we?'

Hale's brow lifted a little at the pronoun. But the question itself he could not deny. He had accepted the benefits; he could scarcely refuse a share in the responsibility now.

'No, we couldn't. Or at any rate, we didn't,' he acknowl-edged. 'What we do with the scheme now will show whether it's justified. We'll have to watch that, Reed.' It was a warning. 'Do you have anything planned yet about how you'll meet that crisis when it comes?'

Sam had, of course. But he was quick to accept the warning. So Hale would go only so far in exploiting the candidates for Immortality, eh? Very well, then, Sam's plans would have to remain disguised until the hour came for action.

'I've thought of several outs,' he said carefully. 'We'll discuss it when we have more time.' He had thought of one safe out and one only, and Hale was a fool, he thought, if he didn't know it. When the promise of immortality showed itself a fraud, there was going to be a tremendous surge of resentment against the men who had made the promise – Hale by implication, along with Sam. Violence would be the result; and you can meet violence only one way. Sam meant to be prepared for that day. If Hale disapproved of his solution, let Hale find a better one or take the consequences. Sam meant to provide for Sam Reed. And if Hale tried to interfere in Sam's plans about that vital subject, there was going to be conflict in Plymouth Colony.

Sam had an uncomfortable notion that Hale might be a more formidable opponent than he had heretofore guessed.

It seemed prudent to change the subject. Sam had found out most of what he wanted to know, but the thing which had ostensibly brought him here remained unsolved, and it, too, was important enough.

'About the Harkers,' he said, 'this time I think we'd better stay in touch with them. We've got more chance of watching out for their schemes if we're working together. And right now, I don't see how they can go on opposing our plans. Even they must know that if colonisation is ever going to succeed, it's got to succeed right here in Plymouth Colony. If this fails, there'll never be another attempt.'

'You're right, of course. I believe all the Keep Immortals must know that by now.'

'Then they'll have to work with us towards the same goal, if their motives are as good as I've been told they are. We're the winners. I think it may be up to us to make the first gesture towards consolidation.'

'Yes?'

Sam hesitated. 'I don't trust myself to do it,' he said with a burst of frankness. 'Zachariah Harker and I are ... well, we don't get along. Whenever I see him I want to hit him. You'd be a smoother diplomat than I am. You're an Immortal. You've known them all for a long time. Will you do it, Hale?'

Hale hesitated in turn. Then, obliquely, he said, 'You're an Immortal too, Reed.'

'Maybe. I suppose so. Not in the same sense, though. That's something I'll have to investigate some day, when I have time. It isn't important now. Will you go?'

Still Hale hesitated. While he stood there, evidently searching for the right phrase, the transmitter in his hand buzzed thinly with excited voices and he put it to his ear, relieved at the interruption.

For a moment he listened, peering towards the distant jungle where here and there a treetop could be seen to sway and go down before the juggernaut onslaught of the invisible crusher at its work.

'Take your binoculars,' he said to Sam. 'Step over to the left there – I think there's a gap where you can see across the quarter-line. You shouldn't miss this – they've run into a siren web.'

Curious, Sam obeyed.

The binoculars seemed to lift the jungle forward and upward in one tremendous jump. The crusher had quartered the island, smashing flat four broad avenues between which wedge-shaped segments of jungle still stood, drooping from the poisonous sprays, already paling from brilliant hues to drab. The nearer segment had already been nearly flattened and Sam could see across it, and across the crushed avenue beyond, into the distant wedge of standing trees where the crusher was ploughing methodically forward.

It was a monstrous thing, heavily mailed, lurching on its caterpillar treads with a ponderous, rhythmic gait not inappropriate to this jungle it moved through. The giant saurians of Venusian landside moved with the same vast, lurching tread, heaving their mailed sides through the trees no less majestically than the man-made juggernaut that had come to destroy them.

Vines wreathed it, hung in great swathes and matted tangles from its shoulders and sides. Some of the vines still feebly writhed against the metal, striking with fanglike thorns at the unyielding plate.

Sam could hear faintly the rumble and roar of the crusher lumbering on its way; the crack of breaking tree trunks came sharply through the air, and now the distant shouting of men running forward to watch the excitement was clear and thin over the distance between.

Then a flash of colour just ahead of the crusher caught Sam's eye, and for an instant it seemed to him that all his senses paused. He did not hear the sounds from below or feel the binoculars pressed on his eyes or smell the heavy discomfort of the landside air, which he was still unaccustomed to breathe. There was only that flare of colour that glowed almost in his face and then faded and blurred to another colour more exquisite than the first.

Sam stood motionless while the two blended together and slid into a third hue clouded all over with paler tints whose motion as they coalesced was hypnosis itself. The colours were almost painful to see.

Abruptly he lowered the binoculars and looked questioningly at Hale. The Free Companion was smiling a little, and there was admiration in his face.

'You're a good man,' he said with some reluctance. 'You're the first person I've ever seen look away from a siren web that quickly. Most can't. You'd be a bad hypnosis subject.'

'I am,' Sam said grimly. 'It's been tried. What is that thing down there?'

'A distant cousin of the happy-cloak organism, I imagine. You remember they make happy-cloaks from a submarine thing that subdues its prey through a neuro-contact and eats it alive – only the victim doesn't want to get away once it's sampled the pleasures of the cloak. The siren web works in the same way, only with a landside variation. Look and you'll see.'

Sam looked again. This time he adjusted the binoculars to bring the coloured thing into very near focus. It was impossible for a moment to see what the siren web really was, for again he experienced that stasis of the senses and could only gaze with painful delight at the motion of its colours.

Then he wrenched his mind free and looked at it objectively. It was a very large web, probably an old one as age goes in these ravening jungles. Judging by the men who still ran towards it behind the crusher, he saw it must be nearly ten feet in diameter. It was stretched between two trees in a little clearing, like a spider web, anchored by strong interlacing cables to branches above the vines below. But in the centre it was a solid thing, like fine membrane stretched taut, vibrating slightly with a motion of its own, and flushing with colour after colour, each more enthralling than the last, pumping faster and faster over the shivering web.

A faint twang of sound floated across the distance to Sam's ears, coming more slowly than sight so that though he saw each sound created by the vibrating cables and membrane, he heard it superimposed upon the next visible vibration. The sound was not music as human beings know it, but there was all the rhythm of music in it, and a thin, singing shrillness that touched the nerves as well as the ears, and made them vibrate ecstatically to the same beat.

The thing was exerting all its siren powers to lure the crusher to destruction. It flashed its most exquisite colours hypnotically in the faceless muzzle of the machine, it shrilled irresistible hypnosis to disrupt the synapses of the wire-linked nerves and paralyse the juggernaut tread.

And for a moment it seemed impossible that even a creature of steel and impervium could withstand the onslaught of that wonderful hypnosis.

If it had not withstood the siren, the men who were running forward now would have been lost. All Sam caught was a distant echo of the humming, but it made his brain work only in flashes, and in flashes the colour of the web wrought its paralysis of the mind. He knew that if he were running with those men behind the crusher he would probably run blindly too, to throw himself into the outstretched embrace of the siren.

'It's happened before,' he told himself dazedly. 'A long time ago in Greece, and Homer wrote the story.'

The whole thing was over in a matter of seconds. To the last the siren flamed and shrilled, spreading out its web in a wide-flung promise of rapture. Then the nose of the crusher lurched forward and touched the centre of the web.

In a flash the membrane leaped forward and closed about it. The cables drew thin and fine, screaming with a last vibration of triumph. And there may have been some faint electrical impulse to shock and paralyse the prey, for even the crusher seemed to hesitate for an instant as the glowing wings of the thing infolded its muzzle. Even the crusher seemed to tremble in every plate and filament at the ecstasy of the siren's touch.

Then the juggernaut lurched on.

The cables drew thinner, thinner, tauter, paling from brilliance to translucent white at the increasing tension. They sang so shrilly the ear could no longer hear, but the nerves felt their last agonised vibration high up in the supersonic chords.

The cables snapped. The siren web clutched convulsively in one last spasm at its metal destroyer, colours flamed over it in impossible discords. Then it went flaccid and dropped limply forward, sliding down the mailed muzzle. The grinding treads caught it, carried it remorselessly to the ground, trampled it under into the debris.

And the thing that slid groundward was an enchanted web, a Nessus-shirt of burning colour. But the thing the caterpillar treads crushed into the green mêlée beneath them was an ugly, rubbery grey mat that squirmed convulsively when the cleats caught it.

Sam let out his breath in a long sigh. He lowered the binoculars. For a moment he said nothing. Then he stepped forward, laid the glasses on Hale's camp table, and proved anew that he was no fit subject for hypnosis of any kind.

'About the Harker interview,' he said, 'when can you get away for the trip?'

Hale sighed, too.

'I can't' he said.

Sam frowned. 'It's important. It's something nobody but you is really fitted for. I wish you could manage it, Hale.'

'There's only one place where I'm really indispensable, Reed. Right here. Nobody else knows landside as I do. I'm no diplomat. You're our contact man. I'm sorry.'

There was more to it than that. Sam felt perfectly sure of it. Hale was dissociating himself resolutely from every aspect of this game of deceit except one – the profit. The man power. That he would accept. The rest was up to Sam. And there was nothing whatever that Sam could do about it.

For the first time an unpleasant idea flashed across Sam's mind. Until this moment he had seen himself as the motivating force behind the colonisation. He had pulled the strings that moved the puppet figure of Robin Hale. But in the final analysis, he wondered suddenly, who was the puppet-master and who the dancing doll?

He shrugged.

'All right. I'll do it if I have to. But don't blame me if I make a mess of it.'

'I won't.'

Sam set his jaw. The matter was not really ended. He knew now where his real competition lay, and he knew the conflict had just begun.

The light was cool and clear as crystal. It was a room for working and thinking and planning. It had been designed by Immortals. The planes and curves were functional, but not obtrusively so; they flowed smoothly into each other, and the crystalline flower sprays and the changing picture designs on the frieze were part of the entire quiet, casual pattern. There was nothing to catch and hold the eye for longer than a moment or two. But where the eye rested on shifting colour or slow-budding, slow-flowering artificial crystal plant, the beholder found an anchor for his shifting thoughts, and could build new ones from that point.

In that cool, quiet place, brimming with a clarity of light that held steady from its invisible sources, Zachariah sat beside Kedre at a long desk. Her tapering fingers, with gilt nails, shuffled through the dossiers before her.

'You had better go to see Reed,' Zachariah said.

Kedre lifted her shoulders in a delicate shrug. 'Landside?' she asked. 'Oh, no!'

'Aren't you the one best qualified to deal with him at this point?'

'Must we deal with him?'

Zachariah nodded towards the desk top. 'You have a plan. But Reed's no fool. Misdirection – he's used that trick himself. We should have one real plan, and one overt one to distract Reed's attention.'

'You don't know what I have in mind.'

'I've got an idea. You must have based it on the theorem that Sam Reed is necessary now but will be dangerous at some later time.'

She nodded.

Zachariah took one of her hands and ran his finger tips lightly across the gilded nails. 'But when? We don't know that. And until then, Sam Reed will make his position stronger and stronger. He may be vulnerable now and invulnerable later. We can't strike now, though. Not if Venus landside is to be colonised.'

'Hale was right, you know,' Kedre told him musingly. 'We did wait too long.'

'Not quite – but we would have. However! One error doesn't mean failure. The question is, who's the pawn and who's the player? Reed thinks he's the player. He must remain so, until—'

'Until?'

Zachariah looked at a crystal plant, not answering till it had gone through its glittering cycle of bud and flower. 'Until he's served his purpose and landside's safe. We can't set a definite time-period. So what we need is a bomb, planted now, which will explode when we set it off.'

'That's my plan,' Kedre said. 'A bomb. The only possible time-bomb an Immortal can use against an Immortal, when we can't read the future.'

'And that is?'

'What can we plant near Sam that will stay with him always, potentially explosive, that won't deteriorate for, say, twenty years? That should be time enough. Sam must *want* that bomb near him. It must be something he will want and need. Something that can be custom-made, to suit Sam's requirements exactly, and especially something that Sam can't possibly suspect. A bomb that must seem so harmless Sam can investigate it thoroughly without suspecting its deadliness, even if he traces it back to its – construction.'

Zachariah chuckled. 'Construction?'

'Birth.'

'Of course. A human time-bomb. As you say, the only feasible one an Immortal can use against an Immortal, under the circumstances. What about the difficulties?'

'I need your help now, Zachariah. We've got to start *before* birth. We've got to plan our time-bomb from the very gene, train him every step of the way, and cover our tracks very thoroughly. I think I know how we can do that. But first – I've been using deduction, and then induction. Here's a brief of pertinent information from Sam Reed's dossier.'

'Not the public—'

'I used our private files, too. Oh, we know more about Sam than he suspects. Psychologically we have him pretty well taped.'

'He'll change in five years. Or fifty.'

'We can make prediction graphs. And some basics won't change. He'll always have a weakness for the colour blue, I know. Our time-bomb will have blue eyes.'

Zachariah began to laugh. Kedre didn't. She made an irritated gesture and picked up a photograph.

Zachariah sobered. He looked at her shrewdly.

'I wonder what your motives are, Kedre,' he said. 'I wonder if you know?'

She said calmly, 'I isolated many facts from Sam's records, and built up a picture of what sort of man he'll want near him in, say, eighteen years. I'm predicting my picture on the success of the colonisation plan, naturally. We'll have to work with Sam on that. Our time-bomb must be specially trained, so his talents and skills will be what Sam needs. Personality and appearance are important, too. Sam's conditioned to like certain types of voices and faces. And to dislike others. Well – I got that picture clear . . . what sort of man we'd need.'

She found another photograph.

'Then I searched in vital statistics for a man and a woman. I checked everything about them – heredity, everything! I can predict almost exactly what their child will be like, especially since it will be conceived and born under certain conditions we'll arrange – not obviously.'

Zachariah took the photographs, one of a young man, the other of a young woman.

'Do they know each other?'

'Not yet. They will. The man is ill. I had to arrange that. I had him infected – he had volunteered for the Colony. We'll keep him here, and we'll arrange for him to meet this girl. But we must never show our hand.'

Zachariah, suddenly interested, bent forward, glancing at various charts.

'What's his work? Oh, I see. Mm-m. Give him something more interesting. Making sure they stay in Delaware will be tricky. I think we can pull the right strings, though. Yes, I'm sure of it. We can arrange for them to meet and marry – but the child?'

'Simple. We already know her fertility period.'

'I mean, what if the boy turns out to be a girl?'

'Then she may have even a stronger appeal to Sam Reed,' Kedre said, and was silent for a little while. Suddenly she pushed the girl's photograph away.

'Psychonamics is the rest of the answers,' she said briskly. 'The child, boy or girl, will have psychonamic treatment from the very start. Secret, of course. Not even his parents will know. There will be mnemonic erasure after every treatment, so the boy himself won't know he's undergoing continued hypnosis. And it'll amount to post-hypnotic suggestion. In the boy's unconscious, by the time he's eighteen, will be a command he can't disobey.'

'To kill?'

Kedre shrugged. 'To destroy. We can't yet tell what will be the most effective treatment. Of course nobody can be hypnotised into committing any act he wouldn't do consciously. The boy must be trained so he'll have no compunctions about Sam Reed. There'll have to be some triggering response – we'll implant that hypnotically, too. He mustn't act until we set off his reaction, no matter what provocation he gets up to that time.'

Zachariah nodded thoughtfully. 'It's good. It's elaborate, of course, too. A Robin Hood's barn sort of plan.' He used the curious colloquialism without even thinking of its vastly faraway origin. 'Are you sure we aren't overestimating the man?'

'I know Sam Reed. Don't forget his background. During his formative years he thought of himself as a short-termer. He's got a tremendously strong instinct for self-preservation, because of the life he lived in the Keeps. Like a wild animal's, watchful every second. I suppose we might kill him now – but we don't want to. We need him. The whole culture needs him. It's only later, when he's dangerous, that we'll want him destroyed. And by then . . . well, you'll see.'

Zachariah, his eyes on a slowly unfolding stone flower, said, 'Yes, it's a pattern, I suppose. Every autocrat knows how precarious his position is. We'd have been better rulers of the Keeps if we'd remembered that ourselves. And Sam will have to be an autocrat to survive.'

'Even now it probably would be very hard to attack him personally,' Kedre said. 'And in ten years – twenty – fifty – he'll be really invulnerable. He'll be fighting every hour, every year of that time. Venus, his own men, us, everything around him. He won't be living in the Plymouth Colony we see on the visors now. Here in the Keeps nothing changes – it's hard for us to adjust our minds to the changes that are going to take place landside. Our own technologies will make his invulnerability possible – protective devices, psychological barriers, screenings . . . yes, I think we'll need something like our time-bomb to make sure of reaching him by then.'

'It's elaborate in one way,' Zachariah told her, 'but I withdraw my Robin Hood's barn simile. In its own way its extremely simple. Once you admit the need for the roundabout approach, you can see how simple it is. Sam will be expecting some tremendously complicated attack from us. He'll never dream we could lack deviousness to the extent that our single weapon is a gun in the hands of a boy.'

'It may take fifty years,' Kedre said. 'It may fail the first time. And the second. The plan may have to be changed. But we must start now.'

'And you'll go landside to see him?'

She shook her gold-coifed head. 'I don't want to go landside, Zachariah. Why do you keep insisting on that?'

'He'll be wondering what we're up to. Well – give him an answer. Not the right one. He's no fool. But if we can make him suspicious of minor things, it'll occupy his mind and stop him from watching us too closely in our major project.'

'You go.'

Zachariah smiled. 'I have a personal reason, too, my dear. I want you to see Sam Reed. He isn't the underdog anymore. He'll have begun to change. I want your reaction to Sam Reed Immortal.'

She gave him a quick, masked glance, the light glinting from her golden hair and golden brows and dazzling from the flicker of golden beads that tipped her lashes.

'All right,' she said. 'I'll go. You may be sorry you sent me.'

Hale studied the site of Island Six's ganglion, the cleared area where the local administration buildings would presently rise. Work progressed. In distant jungles, towards the coast, the rumbling roars of crushers could still be heard, but here there was constructive, not destructive, activity. Tree boles had been hauled away over a four-acre area, and the ground had been ploughed up. Surveyors were already busy.

An old man was stooping down not far away, and Hale strolled towards him as he recognised the Logician. Ben Crowell straightened, his shrewd, seamed face alight with speculation.

'Hullo, Governor,' he said, 'Looks like good soil here.' He crumbled loam between his calloused fingers.

'You're not expendable,' Hale said. 'You shouldn't be here. But I suppose there's no use trying to give you orders.'

Crowell grinned. 'Not a bit. Thing is, I always know what'll happen and about how far I can go.' He examined the loam again. 'Poisoned now, but it'll come back. When an anaerobic bacteria get to working—'

'First we'll flood the soil with bacteriophage,' Hale said. The surveying crew and the diggers were some distance away; they could talk without being overheard. 'One toxic treatment helps, but one isn't enough – there are too many dangerous bugs in the dirt.'

'It's good dirt, though. Almost too rich. Over to the west there it's sour; needs liming. But you can get some nice crops on this island.'

A man wearing a shoulder-tank equipped with a hose, and what seemed to be a gigantic hypodermic syringe came past, moved to a labelled stake, and began working the telescopic 'needle' into the ground. 'One of them, huh?' Crowell said.

'One of the worst. Above ground it's just a creeper. But the root-reservoir's twenty feet long and ten feet down. Only way to kill it is pump it full of poison.'

'Used to be something like that on Earth – Man Underground, we called it. Dunno the scientific name. Only we used kerosene to kill it. Stuff never grew quite as fast on Earth as it does here. Bad now, but it'll be an advantage when we get good crops in. Corn in twenty days, maybe.' He shook his head, clucking appreciatively.

'If we can keep the weeds out.'

'Only one real way. Pull 'em. You might try crab grass, though,' Crowell suggested. 'I'd back crab grass even against Venus creeper, and you know what a strangler that is. Look, instead of letting some of the acres stay poisoned – that don't help the soil – why not put in some crab grass? Brother, it *grows*!'

'I'll check on it,' Hale said. 'Thanks. Any more ideas? Or is that against your rules?'

The Logician laughed. 'Shucks, I can make suggestions. They don't alter the future one way or the other – somebody was sure to try crab grass here sooner or later. It's only the big things I don't interfere with, if I can help it. They may not look like big things at the time, but *I* know.' He peered through a swathe of fallen trees towards the coast. Far beyond, across the bay, was the mainland, where the cliff-like structure of the old Doonemen fort stood. There was activity on that weed-draped, lichen-stained hulk. Bright scarlet flashes blazed out and were gone. Boats kept up a continual traffic from the mainland to Island One and back again.

'What goes on?' Crowell asked. 'Going to work on the fort already?'

'Sam's idea,' Hale said. 'I think he's afraid I'm beginning to take the initiative. I started work on this island without discussing it with him first. So he'll pulling the same trick. That's fine.'

Crowell considered. 'So? What is the setup?'

'He's started to clear the old fort. Quite a job, and we weren't ready to tackle the mainland yet – but I think it'll be O.K. I'd say otherwise if the fort weren't already there. The Doonemen built it the right way. I remember—' He, too, looked towards the shore, his face changing a little. 'There was always a maintenance crew on duty. The jungle was always ready to eat us up, if it could. The plants and the animals. But the Keeps gave us equipment then, UV batteries, heat rays, acid sprays. The Free Companions always had two fights going on. One was irregular; wars against other Companies. But the fight against the jungle never stopped.'

'Maybe Sam's bit off more than he can chew,' the Logician suggested.

'No. He's got the equipment and the man power. Once he clears the fort, once he sets up his maintenance machinery, he can keep things running. He can't move back inland yet, but he doesn't want to. He's going to use the fort as an additional base, he says, and start working along the archipelago till he meets me. That'll save time – our working from both ends of the island chain. It's a good idea.'

'Got enough men?'

'Five thousand,' Hale said. 'It's enough, but not too much. We're a little crowded yet, but we've got to have the man power reserve to fall back on for emergencies. Never know when you have to throw in shock troops against the jungle.

And every mile we clear means losing a crew left to maintain it. Five thousand, and more coming when we have room to house and use them.'

'No rumpus yet?' Crowell asked.

Hale looked sharply at him. 'Expecting trouble?'

'Don't have to be prescient for that, son. Five thousand men doing hard work, and more coming – promising 'em immortality won't keep 'em quiet indefinitely. A fella has to go to town Saturday night and raise a bit of hell.'

'What do you know about that immortality business?' Hale asked, with a glance around.

The Logician merely grinned.

Hale looked towards the distant fort, where the red flashes of flame-splashers were burning the old walls clear. He said, 'You know, and I know. Nobody else can be sure, except Sam. But his story is that you can get immortality from a radiation that exists on Venus. Well – you were born on Earth!'

'Oh, there was a certain amount of radioactivity flying around on Earth just before it blew up,' Crowell said.

'There'll be trouble, though. You know one danger. It could happen here. That time, man left Earth and came to Venus. If it should happen again—'

'Kind of like a hermit crab. When it outgrows its shell, it crawls out and finds another. Mistake to stay in a shell that's too tight. Lots of things might make it tight. Growing too fast – which was what happened on Earth. These people—' Crowell waved towards the crew of workers. 'Could be they're outgrowing the Keeps, only they never knew it. A man needs a lot of things, all in all.'

'Are you going to stay in the colony?' Hale asked abruptly.

'Guess so, for a while. I'm a dirt farmer at heart. Why?'

'Oh, not because you're the Logician. You're an Immortal. So am I. The short-termers – you can't let yourself get too closely involved if you're immortal. The Keep Families ... Sam ... you're the only man on Venus who's my kind.'

'We both spent the best parts of our lives under the sky, son,' Crowell said. 'And with our feet on good brown dirt. Not the longest part of our lives, but the best part. With me it was Earth, with you it was Venus, but it comes to the same thing. I know what you mean. I can feel at home with you, though sometimes you sure act like a cussed fool.'

They watched the workers again. After a while, following a new chain of thought, Hale said, 'We'll have to militarise. Sam suggested, but I was thinking about it for some time.'

'They don't look sharp, for a fact,' Crowell said, examining the nearest crew.

'It isn't only that. We've really got a military setup here already, basically. Military discipline and organisation. Like the old Companies, in some ways. But there ought to be uniforms, and what goes with them.'

'Think so?'

'If you take away a man's freedom, you've got to give him a substitute, even if it's only a sop to Cerberus. Let him have safe outlets for his individuality. If he can't wear flimsy celoflex – and he can't here, he needs tough protective fabrics – give him a smart uniform. Service insignia, too, and insignia of rank. Recreational facilities – but organised and controlled. Promising immortality won't be enough, and militarisation won't either, but together they'll postpone the blowup a little longer. With the Free Companions it was different; we knew what to expect when we joined up, and we joined because we wanted to, not because of any rewards except the life itself – it was the life we wanted. These recruits now – I think militarisation will have a good psychological effect.' Hale, without seeming to do so, was watching the Logician very closely. 'What I'm wondering is why Sam suggested the idea. I'd like to know *all* his motives for doing so. His future plans.'

Crowell chuckled. 'I expect you would, son. I expect you would.'

Hale kicked the brittle wing-cased body of a foot-long beetle and watched it fly spinning across the clearing towards a heap of other glittering dead insects shovelled aside for disposal. One of the first results of the poison sprays on every island was the clattering rain of beetles that dropped like iridescent hail from the foliage, some of them large enough to stun the men beneath.

'You could tell me,' he said stubbornly. 'You could if you would. It would save so much—'

'Now there's where you're wrong, my boy.' Crowell's voice was suddenly sharp. 'Seems to me I've mentioned before that seeing the future doesn't mean a man can change it. That's always been the fallacy – thinking that if you know what's going to happen, you can avoid it. Let me give you a little lecture son, on the problems of being prescient.'

Crowell hitched his belt and dug a toe into the sod, turning over the rich dark soil appreciatively, spreading it flat beneath his shoe sole as he talked. And his diction changed with his subject.

'The truth is, generally speaking, the superficial currents of events don't mean anything. The big tides are important, but by the time they're big enough to notice, they're too big to be altered. A sea wall wouldn't do it. Because what makes the tide itself, that keeps pounding and pounding away?

'The minds of men—

'Back in the Twentieth Century a lot of men knew what was going to happen to Earth. They said so. They said it loud and often. And they were men who had earned public respect. They should have been believed. Maybe they were, by a lot of people. But not enough. The minds of men kept right on working in the same set patterns. And so we lost Earth.

'If you've got prescience you've got to stay a witness – no more. Remember Cassandra? She knew the future, but the price she paid for prescience kept her harmless – nobody would believe her. Prescience automatically cancels out participation. You see that certain prearranged factors add up to a certain equation. THOSE FACTORS. Add another factor – your interference – and the equation is changed too. That's the imponderable – your own interference.

'You see why oracles have got to speak in riddles? There've been plenty of prescient folk in history, but they had to speak vaguely or what they said wouldn't come true.

'Look now. Suppose two major possibilities exist for you. You go down to Nevada Keep tomorrow and put across a deal that nets you a million credits. Or you stay home and get killed. Well, you come to me and ask me whether to go or stay. And I know these two possibilities are right ahead of you. But my hands are tied.

'Because both results depend entirely on your personal motivations and reactions. In possibility A, you'll have gone to Nevada Keep without consulting me, and with certain reaction-basics already existing in your mind. *Under those conditions*, reacting in exactly a certain way to a given set of circumstances, you'll make a million credits. But you consult me. I tell you, say, go to Nevada Keep.

'And you do go – but with a different psychological quotient. I've advised you to go. Ergo, you decide something nice is waiting for you there and you go with a passive attitude, waiting to stumble over a bag of gold, whereas your earning your million credits depends on alert aggressiveness. You see?

'Or here's another possibility. Unconsciously you don't want to go. You rationalise my answer to the point where you stay home, deciding I'm a liar, maybe, or that my advice was really to stay, not go. So you get killed.

'So my job is to keep the factor constant as given, without changing them by introducing the catalyst of my own oracle. I've got to do it subtly, gauging your psychology. And that's tricky. I have only limited information to go on. Prescience works by rules of logic basically. It isn't magic. Knowing you, I've got to find certain ideas, semantic groupings that will influence your decision without your knowing it, without altering your original emotional attitude. Because that original attitude is one of the factors in the final equation my prescience has foreseen.

'So I can't say, "Go to Nevada Keep!" That would mean you'd go passively. I've got to phrase my advice in cryptic terms. Knowing what I know about you, I might say, "The kheft tree has blue leaves", and you might be reminded of certain affairs – apparently natural, spontaneous thought-process on your part – which will create a desire to get away from home temporarily. That way I sidestep – if I'm deft enough – introducing any new element into your original psychological pattern as of that moment. You go to Nevada Keep, but ready to react according to the original pattern.

'You make your million credits.

'So now you know why oracles speak in riddles. The future depends on imponderables which can so easily be changed by a word. THE MOMENT AN ORACLE PARTICIPATES, PRESCIENCE IS LOST.'

The Logician stamped his turned clod flat Then he looked up and smiled wryly. 'Also,' he said, 'this presupposes that it's advisable, in the long-term view, that you should make that million. It may be better for you to stay home and be killed.'

Hale was looking at the flame that washed the walls of Doone Fort clean. He was silent for a while. 'I suppose I see what you mean,' he said finally. 'Only – well, it seems hard to stand this close to all my answers and not be able to get at them.'

'I could hand you an answer to every problem you'll ever meet, all written out in a little book,' the Logician said. 'So you could flip the page and parrot out your answer whenever you needed one. What good would that do? You might as well be dead to start with. And I'm an oracle only within certain limits. I can't answer all questions – only those I've got full information about. If there's an unknown factor – an x factor – I can't foresee anything reliably about that question.

'And there is an x factor. I don't know what it is. I realise now I'm never going to know. If I did, I'd be God and this would be Utopia. I recognise the unknown quality only by its absence, its influence on other factors. That's none of my business or yours. I don't let it bother me. My business is to watch the future and not interfere.

'The future is the mind of man. It wasn't atomic power that destroyed Earth. It was a pattern of thought.

'It's easier to control a planet than to control that dust-mote there, blowing around unpredictably on currents we can't even feel. Blowing on a current created by your motion when you reach out to control the dust-mote – which is a thought – and the future of mankind.'

Curve beyond great white curve, the walls of Doone Fort stood pearly against the jungle. To Sam, looking up at them from the cleared white floor of the *enciente*, they seemed tremendously tall and powerful. Curve upon thick, smooth curve, they seemed to beat back the forest, to encircle in a jealous embrace the foothold of life within them. Their lines were the lines of waves and of all things carved by waves, instinct with a meaning men can recognise without in the least understanding.

Three stories high the smooth, rounded walls rose, broken by windows that glittered with interlacing screens of light to filter out the bugs visible and invisible. These forts had been built on much the same scheme as medieval castles, to withstand attack from ground-level, horizontally, by men, and by air from bacteria and flying things as medieval men built to withstand flights of fire-arrows. There was a close parallel, for attack by planes had been unknown in the early days on Venus. The Free Companions respected each other's forts. And air travel then as now was too wildly erratic, dependent on currents and torrents of wind too dangerous to attempt.

There was a great deal of activity here. Around the great curve of the *enciente* the barracks and shops stretched, seething with men. In the higher buildings at the inland end were the hospital, the labs, the officers' quarters. The outer walls curved down to enclose a small harbour with a heavily fortified barbican giving on to the piers outside.

A flurry was in progress at the open barbican, though Sam had not yet noticed it. Men and women already browning from the filtered sunlight paused in their activities and stared frankly, drawing back out of a respect generations implanted in their forebears to let the Immortals through.

Kedre came up the courtyard serenely, smiling at the watchers, now and then greeting someone by name. Her memory was phenomenal; Immortals cultivated the faculty. Her adaptivity was phenomenal, too. In Keep attire she might have looked garish exposed to daylight, but she was too wise to attempt it. She wore a long straight cloak the pearly white of the Fort itself, and her head was swathed in a white turban very cunningly wrapped to make the most of her aloof beauty. White in a sunny world would have been blinding; here Fort and Kedre alike glowed nacreous in the misty day, gathering all light to themselves.

She said composedly, 'Hello, Sam.'

He clasped his hands before him and bowed slightly in the semi-oriental gesture of greeting that had for so long replaced the handshake. It was his first recognition of her existence, done formally and this time between equals. He could afford it now.

She laughed and laid her narrow hand on his arm. 'I represent all the rest of us down below,' she said. 'We hope we can work together in peace from now on. I . . . heavens, Sam, how can you breathe this air?'

It was Sam's turn to laugh. He whistled, and a young man who had been following him with a notepad and stylus came up from the respectful distance to which he had retired. 'Bring a pomander,' Sam told him.

The boy came back at a run, and Sam put the perforated ball of plastics into Kedre's hand. It was filled with fresh flower petals and the warmth of the palms released a heavy cloud of perfume that made the air seem pleasanter to breathe.

'You'll get used to it,' Sam assured her, smiling. 'We all do. This is an honour I hadn't expected so soon. I'd meant to call on you first.'

'You're busier than we.' She said it graciously, and then pulled a little at the arm she held. 'Do show me around. I'm so curious. I've never seen the inside of a Fort before. How beautiful it is up here! If only you could do something about this unbreathable air—'

'Wait a while. Wait twenty years. These jungles are thick now. They give off too much carbon dioxide, for one thing. But wait. It's going to be better.'

She walked beside him slowly, her spotless cloak-hem brushing the white pavement. 'I believe you, Sam,' she said. 'We rather incline now to thinking you were right. This is the time to colonise, not a generation ahead. Your methods were abominable, but the end may justify them. I'm sure it will if you'll let us work with you. You're a headstrong fool, Sam. You always were.'

'You didn't object to it forty years ago. I haven't thanked you for switching the dream-dust for me, Kedre. Or for having me looked after while I was – asleep.' He said that without so much as a glance at her, but from the sudden twitch of her finger on his arm, and the way she paused to look up, he knew he had guessed wrong.

'But Sam, I didn't. I tried, but you'd disappeared. Do you mean you don't know where you were all that time? I'll put my men to work on it – maybe we can find out something.'

'Do if you like. I doubt if they can turn up anything my men couldn't.'

'But Sam, that's ... it's almost frightening! Because we know someone did take care of you. You couldn't have vanished for forty years like that without ... Sam, who could it have been?'

'I'll find out, some day. Forget it. Look – this is the jungle. The real thing, not just something on the screen. What do you think of it?'

They had mounted the white outer stairs leading to the battlements. Now Sam paused and leaned on the parapet, looking down at the belt of raw ground surrounding the Fort, and the solid walls of greenery beyond it. Sounds and scenes and subtle motions came from the undergrowth that were frightening because they were still so mysterious. Man had not even scratched the surface of the Venusian jungle yet and all its ways were alien and strange.

Kedre gave it one glance and then turned her back. 'I don't think about the jungle at all. It isn't important. This is.' She gestured towards the teeming courts below. 'You've got a tremendous job to do, Sam. And you're almost single-handed. I know Robin Hale handles the actual working parties, but that's the least part of it. Will you let us share your work? We've had a great deal of experience, you know, in handling men.'

Sam laughed. 'Do you think I'd trust a one of you?'

'Of course not. And we couldn't trust you. But working together, we'd keep an eye on each other. You need a check and we need impetus from you. How about it, Sam?'

He looked at her in silence. He was remembering the moment before the dream-dust shut out all sight and sound, her face watching him from the visor screen and her hand giving the order for his extinction. He knew she must be here now for some motive more devious than the overt one. His mistrust of all other human beings and of the Immortals in particular, was profound. And his mind, which until now had been tentatively half-open towards co-operation, dubiously began to close. Sam's early training had been too complete. It was not in him to trust anyone.

He said, 'It wouldn't work. Our motives are too different.'

'We'll be working towards the same goal.'

'I couldn't do it. I've always worked alone. I always will. I don't trust you, Kedre.'

'I don't expect you to. But have it your way. Remember this, though – we both want the same thing, successful colonisation of the land. Whether you like it or not, we'll be working towards the same end, down below. And Sam – if after a few years have gone by we find we're at cross-purposes again, remember, it will be you, not we, who have gone astray.' There was a warning in her voice. 'When the time comes – and it will – there's going to be trouble, Sam.'

He shrugged. He had just taken, though he did not know it, the first definite step towards the isolation of the mind and body which in the end was to mean his downfall.

'So it's taken five years,' Ben Crowell said. 'Just about what I figured.'

The man walking beside him – Platoon Commander French – said: 'You mean – us?'

Crowell shrugged noncommittally and waved his hand. He might have been indicating the darkness beyond the rampart on which they walked – the pillbox-dotted, cleared lands in which a man might walk for three days in a straight line in safety. It had taken five years to clear seventy-five miles, a great bite taken out of the jungle with the fort as the focal point.

Nothing could be seen now. Floodlights, with charged wire-mesh shields to guard against phototropic bugs, showed part of the ground outside the wall, but in the dark beyond the safety area stretched far inland. The fort had changed too. It had expanded till it crouched on the shore like a monstrous armoured beast, so huge that if it had been alive, it could never have walked the earth of Venus.

Curious – earth of Venus. A paradox. Mankind would always carry with him his terrestrial heritage, though he carried his colonies beyond Cygni. The old words, the old thoughts—

The old motives.

Platoon Commander French touched Crowell's arm, and they turned towards a sloping ramp, past the masked muzzle of what seemed to be a strange sort of gun. French indicated it.

'See?'

'What about it?'

'Oh, you'll find out. Come on.'

As always, the courtyards teemed with activity under bright lights. Crowell and French walked through the tumult briskly – only furtiveness was suspect, and their openness was a good mask. They entered an outbuilding. French took the lead.

The fort was a labyrinth now. Technically the chamber the two men entered presently was classified as a storeroom, but it served a different purpose at the moment. Nearly fifty men were here, drawn from all levels of colony life. Somebody gave a soft challenge.

French said, 'Hello, Court. This is Ben Crowell. I'll vouch for him. Sit down over here, Crowell – and listen.'

He moved to the front of the room, holding up his hand for attention. 'All set? Shut the door. Got the guards posted?'

A man said, 'Step it up, French. Some of us have to be back on duty pretty soon.'

'This won't take long. Listen. There's about a dozen new men here tonight – right? Hold up your hands.'

Crowell was one of those who raised his arm.

'All right,' French said. 'We'll be talking most for your benefit. You're all convinced already, or you wouldn't be

176

here. And you won't do any talking to the wrong people after you get out of this room – we chose you carefully.'

He hesitated, looked around. 'The main thing – is there anybody here who still believes in Reed's immortality gag? That phony Fountain of Youth?'

A voice said, 'There's no proof either way, is there, commander?'

French said, 'I came here five years ago. I was twenty then. Island Five had just been cleared. Everybody was talking big – big plans of the future. Immortality for everybody. The treatment was supposed to take six or seven years.'

'Well, it's only been five for you, hasn't it?'

'You don't have to wait a hundred years to be sure. Some of us have been seeing Keep doctors. We're getting older. All of us. There's a way of checking – the calcium deposits in the blood vessels, for one thing. Those treatments of Reed's are fakes. I know I'm five years older than I was when I first hit Plymouth, and the same thing goes for the rest of you. Reed's crossed us up. Look at his record – you can't trust him an inch. Five years I've been sweating up here, when I could have been back in my Keep taking it easy.'

'I kind of like it landside,' Ben Crowell put in, stuffing tobacco into his pipe.

'It could be all right,' French admitted, 'but not under this setup. All we do is work. And for what? For Sam Reed and Robin Hale – building, building, building! Hale's an Immortal; maybe Reed's going to live seven hundred years too – I don't know. He doesn't seem to get any older. Maybe he did find the Fountain of Youth, but if he did, he's kept it for himself. Know what that means? We work! We work till we die! Our children work too, when their time comes. And Sam Reed just hangs around and waits a few hundred years till we've done his job for him and fixed him up a nice, comfortable setup that's just what he wants. Well – I don't see the profit!'

A new voice said, 'You're right. I agree. But Reed had to get the fort built strong. You were here five years ago; you know what it was like.'

'He's in too much of a hurry. Discipline – there's too much of it. He's got plans of his own, and we're not told what they are. Colonising landside isn't all of it. Sure, we needed that fort five years ago – and we needed it strong. But what about all this top secret armament work? Nobody's supposed to know about the new gun emplacements on the walls – the electric-spray blasters, and the gas throwers. But they're being set up.'

'The jungle?'

'Seventy-five miles away now!' French said. 'And some of these new weapons – they don't make sense! Kalendar, you're a logistics man. Tell 'em.'

Kalendar stood up, a short, swarthy figure in a neat blue uniform. 'They'd be useful for defence against human enemies. They could fight off and smash an onslaught by tanks, for example. But they're more powerful than we need even against a thunder-lizard. Besides, there are long-range cannon being cast and set up – they've got everything from radar calibration to video reactors. They'll throw a shell five hundred miles away and hit the target. What are they going to be used against? Another battery aimed at the fort? And our new plane construction programme – you don't colonise by plane!'

'Exactly. What's Reed expecting?' French asked. 'Attack from the Keeps? The Keeps don't fight. They're living a life of glory down there, taking it easy, while we work ourselves to death.'

A low growl of resentment arose. These men didn't like the people of the Keeps – jealousy, probably. But the sound hinted at something new on Venus, just as this secret meeting foreshadowed a result Sam had not expected. For Sam had always been used to dealing with Keep people, and this was a new breed of men.

Ben Crowell puffed at his pipe and watched interestedly.

There was a burst of argument now, violent and angry. The plotters talked a lot – naturally! It was an escape from discipline. They were talking out their emotions in hot argument instead of in action. When they stopped talking, the volcano would probably erupt.

Ben Crowell settled himself more firmly, his back against a packing case.

'—whatever Reed's planning—'

'—let the Keep people do some work—'

'—how much more time are we going to give Reed?'

'How long are we going to sit and take it?'

French hammered for silence.

'We've got several plans. But we've got to figure well ahead. Suppose we kill Reed—'

'That wouldn't be easy. He doesn't take chances!'

'He can't win if most of the colony's against him! And it will be. We've got to spread our organisation. Once we get rid of Reed – and Hale – we'll be on top and able to stay there. We'll have the fort. And there isn't a thing on Venus that can smash the fort!'

'Hale's no fool. Neither is Reed. If they get wind of us—'

French said: 'Every man takes a lie-detector test before he leaves one of our meetings. No traitors live.'

'I haven't lived a thousand years without figuring out how to fool a lie-detector,' the Logician said to Hale.

Hale turned away from his light-latticed window that looked down so far on the walls which had once seemed so high to them all. He said coldly, 'I know you were at that meeting. I have spies, too.'

'Did your spy recognise me?'

'He didn't recognise anybody. He got there afterwards. But he smelled pipe smoke and that rank tobacco of yours. Anyway – I know a little about what goes on around here.'

'What, for example?'

'I know when discipline begins to fail. When men are sloppy about saluting. When they don't polish their brassards. I learned discipline in the Free Companies. I saw the crack-up start in Mendez's company before his men killed him. I noticed signs of trouble here months ago. That's when I put my spies to work. I knew what to expect, and I was right. It's beginning.'

'What?'

'Mutiny, I know a few of the ringleaders – not all.'

'Does Sam Reed know?'

'I've discussed it with him. But – I think he discounts the danger. He's been guarding himself so thoroughly he mistakes personal safety for colony safety. I want you to tell me what's going on. I know you can. If you don't, I can get the information elsewhere, but I'd like to discuss it with you if you're willing.'

'I know you can find out elsewhere,' Crowell said. 'I'll be glad to talk. I've been waiting for you to ask me, hoping you would, because I couldn't volunteer anything without upsetting the pattern. I got into this passively, you know. Guess I looked like a malcontent. God knows why. No, I do know. Do you?' He squinted at Hale over the hand that cradled his pipe.

Hale shook his head. 'No, I ... wait. Maybe I do.' He strolled to the window again and looked down at the busy courts. There was much more of a pattern to the activities in Plymouth Colony than there had been five years ago. Discipline had stiffened into iron rigidity. It seemed to the average man that as the need for discipline lessened with their growing conquests of the land, the meaningless forms of it grew more and more inflexible.

'Sam has his reasons,' Hale said, looking down. 'I don't know what they are, but I can guess. His time's running out. The balance is going to shift pretty soon. Men are losing faith in immortality and beginning to wonder. Sam knows the balance is tilting already, but I don't think it's dawned on him what he's weighing in the balance. Men. And not Keep men any longer. Men like you and me, who know what independence means. No wonder they spotted you for a malcontent. You've lived in a world where every man had to shift himself or go under. So have I. I suppose the marks of it are plain.'

'Right.' Crowell grinned. 'Keep people want their leaders to do their thinking for them. Our men landside have had to think for themselves. Those who didn't – well, they just don't survive. It's the old pioneer feeling come back, son, and I like the feel of it. It means trouble, but I like it.'

'Trouble is right. Serious trouble, unless we move at the right time.'

'Now?' Crowell was watching the Free Companion keenly.

'Not yet,' Hale said, and the Logician's smile was faint, but satisfied. 'No, not quite yet. Partly I want to sound this thing out, see how far it's going to spread. Like the Man Underground plant, you've got to locate the root. And partly – I don't know, exactly. I've got a sort of feeling that something's working out in these mutinies and plots that shouldn't be crushed. It's the pioneer spirit, all right, and I feel the way you do. I like it. Mutiny isn't the answer, but mutiny's a good sign, in a way.'

'You going to let them go ahead, then?'

'No. I can't do that. At this point they still need Sam and me, no matter what they think. Let the mutineers take over and they'd wind up down in the Keeps again, sinking back into the old apathy. This is a crucial period. Sam's got some sort of plan I don't understand yet, but I'm betting on Sam to come out on top. Sam can take care of himself. His reaction to the mutiny, if he took it seriously, would simply be to stamp it out. And at this point that might mean stamping out the independent spirit of pioneering along with it. I'll have to think it over, Crowell. No use asking you for suggestions, is it?'

Crowell peered intently into his pipe, which had gone out. He poked ineffectually at it with a calloused finger. 'Well,' he said slowly, 'I don't think you need much advice, my boy. You're on the right track. Don't interfere any more than you've got to. There are natural processes at work levelling themselves off and the longer they operate on their own, the better. You know something? I think just living up here landside has done one mighty big service to these people. They've discovered Time again. Down below day and night don't mean much. One season's pretty much like another. But here, you *see* time passing. You get the sense of its being later than you think. These boys and girls started out with the idea they were going to live forever. They had a long-term view. They were willing to work for a colonisation they hoped to enjoy themselves, in person, two-three hundred years from now. But that's passing. Time's passing. And they're suddenly waking up to it. No, I'd let these natural forces level off if I were you. As you say, Sam Reed can take care of himself.'

'I'm going to let him,' Hale said. 'You'll keep an eye on these meetings, then? I know they've got a lot of schemes under way, but nothing's near completion yet, is it?'

'They're still blowing off steam. They'll act, but not for a while.

'Spy away, then. I won't move until I have to. I'll wait – that is, unless Sam moves first.'

Sam moved first.

As usual, he timed himself carefully, integrating every detail, and his action was spectacular, which made a few people wonder what Sam had up his sleeve. But, of course, they couldn't be sure. Some of them never were sure, even after the fantastic gambit was played. As a gambit it was effective – it was check, though not quite checkmate, and the arena from now on would follow even more closely the imagery of the old poet and his great translator – a checkerboard of nights and days. As for the Opponent – the Unseen Player – not even Sam had penetrated that mysterious symbolism. Who *was* the Player? The Harkers? Venus? Another part of Sam?

He knows about it all. . . . He knows . . . he knows . . .

It was a chilling thought, but, Sam realised, there wasn't anybody who 'knew about it all'. Certainly not the future, and even the present was difficult enough to interpret in every detail and trend.

Still, he was ready; zero hour had struck, since he had got word certain secret arrangements of his own had been completed. He was in one of his private offices in the great tower he reserved for his own use. Part of that tower was top secret. But this office wasn't; port windows looked seaward towards the archipelago, now covered with farms and little settlements, though the protective pillboxes remained.

He avoided Hale's gaze. He was examining a flat cube on the table before him. It was like a very deep picture frame. But what it held was a siren web, flushing slowly from rose to deep scarlet. Sam opened a silver box on his desk, took out an insect, and fed the siren web through a miniature hinged door. A faint odour of perfume escaped at the same time, and there was a low rhythmic humming.

'Put it away,' Hale said. 'I've smelled that odour too often! What about Crowell?'

Sam slid the siren web frame aside. 'I didn't know he was working for you. He was one of the mutineers, that's all. So I had him arrested with the others.'

'Why did you act without telling me? Why wait till I was forty miles away on an inspection trip?'

'You got here in half an hour,' Sam said. 'Anyway, I had to move fast. I've found out that there's more to this plot than you ever suspected, from what you've been telling me about it. Crowell may be your man, but he's an inefficient spy.'

'I want him released.'

Sam shrugged. 'Of course. But his usefulness is over, isn't it?'

'Not necessarily.'

'A visor call would have done the trick. You needn't have rushed back here.'

Hale said, 'I didn't want any chance of a slip-up. Crowell's got to be released. Accidents do happen. The wrong order, the wrong interpretation by a guard—'

'I've never seen you so concerned about any one individual. Why is Crowell so important?'

Hale hesitated. Finally he said, 'Well – I trust him.'

Now it was Sam's turn to pause. He said softly, 'Trust? You mean you'd trust him with a gun behind your back?'

Hale nodded.

'Maybe some day I'll find a man like that,' Sam said wryly. 'So far I haven't. Well, let's get Crowell released. It's almost time for the trial.'

'You're holding it today?'

'Yes. I've found out so much – unexpectedly – there are dangers. Worse ones than we'd suspected. Our enemies are better armed than we know. Perhaps they've got Keep backing. I don't know. But I haven't time to tell you now; I've arranged for Venus-wide videocasting of the trial, and the

Keeps will be tuning in in a few minutes. Come along. You'll find out what the setup is.'

But he paused long enough to feed the siren web another insect. Hale said, with strong distaste, 'Where did you get that thing?'

'Oh, it's a trophy.'

'Young one. Going to keep it? It'll grow—'

'I expect it to.'

'It'll grow dangerous. It's a siren web, Sam.'

Sam said, 'Still, imagine it twenty feet across. Up on the wall there—'

'With you walking into its mouth.'

'I'm not a good hypnosis subject, remember? Anyway, I'll take precautions when it really gets big. Polarised glass or stroboscopic attachment, a special filtering tonometer for its siren song, some gadget to cut the scent to safety level – the trial's starting. Let's go.'

They went out together.

Hale said, 'How many mutineers have you rounded up?'

'About seventy. Some of them will be useful in the right places. Others are too dangerous to let live—' Sam stopped abruptly. He had almost said too much.

Crowell's release came first, but afterwards they went to the room where the trial was to be held. Batteries of visor screens were already set up. There were guards, plenty of them. And the seventy-odd prisoners, unmanacled, were herded together in a railed pen.

Sam started talking abruptly. He was talking to the colony and the Keeps as well as to the prisoners. He began by describing the activities of the malcontents, his growing suspicion of an underground organisation in the colony – 'a colony expanding every hour, succeeding in conquering landside so in a day to come men will be able to live under the open sky – every man and woman on Venus!'

He had arrested the plotters. But the plot had ramifications stretching deep underground. There had been a great deal of secret theft – theft of vital equipment, technological equipment, even materials for weapons. Why?

The screens focused on the prisoners.

'You men are cat's paws,' Sam told them. 'Originally you were the ones who started this potential rebellion, but someone else has taken it over. Someone who has kept his identity completely secret. Either you don't know who he is or you won't tell me. You've been questioned. Who is your secret leader?'

Silence.

'What are his plans? Is he a Colony man?'

Silence.

'We have proof. The equipment went somewhere. And there's other evidence. We'll find him, and the rest of his band; he's a menace not only to the colony but to the Keeps. If such a man should seize power—'

The menace hung unspoken over Venus.

'We will find him eventually. We ask the Keep's co-operation in this. But now – you men have been guilty of treason. You plotted to overthrow the colony government and take control. After that, you intended to rule the Keeps as well.'

A man thrust himself forward from the other prisoners. His voice cried thinly across the visors.

'I'm older! We're all older! Where's the immortality you promised us?'

Sam said contemptuously, 'I'm not a fool, Commander French. I've known for a long time that this plot was going on, and I knew of the men involved. Why should I give people like you immortality – to plot further? None of you have been given the immortality radiation treatment for many months. You had nominal treatments, to quiet your suspicions – but immortality isn't for traitors!' His face hardened.

'Governor Hale and I have been waiting, hoping to locate the top man in your organisation. Certain events forced us to move now. We still intend to get the top man and render him harmless to civilisation, but the present problem is what to do with traitors.

'I condemn you to death.'

The silence began and ticked on and on – longer on landside than in the Keeps. For the colonists knew time now.

Sam made a little gesture.

'You will be taken under escort back to whatever Keeps you may elect. None of you may return. The colony is closed to all of you. So is the immortality treatment. You had your chance to live for a thousand years, and you chose a traitor's way instead.

'You will not be harmed. You will be taken back to the Keeps – and be free. Until you die. And you will die not in a thousand years from now, but in thirty, forty, fifty, perhaps. I withdraw the boon of immortality from you, and therefore I condemn you to death by natural causes.

'Go back to the Keeps. We don't want you here.'

He brought his hands together in the conventional gesture.

'The trial is over.'

Trial: A testing of capacity—

'Message to all Keeps: You will no longer pay korium ransom to Plymouth Colony. You will pay it to the Venusian Provisional Government. We are taking control of the planet. We have means to enforce our demands. Message to the Plymouth Colony: ground all your planes or be destroyed—'

Triangulation couldn't locate the source of the message. It kept moving. And it was always at sea. Apparently the call was being shifted rapidly from transmitter to transmitter – planes, perhaps, though no radar apparatus recorded unauthorised planes in the Venusian atmosphere.

Sam's answer to the challenge was brief – 'Surrender!'

'We have means to enforce our demands—'

Sam's face appeared on all vision screens, in the Keeps and in the colony.

'An all-out offensive has been organised from Plymouth Colony. For the first time the mutineers have come out in the open. Now we can find and smash them. We *will* find them. Television reports on our progress will be relayed as we proceed. Special ships and plane crews are being sent to guard the sea areas above every Keep. We are taking all possible precautions. Unauthorised plane approaching Plymouth Fort has been fired on; it is retreating southward. I must direct certain operations; one of our Operations Officers will take over and keep you informed.'

Sam was in his tower. He was alone. For months he had superintended the installation of one-man apparatus. Some tasks he could relay, but the main job depended on him alone. It would be no easy task.

The skip-source message came from the Venusian seas.

'Ground your planes, Plymouth Colony! You can't survive atomic attack!'

Every listener thought suddenly of the memorial eidolon in every Keep; the black-plastic shrouded sphere of the lost Earth. Atomics on Venus – for warfare? Atomic power that could so easily become uncontrollable.

Visors showed infrared and radar jungle vistas as Sam's planes quartered landside and the sea, delicate instruments probing into the black secret fury of native Venus, searching efficiently for the marauders who called themselves the Venusian Provisional Government.

'This is an ultimatum. You have forty-eight hours. At the end of that period, one of the Keeps will be destroyed.'

Atomics!

That was the old, terrible fear. That was the terror that had come down in the race through seven hundred years. And in the Keeps the years had meant nothing – had been as meaningless as the hourless days.

Forty-eight hours?

Time had come to the Keeps at last.

Two planes were shot down before they got too close to the fort. Tractor rays eased them to the ground, and there were no explosions. But the threat of the atomic warhead moved closer.

Sam said: 'In our all-out effort, we have recalled our men already assigned to the colony expansion effort – our newest venture.' His tired, strained face gave way to a view of a wide, cleared area on a seacoast, with its familiar jungle backdrop. Some huts had already been constructed, and others stood half-completed, the plastic layers only partly sprayed on the custom-shaped balloon foundations. Piles of equipment were neatly lined up. But orderly crowds of men were moving toward the motor-powered barges beached to receive them.

'The mutineers have not yet been located. Our planes are proceeding with their search—'

The patterns of radar gave place to depthless, infrared jungle, seen from far above. It shifted back to the radar matrix as the plane swept on, probing with all the marvellously keen sensory equipment technology had given it.

'Forty-seven hours. You have forty-seven hours. Plymouth Colony, ground your planes. We have atomic power and we will not hesitate to use it—'

Time . . .

'You have forty-six hours—'

And fear swept the Keeps. Crowds seethed the Ways, gathering at the cloverleaves where the big visor screens were set up. Zachariah Harker said to Kedre:

'The body politic is more than a figure of speech. The Ways, you know, are like the circulatory system. When too many people gather, forming – well, blood clots – then there's danger of an aneurysm.'

'Zachariah—' Kedre said.

He took her hand.

'I don't know. I don't know, my dear. I'm trying to think. We still have forty-five hours.'

'You have forty-four hours.'

'Another attacking plane has been shot down and eased with tractor beams thirty miles from Plymouth Fort. No atomic explosion resulted. This plane was radio-controlled. The robot-guide signals were relayed from constantly shifting areas at sea.'

Hale looked at the Logician.

'Things level off,' Ben Crowell said packing his pipe.

'It's all right for you to talk. You know the answers. I don't.'

'Time to look for real trouble is when you don't see any,'

Crowell pointed out. 'You might see some harmless-looking plants, little ones, and you wouldn't think there's a Man Underground root twenty feet long hiding 'way down, waiting for the right time. Right now—' He glanced at the Keep announcer on the nearest screen. 'Well, you don't see me interfering, do you?'

'No. And you ought to be more excited, with atomic war threatened. Even the Free Companies outlawed atomics for offence.'

'You have forty-three hours,' the screen said.

'You have twenty-four hours.'

'You have twenty hours.'

'You have sixteen hours.'

'Sam Reed speaking. We've found the skunks!'

The screens showed jungle, seen from high above – green, luxuriant, writhing with life. No more than that. Then the bombardment began, acid, flame, rays, and the fury of man's own weapons crashed against the fury of Venus.

The jungle green blackened. It writhed in torment. It flung up huge ropes of screaming vines. Clouds of flying things poured away from the centre of that circle of awful holocaust. The towering, pillarlike neck of the thunder-lizard curved up; the red maw opened. The hissing shriek of the saurian rose high and keening through the dull, incessant roar of the blasting rain from above.

'Surrender! We'll destroy the Keeps – we won't hesitate – stop your attack—'

There was only raw, blackened, steaming earth now where there had been jungle.

The soil melted and crumbled. It flowed like lava. A white-hot lake began to grow. Pressure-jets blasted down, forcing the molten rock out from its lake in a flashing, incandescent spray. And something seemed to rise from the turgid steaming depths. As the molten level sank, a grey, rounded surface emerged.

Sam's face flashed on to the screens.

'You are seeing the secret headquarters of the mutineers,' he said. 'You will see it destroyed now.'

A voice shouted: 'We'll destroy the Keeps! Stop your attack—'

The grey dome stood sullenly in the white-hot lake.

The black torpedo shape of a bomb dropped. The grey dome was tough. But then another bomb dropped.

And another.

The first explosions had not mushroomed before the next missile hit. Then the next. And there was no cessation, no pause in the terrible regularity of the pin-point bombing. Hammer-blow after hammer-blow struck. Four – five – six –

Sam dropped forty-eight bombs, one for each hour of the deadline the Venusian Provisional Government had given him.

The screens showed smoke. When at last the smoke cleared – they showed such ruin as not even the fury of Venus's jungles, could achieve. The Man Underground was rooted at last.

And twenty submarines discharged extremely specialised torpedoes at the impervium domes shielding the Keeps.

Six hours later Zachariah Harker was speaking to the Keeps.

'The mutineers were destroyed by Sam Reed. But they had a suicide fleet. As they died, they had their revenge. The impervium dome above Delaware Keep has been radio-activated. The same holds true for all the Keeps. One moment—' He turned away, and presently returned.

'I am told that new messages have recently been received – the mutineers were not all destroyed. Apparently there were some survivors. They are harmless at the moment, but they comprise a permanent threat until they, as well as their organisation, is eradicated. Completely. Meantime, their revenge is effective. Within a week the danger level will be reached, and the Keeps will be uninhabitable.

'Do not be immediately alarmed. There is no chance that the activated impervium will reach critical mass. But there is no way of halting the atomic reaction, and after a week has passed, the Keeps will be slow death traps. Only one solution seems practical. There is no time to build new impervium domes undersea – yet. But it may be done on landside. Here is Sam Reed; let him tell you his plan.'

Sam's face appeared.

He said almost casually, 'We did our best, but the skunks had the last word. Well, you've got to leave the Keeps – all of you – or die. I told you, I think, that we had been planning colony expansion. We've cleared a great deal of ground in preparation for that, and have already set up some equipment. It's yours. We'll stay in Plymouth or start new colonies. The land we cleared, and the equipment, is at your service. In this hour of disaster, we'll have to work together; we're one race.

'In a week you can transport the *matériel* you'll need. It won't be an easy life, but it'll be life. We of Plymouth Colony stand ready to help you to the fullest extent. Good luck.'

Someone else appeared on the screen; Sam and Zachariah began talking on a private beam.

'Can you evacuate the Keeps in a week?'

'Easily. Since we have to.'

'All right. We'll have to work together – for a while at least. Kedre proposed that once, and I said no. But now I'm proposing it. We'll send special officers to advise you on what equipment will be required. In cleared areas, the first problem will be medical. We'll supply medical administrative officers. You've got to stay alive and healthy, and you're not acclimated to landside life. Don't count too much on impervium domes. We haven't wiped out the mutineers, and what they can do once, they can do again. When you're under impervium, you're vulnerable. If the survivors get organised again—'

'Landside life will be hard on the old and infirm.'

'The strong men will have enough to do. There will be plenty of maintenance jobs that won't require physical fitness. Jobs that have to be done. Give those tasks to the old and infirm; that way, you'll release the strong ones for work that takes strength. You'll have a lot of clearing and building to do.'

'Our technicians estimate the half-life of activated

thorium at twelve years. We can return to the Keeps after twelve years.'

'But you'll have to live until then. And don't forget the survivors – the ones we didn't blast. They could reactivate the Keep domes, unless we catch them first. Twelve years is a long time.'

'Yes,' Zachariah said thoughtfully, looking into his grandson's oblivious face. 'Yes, I expect it will be a long, long time.'

And the Lord said. ... Depart and go up hence ... unto the land which I sware unto Abraham ... a land flowing with milk and honey ... And the children of Israel went into the midst of the sea upon the dry ground, and the waters were a wall unto them on their right hand and on their left.
        – EXODUS

Seven hundred years ago the last exodus of the race of man took place. Today it began again. The vast mass migration was too complex for any single mind to encompass, and the people who looked back on it later remembered only intolerable confusion of the mind – hysteria, near panic, blind rebellion against destiny, but concerted, obedient motion as an overall pattern. The people of the Keeps had learned docility the easiest way of all. Now they did as they were told, grumbling, frightened, unwilling, but obeying the orders of anyone who spoke with enough authority.

No one would have believed, beforehand, that so tremendous an exodus could take place in the time allotted. No one, looking back, quite understood how it had been accomplished. But accomplished it was. That incalculable weight of inertia in people contentedly settled for seven hundred years in one place required an even more incalculable weight in the scales to tip them over into action—

And they had that weight. The nucleon. Weightless by any comparable scale of physical value, still it tipped the balance as no other thing could. There was one old, old terror in the mind of every man who had ever looked up from the moving Ways and seen the globe of lost Earth hanging in the centre of every Keep, shrouded in its symbolic pall.

They moved.

Kedre looked around her beautiful quiet room for the last time. It was a long look, quiet, like the room.

'We won't come back,' she said. Zachariah, waiting at the door for her, said patiently, 'Why?'

'You know we won't. And it's a good thing. I hate Sam Reed. He's always forcing me to face unpleasant truths for perfectly irrelevant reasons of his own. He isn't doing this because it's time and past time for the sake of the race. He's doing it because he told a monumental lie and couldn't think of any other out.'

'I wonder if we'll ever be able to prove it?'

Kedre shrugged. 'If we could, it wouldn't matter, now. We know Sam's methods. Once before when he was in a desperate spot he took desperate measures. We've expected it again ever since. I didn't give him credit for such misdirection, but Sam's learning fast. No, I don't suppose it ever can be proved.'

'Are you ready, my dear? The lift's waiting.'

'All right.' She sighed, turning to the door. 'I shouldn't feel as if I'm going out to die. I'm just now going to vindicate my own existence by starting to live! It'll be uncomfortable and I suppose dangerous, though I mind danger less. But it's something that's needed doing for longer than I like to think. Only – Zachariah, it's so horribly ignoble to be *forced* to do it!'

He laughed. 'I feel the same way. I suppose the first invertebrates who crawled up out of the prehistoric seas felt just as we do – hating every minute of it. It's time mankind crawled out of the water and stood on dry land again, but even Sam Reed can't make us like it!'

'He'll be sorry.' She buckled the cloak at her throat and crossed the room on lingering feet, pressing each step into the resilent flooring she would probably never walk again except out of curiosity, perhaps a century from now. 'How strange it will all look then,' she thought. 'Dark and stifling,

I expect, after so long in the free air. We'll wonder how we ever stood it. Oh dear, I wish Sam Reed had never been born.'

Zachariah held the door for her. 'Our plans will still go forward, landside,' he said. 'I checked about your . . . your time-bomb. Parents and child are safe up there, in a sheltered job.'

'I wish,' Kedre declared, 'that it had been a boy. Still – this may make a better weapon, after all. And it isn't our only weapon, of course. *Sam has got to be stopped.* We may have to use weapons as disreputable as the ones he's used against us, but we'll stop him. We have time on our side.'

Zachariah, watching her face, said nothing at all.

'I knew you were up to something,' Hale said, 'when you let all those mutineers go. It isn't like you to let anything go you can use.'

Sam looked at him under meeting brows. 'You wanted to colonise landside,' he said uncompromisingly. 'Well, this is it.'

'Robot submarines, robot planes, remote control – and a long-term plan,' Hale said musingly, and shook his head. 'Well, you've done it. No one else in the world could have, but you did.'

'After twelve years,' Sam told him calmly, 'they'll be pretty well acclimatised. After another twelve – and maybe another – they're going to like it up here so well you couldn't drive them back. Remember you told me once what makes pioneers? Push plus pull. Bad home conditions or a Grail somewhere else. The Grail wasn't enough. Well—' He shrugged.

Hale was silent for almost a minute, regarding Sam with his steady stare that had seen so much on Venusian landside before now. Finally he spoke.

'Remember what happened to Moses, Sam?' he asked gently, and then, like a classic prototype, turned and went out of the room, not staying for an answer.

The race struck roots and grew. Slowly at first, reluctantly, but with gathering vigour. And down in the deserted Keeps, in the first few days after the departing thousands had gone, for a little while life still moved through the strange new silence of the dying cities.

There were those who did not choose to leave. Some of the old people who had always lived here and could not face life above water, some of the ill who preferred the slow, comfortable death that had been provided for them. Some of the drug addicts. Silently in the deathly silence they moved through the empty shells. Never before since mankind first colonised Venus had such silence dwelt beneath the domes. You could hear the slowing Ways sighing on their rounds. You could hear strange, vague underwater noises transmitted from the great sounding boards of the city shells. You could hear sometimes the shuffling footsteps of some fellow wanderer.

But after a little while all footsteps ceased, and all sounds except echoes from the seas outside.

The thick walls shivered in the thunder of bombardment. In Sam's hand the stylus danced upon the suddenly shaking paper. His desk top shook, and the chair he sat in, and the floor quivered rhythmically and was still. Sam grimaced without knowing it. This was the third day of the bombardment, and he had shut his mind to the minor irritations of the unstable walls.

A young woman in a sleekly severe brown tunic bent forward, watching him write, her black hair falling in short straight wings across her face. She pulled the page off the pad almost before his stylus had finished writing, and went quickly across the trembling floor to her own desk. There was a televisor on it, and she spoke rapidly, in a soft, clear voice, into the transmitter. In a dozen other visors scattered about the vast, beleaguered fort her tanned face was the target for intense attention as Sam's lieutenants received their latest orders. In a dozen visors her violet-blue eyes looked out narrowed with intentness, her velvety voice gave incongruously stern messages.

'All right,' Sam said wearily when she had finished. 'All right, Signa, send in Zachariah now.'

She rose with a smooth precision of motion that was

beautiful to watch, and went quickly across the floor. The door she opened led not directly into the waiting room beyond, but into a little space lock that could be bathed at a touch by searcher beams to catch the presence of any weapon a man might try to smuggle past it. Sam took no chances. It didn't seem to matter much now – perhaps he had too long mistaken personal safety for group safety. The bombardment roared again and for the first time a long delicate crack went flashing like slow lightning down one wall. The space lock would seem futile enough when the walls themselves began to go. But for a little while longer it must be used.

Two guards came in at Signa's beckoning, and paused perfunctorily in the lock and stood back for their prisoner to take his turn in the invisible bath of the beams. Two more guards came after.

Zachariah had a cut lip and a darkening bruise on one side of his ageless face, but he looked remarkably confident in spite of his manacles. Except for his tan he had changed little. He was still head of the Harker clan, and the Harkers were still the most influential family on Venus. But if Sam's coup in capturing the leader of the attacking forces meant anything, Zachariah did not show it.

Twenty years had not been a very long time.

The Keeps were still uninhabitable. The change-over to landside living had come very gradually, but it was complete now. The signal for completion had been sounded on that day when instruments first showed that the atmosphere of Venus had at last shifted over to an ecology balance that matched Earth's. Crab grass and earth-native herbs with a high oxygen output had finally tipped the scale. From now on, this continent could be left to itself, botanically speaking. For the plants had changed the air. The heavy carbon dioxide atmosphere in which Venusian flora flourished would foster them no longer. What is normal for Earth-born plants is poison for the Venus-grown things that were so often neither plant nor animal, but a deadly symbiosis of the two.

It was this shift that the spreading colonies had been awaiting.

It was this war that came of the shift.

'Zachariah,' Sam said in a weary voice, 'I want you to call off your men.'

Zachariah looked at him narrowly, not without sympathy, trying as he had so often tried, in vain, to trace some likeness to the Harker blood that ran in them both. 'Why should I do that, Sam?' he asked.

'You're in no position to bargain. I'll have you shot unless this attack's stopped by noon. Step over here – you can use my telecaster.'

'No, Sam. You're finished. This time you can't win.'

'I've always won before. I can do it again.'

'No,' Zachariah said, and paused for a moment, thinking of those many times in the past when Sam had won – easily, scornfully, because of his impregnable defences built up so cannily in years of peace. When the Immortality bubble broke completely, there had been rash, furious, tragically futile assaults upon this great white fortress that sheltered the most powerful man on Venus.

'We aren't guerillas,' Zachariah said calmly. 'We've been building up to this attack since the day you pirated our korium with the death-bomb threat. Remember, Sam? You haven't made many mistakes in strategy, but you should have checked the equipment we took landside with us when we left the Keeps. A lot of it was stuff we're using now.' He looked at the jagged lightning-streak that was creeping down the wall as the bombardment went on. 'This time we've got you, Sam. You've been building for defence a long time – but not as long as we've built towards this offence.'

'You're forgetting something.' Sam's head ached from the incessant vibration. It made talking difficult. 'You're forgetting yourself. You aren't really willing to be shot rather than call off the attack, are you?'

'That's something you couldn't understand, isn't it?'

Sam shook his head impatiently. 'You'd have attacked twenty years ago if you were as strong as you pretend. You aren't fooling me, Harker. I've never been licked yet.'

'We've needed you – until now. You've lived on sufferance, Sam. Now it's over. This bombardment isn't only guns. It's the . . . the pressure of human emotions you've held down too long. You've tried to bring progress to a full stop at the level of your choosing, and you can't do it, Sam. Not you or anybody. For twenty years that pressure's been building up. You're finished, Sam.'

Sam slammed the vibrating desk top with an angry fist. 'Shut up!' he said. 'I'm sick of talk. I'll give you sixty seconds to make up your mind, Harker. After that – *you're* finished.'

But there was in his mind as he said it a nagging uneasiness he could not quite name. His unconscious mind knew the answer. It nagged at him because Zachariah's capture had been too easy. Sam's conscious awareness had not recognised the incongruity yet; perhaps his vanity would not permit it. But he knew something was wrong about the setup.

He glanced nervously around the room, his eyes pausing for a moment, as they so often did, on the blue-eyed girl at the desk across the room. She was watching everything in alert, tight-lipped silence, missing nothing. He knew he could trust her. It was a heart-warming assurance to have. He knew because of the exhaustive psychological and neurological tests that had winnowed out all applicants except the half-dozen from which Signa had been chosen.

She was eighteen, Keep-born, landside-bred, when she first entered the Fort as a clerical worker. All of them were screened throughly, of course. All of them were indoctrinated from the first with the precepts Sam's psychologists had worked out. But Signa rose faster than most towards the top. Within a year she was an assistant secretary in the restricted building that housed administration. Within six months from then she was a secretary with an office of her own. And then one day Sam, looking over applicants for his personal staff, was rather surprised to find a woman's name among those with top-flight test ratings. One interview clinched the appointment for her.

She was twenty-five now. She was not Sam's mistress though few in this Fort would have believed it. Periodically she underwent further tests, under narcosynthesis, to make sure her emotional reactions had not changed. So far they had not. She was utterly to be trusted and Sam's efficiency would be halved, he knew, if he had to work without her now.

He could see that something was troubling her. He knew her face so well the slightest shadow on it was recognizable. There was a crease between her brows as she looked at Zachariah, and an expression of faint uncertainty, of puzzled anticipation flickered in her eyes.

Sam looked at his wrist. 'Forty seconds,' he said, and pushed back his chair. Every eye in the room followed him as he went over to the far wall, the wall where the long crack was widening, and flicked a switch in a six-foot frame. A shuttered screen, filling the frame, began to open slowly. From behind it a faint, sweet, infinitely seductive humming swelled. Sam was reaching for the lid of a box set into the wall beside the frame when a buzz of Signa's visor interrupted him.

'For you, Sam,' she said in a moment. 'Hale.'

He flicked the switch again, closing the screen, and went rapidly across the room. The Free Companion's brown unaging face looked up at him from the tilted visor.

'You alone, Sam?'

'No. Wait, I'll switch to earphones.'

The face in the screen grimaced impatiently. Then, at Sam's signal the face vanished again and Hale's voice buzzed in his ears, unheard except by Sam.

'There's been a breakthrough,' Hale said crisply.

'How bad?'

'Bad enough. Vibration did it. I told you I thought that plastic was too rigid. It's down in the lower courts. They've already manned some of our own guns and swivelled them around. The upper bailey's going to start getting it in about five minutes. Sam – I think there's been a leak somewhere. They shouldn't even know how those needle guns work. But they do.'

Sam was silent, his mind flickering rapidly from possibility to possibility. Hale himself was as suspect as any. It had been a long, long while since Sam had trusted the Free Companion. But he had made grimly certain of Hale's loyalty by insuring that public opinion bracketed the two men together. Hale profited by Sam's methods. Sam made sure all Venus knew it. He made sure that Hale's part in originating unpopular ideas – from the Immortality swindle on down – was fully publicised. It was fairly certain that Hale would have to back Sam up in all he did, if only to save his own hide.

'I've got Zachariah here,' he said into the transmitter. 'Come up, will you?' He slipped off the earphones and turned back to his prisoner. 'Your minute's up,' he said.

Zachariah appeared to hesitate. Then he said, 'I'll talk to you, Sam on one condition. Privacy. We'll have to be alone for what I have to say.'

Sam opened his desk drawer, took out a flat pistol and laid it on the vibrating desk-top, his palm over it. 'You'll talk now, Zachariah Harker,' he said, 'or I'll shoot you. Right between the eyes.' He lifted the pistol and regarded Zachariah down its barrel, seeing the serene Immortal face half blocked out by blued steel.

Silence. Then from far off, muffled by walls, the unmistakable piercing wail of a needle-gun bolt split the air of the inner fort. Impact, dull thunder, and a long sliding crash. The walls shook briefly to a new tempo and the crack widened at Sam's back.

Zachariah said, 'You'd better let me talk to you, Sam. But if you'd rather shoot – shoot. I won't say it until we are alone.'

Sam's hesitation was not very long. He knew now he was more shaken than he had realised until this moment, or he would never have surrendered to a bluff. But he let the pistol sink slowly, and he nodded.

Signa rose. 'All right, guards,' she said. They turned and went out through the still activated searcher lock. She put her finger on its switch and looked inquiringly at Sam. 'Shall I go, too?'

'No,' Sam said. 'Not you.' His voice was firm.

'Sam, I . . . I'd rather go.' She sounded oddly puzzled and distressed. It was Zachariah who spoke first.

'You stay, please,' he said. She gave him another of her strange glances, uncertain, troubled.

Sam watched them, leaning his hands palm down on the desk and feeling the almost continuous vibrations of the bombardment. The air was pierced now and then by the screaming needle beams, and he did not like to think what was happening to his inner ring of defences around the upper bailey.

"All right,' he said. 'What is it? Talk fast, Harker. I'm in a hurry.'

Zachariah, hands still manacled behind him crossed the room and stood looking out the bank of windows that framed a vista of distant sea.

'I'll show you,' he said. 'Come over here.'

Sam came impatiently across the shaking floor. 'What? What is it?' He stood beside the Immortal, but a safe distance away, for caution was second nature to him, and looked down. 'I don't see a thing. What is it?'

Zachariah whistled the opening bars of *Lilibulero* . . .

The room exploded with thunder.

Sam found himself reeling, choking, gasping for breath, with no clear idea of what had happened. *A needle beam,* he thought wildly. But then the whole room would be a shambles, and it was only himself, leaning one shoulder against the wall, shaking his head dizzily, breathing hard, who seemed affected.

He looked up. Zachariah still stood by the window, watching him with a kind of hard restrained pity. The room was untouched. And there was something the matter with Sam's shoulder.

That was where the blow had caught him. He remembered now. He put up an unsteady hand to numb the area and then looked unbelievingly at his palm, filmed with clear red. Something moved across his chest. Incredulously he bent his head and saw that it was blood. The bullet must have come out just under the clavicle.

Signa's soft, clear voice gasped, 'Sam . . . Sam!'

'It's all right . . . it isn't bad.' He was reassuring her even before he lifted his head. Then he saw her standing behind his desk, the flat pistol held in both hands. She was staring at him with great, terrified eyes and her mouth was a Greek square of strained effort. Her stare shifted from Sam to Zachariah and then back, and the incredulity in it was very near sheer madness.

'I . . . I had to do it, Sam,' she said in a harsh, thin whisper. 'I don't know why – there must have been a reason! I don't understand—'

Zachariah broke in, his voice gentle. 'It wasn't enough, Signa,' he said. 'You'll have to try again, you know. Quickly, before he can stop you.'

'I know . . . I know.' Her voice was a gasp. Normally she was a good shot, fast and easy, but she brought the pistol up in both hands, steadying it like a schoolgirl, squinting past the barrel. Sam saw her finger begin to draw up on the trigger.

He didn't want to do it. He would almost rather have risked the shot. But he dropped his right hand to his side, found through cloth the outlines of the tiny needle gun in his pocket, and shot from the hip without taking aim.

He did not miss.

For one long last moment, afterwards, her eyes were wide and brilliantly violet, staring into his. Sam scarcely heard the thud of the dropping gun. He was meeting her blue stare and remembering another blue-eyed girl, very long ago, who had faced him like this and puffed oblivion in his face.

He said, 'Rosathe!' as if he had just remembered the name, and swung around towards Zachariah. It was the same triangle, he thought – Zachariah, Rosathe, Sam Reed – sixty years ago and now. There was no difference. But this time—

His fingers closed on the needle gun again and its bolt hissed again across the room. Zachariah, seeing it coming, made no move. But when it came within six inches of his chest it seemed to explode in midair. There was a scream of expended energy, a flare like a miniature nova, and Zachariah smiled unhurt into Sam's eyes.

What he said made no sense. He still looked at Sam, but he lifted his voice and called, 'All right, Hale, it's up to you.'

There was a challenge in his words. Sam had no time to puzzle it out. He set his teeth grimly and tugged the needle gun from his scorched pocket, lifted it towards Zachariah's face. There at least the Immortal could not be wearing armour.

He never pulled the trigger. From somewhere beyond him a familiar voice said wearily, 'Harker – you win.' And a searing light flashed blindingly into Sam's eyes.

He knew what it was. He and the Free Companion carried the little riot-breaker flashes instead of deadlier weapons for discipline. Blindness was not usually permanent after that glare had burned a man's eyes, but it did not pass quickly.

In the sudden darkness that had engulfed the room Sam heard Zachariah's voice saying, 'Thank you, Hale. I was pretty sure you would – but not quite. That was close.'

The Free Companion said, 'I'm sorry, Sam.'

And that was the last thing Sam heard in Plymouth Colony.

And Moses went up from the plains of Moab ... and the Lord said unto him, This is the land ... I have caused thee to see it with thine eyes, but thou shalt not go over thither ... And Moses died there in the land of Moab, but no man knoweth of his sepulchre unto this day. – DEUTERONOMY

There was a swimming dark, and the roaring of winds. And then vague patterns of light that were presently a face – the head and torso of an old man, a shrewd-faced, wrinkled old man Sam recognised. Beyond him was a bare alloy wall, and a dim light came from somewhere.

Sam tried to sit up, failed, tried again. He could not move. Panic leaped in his mind. The old man smiled.

'Take it easy, son. This is the way it has to be.' He was packing tobacco into his pipe as he spoke. Now he held a flame to it, sucked the fire down into the bowl, blew out smoke. His mild gaze focused on Sam.

'Had to tell you a few things, son,' he said. 'Just in case. You're good and healthy again, in case you're wondering. You been here a few weeks, resting up, getting cured. Nobody knows but me.'

Where? Sam tried to move his head enough to see the

source of the light, the shape of the room. He could not.

'I got this hideout ready quite some while ago,' Crowell went on, puffing. 'Figured I might need it for something like this. It's under my potato patch. I'll be hoeing spuds on this parcel of land for a good long spell yet, I figure. Maybe a hundred years, maybe five hundred. That's right. I'm an Immortal. Don't look it, do I? But I was born on Earth.'

He blew out blue smoke. 'Earth had a good many fine things – the old place. But I could see what was coming, even then. I could see you, Sam Reed. Oh, not your name or your face, but I knew you'd be along. A man like you always is, at the right time. I can figure out the future, Sam. It's a talent I got.

'Only I can't interfere or I'll change the pattern to something different – what it'll be I can't tell for a while, after I've stepped in.'

Same made a frantic effort to stir one finger. Coloured flecks of light danced before his eyes. He scarcely heard as the old man rambled on.

'Easy now,' Crowell said quietly. 'Just try to listen for a bit. I'm the Logician, Sam. Remember the Temple of Truth? You didn't believe the oracle at first, did you? Well, I was right. I was the machine, and I don't make mistakes, at least, not that kind.

'You were in the Temple for forty years, Sam. You wouldn't remember that, either. You were dream-dusting.'

Dream-dusting? Sam's attention came back sharply. Was this the answer he had sought so long, given casually now, when it no longer meant anything! Crowell, the unknown guardian? But how – why—

'Zachariah was out to kill you. I could see that. I could see he'd succeed, unless I interfered – which upset the apple cart considerable. After that I couldn't figure out the future quite so close, till things evened up again. That's one reason I waited forty years. It's why I let you wake up in an alley, broke and disgraced. To even the scale, son. The way things are, when I give a good present I've got to give a bad one too, or it won't come out right.

'You had your troubles to straighten out then, and when

you finished, the pattern was all set again. I could see what was coming.'

Sam did not care. If he could only break this paralysis. He must – he must! Always before now he had drawn upon some deep reserve of strength no other man possessed. And it must not fail him now.

But it was failing him.

'You're not Sam Reed, you know,' the Logician was saying. 'Remember Blaze Harker? He had a son. Blaze was starting to go crazy then, or he'd never have hated the baby enough to do what he did. You know what it was, don't you? You grew up looking like a short-termer, but your name wasn't really Reed.'

Blaze Harker. Blaze Harker, his face distorted, struggling in the strait-jacket—

I let him go! I could have killed him! He was the one – I let him go—

Blaze Harker!

Harker!

Sam – *Harker!*

'I couldn't tell you before,' Crowell said. 'It would have changed the future, and I didn't want it changed that way. Up till now we've needed you, Sam. Once in a long while a fella like you comes along, somebody strong enough to move a world. Oh, I guess other men had qualifications – like Rob Hale. Only Hale couldn't have done it. He could have done part, but there are things he never could make himself do.

'There's nothing you wouldn't do, son – nothing at all – if it would get you what you want.

'If you hadn't been born, if Blaze hadn't done what he did, mankind would be in the Keeps yet. And in a few hundred years, or a thousand, say, the race would have died out. I could see that ahead, clear as could be. But now we've come landside. We'll finish colonising Venus. And then we'll go out and colonise the whole universe, I expect.

'You're the one who did it, Sam. We owe you a lot. In your day you were a great man. But your day's over. You got your power by force, and you're like most dictators, son, who reach the top that way. All you could think of was repeating the things that made you a success – more fighting, more force. There wasn't any way but down for you, once you'd reached the top, because of the man you are. You had the same drive that made the first life-form leave water for land, but we can't use your kind any more for a while, Sam.'

Drive? It was fury. It burned with blinding white violence in him, so hot it seemed strange the fetters of his paralysis were not consumed – it seemed strange the sheer violence of his rage could not send him headlong across the room at Crowell. To get above ground – smash Hale, smash the Harkers –

The Harkers. But he was a Harker, too.

Crowell said, 'Men like you are mighty rare, Sam. When they get to the right position, at the right time, they're the salvation of the race of man. But it's got to be the right time – a time of disaster. The drive never stops, in a man like you. You've got to get on top. You've got to, or die.

"If you can't conquer an enemy, you'll conquer your friends. Up to now the enemy was Venus, and you licked it. But what have you got to fight now?'

'Man.'

'There's going to be a good long time of peace, now. The Immortals have taken over. They'll rule well. You've left them a good foundation to build on. But it's time you bowed out.'

Suddenly Crowell chuckled. 'You thought you were telling a lie, Sam, when you promised immortality was up here land-side, didn't you? It was the truth. They'll get their immortality. Ever think of that? Man was dying in the Keeps. Up here he'll live on – well, not forever, but long enough, long enough. The race has got immortality, Sam, and you gave it to 'em.'

He puffed again at the pipe and looked down reflectively through smoke at Sam. 'I hardly ever interfere with the running of things,' he said. 'Only once I had to kill a man. I had to. It changed the patterns so much I couldn't see the future for a long time after, but I'd already seen enough to know what would have happened if the man kept on living. It was bad. I couldn't think of anything worse. So I killed him.

'I've interfered again, because I know what the future would be like with you in it. This means I won't be able to guess what's coming for quite a spell. After that things will level off and I can take a look.

'This time I'm not killing. I learn more as I get older. Also, you're an Immortal. You can sleep a long, long while without losing anything. That's what you're going to do, son – sleep.

'And I hope you die in your sleep. I hope I'll never have to wake you up. Because if I do, it'll mean things have gone mighty bad again. You and I are long-termers. We'll still be around, barring accidents, for quite a stretch yet. And plenty of bad things can happen.

'I get glimpses. Nothing's set yet – too far ahead. But I see possibilities. The jungle could come back. New life-forms may mutate – Venus critters are tricky. And we won't stay on Venus forever. This is just the first colony. We'll go on out to the planets and stars. There may be trouble there, too, sooner than you'd think. Maybe something will try to colonise our worlds, as we colonise theirs. There's peace and there's war, and it's always been that way, and I guess it always will.

'So maybe we'll need a man like you again, Sam.

'I'll wake you if we do.'

The shrewd brown face regarded him from coils of smoke. The friendly, remorseless, judging eyes considered him.

'For now, though,' Crowell said, 'go to sleep. You've done your job. Sleep well, son – and good night.'

Sam lay motionless. The light was dimming. He could not be sure if it were his own vision that dimmed.

There was so much he wanted to think about, and so little time for thinking. He was Immortal. He must live—

Sam Harker, Immortal. Harker. Harker.

He heard the music of carnival ringing through Delaware Keep, saw the bright ribbons of the moving Ways, smelled drifting perfume, smiled into Kedre's face.

There was a second of desperate urgency, as though he

clawed at the edge of a crumbling cliff, while life and awareness fell to pieces beneath his hands.

Darkness and silence brimmed the buried room. Here the
Man Underground slept at last, rooted deep, waiting.

EPILOGUE

Sam woke—